Praise for the work

And Then There Was Her

This book really was a joy to read. As soon as I started reading this book I was hooked. I loved the premise. I loved the setting of a winery. There is something so romantic about it, and Shepard writes beautifully so you feel like you can taste the grapes and even feel the soil. I thought all the characters were well done. This was the right book at the right time and it's going on my 2020 favorite list.

-Lex Kent's Reviews, *goodreads*

The romance is very delicately written, a well-balanced slow burn with some spectacularly hot moments too! I could have written thousands of words on how much I love this book, the intricacy of the imagery, how much I want to punch Kacey, and how I can relate to the pain and doubt etched in Madison's soul. Anyone who has ever been made to feel "less than" will be touched by this narrative.

-Orlando J., *NetGalley*

I adore an age-gap romance, and this slow-burn story is incredibly romantic. There's something about the writing that is lush and elegant and beautiful, and it really suits the story that is set in a gorgeous vineyard. I highly recommend this gorgeous book for anyone looking for an escape.

-Karen C., *NetGalley*

This book plucked the strings of my romantic side on multiple occasions. I highly recommend this book to the romantics out there and even the aspiring romantics who just need a little encouragement.

-*The Lesbian Review*

Across the Dark Horizon

This is a well written and very fast-paced book. It is not overly long and there is quite a bit of action crammed into the pages. Shepard builds great tension throughout the book through both the plot and the bourgeoning relationship between Charlie and Gail. ...the result is heart-pounding excitement throughout!

-The Lesbian Review

Bird on a Wire

This is the second novel by Tagan Shepard. I said for her successful debut that it is a sign that many more fine books are yet to come. I am glad that I was right...With all main elements done well, this makes for another very good book by this author. Keep them coming!

-Pin's Review, *goodreads*

...She has become an author that I will automatically read now. If you are looking for a good drama book with a little romance, give this a read.

-Lex Reviews, *goodreads*

Visiting Hours

...*Visiting Hours* is an emotional tale filled with denial, pain, struggle, commitment, and finally, more than one kind of deep, abiding love.

-Lambda Literary Review

Queen of Humboldt

The story is told from both Sabrina and Marisol's perspectives and is nonlinear in that some of the chapters are flashbacks. I found these glimpses into the past to be a great way to introduce some much needed character history as well as helping to understand and sympathize with Marisol. This structure can sometimes be confusing, but Shepard does a great job using this device and I never felt disoriented or lost. It is a pulse pumper with a ton of action that will keep you excitedly flipping the page to see what is coming next.

-*The Lesbian Review*

Wonderful. Spectacularly good. The characters in *Queen of Humboldt* are very well crafted and even when they are not necessarily at their best, they are still very sympathetic. I would, and indeed will, highly recommend this book to anyone and everyone. Her ability to capture emotions and reel the reader into her world is part of what makes Tagan Shepard's books so beautiful to read.

-Orla S., *NetGalley*

Queen of Humboldt does not disappoint. This is a second-chance romance with a dose of opposites attract and almost a taboo feel thrown in for good measure. Be sure to pay attention to the chapter headings where a year is involved, because there are flashbacks interspersed and the timing definitely matters. I don't want to give any of the story away because this one is a doozy. A true roller coaster ride that ends with a bang.

-Karen R., *NetGalley*

Talk about an action book! I think I'm still trying to catch my breath over here. While Shepard writes mostly contemporary romances (and one futuristic book) I was excited to see her mix it up again with an action-romance. And when I say action I mean ACTION! I was completely glued to my seat. For me a read like this is just really fun and super entertaining. ...It's a "buckle your seat belt and hang on for the ride" kind of read.

-Lex Kent's Reviews, *goodreads*

Well, this came out of left field. I honestly wasn't sure about this one, because of the darker themes it promised, and it is hard to really balance that grit out with some hope. But dang, this is done so well. Marisol's character and life is well plotted, utilizing flashbacks to help slow down the breakneck pace a bit. I love that there are hints for what Marisol is doing in the shadows of her criminal enterprise, but when its revealed, its done so well that it doesn't lose any of its punch. Shepard avoided switching between Marisol's and Sloane's perspectives too much, giving most of the storytelling duties to Marisol, and it works well. Marisol is a compelling narrator and having events playing out through her eyes was great.

This is dark, pretty violent, but is also full of hope and goodness. Sloane and Marisol are well balanced characters, and one of the few examples where they don't have to grow that much to make them compelling. It is well paced, with some really great action sequences, some slower moments, and some truly emotionally impactful ones. This was a lovely surprise, and is quite possibly my favorite book this month.

-Colleen C., *NetGalley*

Swipe Right

Other Bella Books by Tagan Shepard

Across the Dark Horizon
And Then There Was Her
Bird on a Wire
Queen of Humboldt
Visiting Hours

About the Author

Tagan Shepard (she/her) is the author of six novels of sapphic fiction, including the 2019 Goldie winner *Bird on a Wire*. When not writing about extraordinary women loving other extraordinary women, she can be found playing video games, reading, or sitting in DC Metro traffic.

She lives in Virginia with her wife and two cats.

Swipe Right

TAGAN SHEPARD

BELLA
BOOKS
2021

Bella Books, Inc.
P.O. Box 10543
Tallahassee, FL 32302

Printed in the United States of America on acid-free paper.

First Bella Books Edition 2021

Editor: Cath Walker
Cover Designer: Heather Honeywell

ISBN: 978-1-64247-244-8

Acknowledgments

Penelope is one of those rare characters who arrived in my head fully formed and she changed very little from inception to the final draft. My only struggle came in portraying a woman living with Ehlers-Danlos syndrome in a way that was both authentic and empathetic. For that, I turned to my friend, Renee. She graciously gave up her time for an interview before I wrote and as a sensitivity reader after. I am deeply indebted to her for that.

While there is no universal experience, I hope people living with chronic illness see a piece of themselves reflected in Penelope. I would encourage anyone who reads this book to also read Own Voices literature from disabled authors. My personal recommendation is *Unbroken: 13 Stories Starring Disabled Teens* edited by Marieke Nijkamp.

As always, my excellent beta readers have cheered and challenged me into making my story better. Thank you to Celeste, Cade, and Kate for your insightful and indispensable feedback.

The team at Bella Books is one of the best in the business and I am proud to call myself a member of the Bella family. Linda and Jessica Hill make my dreams come true with every new book and I am eternally grateful. Cath Walker has almost single-handedly molded me into the writer I am today with her encouragement and the occasional bit of tough love. Her hard work has finally borne fruit as this is the first manuscript in which I have correctly conjugated the verb "to lie" every time!

My thanks to David Rotan, both for his excellent work selling our townhome and for insight into the Northern Virginia real estate market. Also to Monica and Chrissy for sharing your online dating horror stories and triumphs.

Most importantly, to Cris, the love of my life. Every single day for twenty years I have felt your love, your support, and your encouragement. Your smile has dragged me out of more writing funks than I care to admit. Your arms have always been there to hold me when I want to fall. You are my home.

Dedication

For Renee
I see your stripes

CHAPTER ONE

"I know it's Tuesday and you don't leave the house on Tuesday, but I need your help." Pen had picked up on the second ring and she hadn't hung up yet. That was a good sign. "Get over here."

"Sure, what's up?"

"I'm horny."

I heard a scuffle on the line like she'd dropped the phone and scrambled to pick it back up. She sounded a little more alert when she answered, "Whoa, we aren't that sort of friends."

"I don't mean it like that," I said, pacing around my cramped living room. Taking a deep breath, I steeled my nerves and blurted, "I need your help making a dating-app profile."

There was a split second of silence, followed by a roar of laughter. I'd expected it, but I still didn't like it. I made two full, fuming circuits around the couch as she laughed. When she finally quieted to a soft chuckle I said with as much dignity as I could muster, "Fuck you. Get over here."

I could hear the pout in my voice and obviously Pen heard it, too. There was a genuine kindness in her tone which reminded me that, under all the bravado, my best friend was a caring person. "Sweetie, you don't need that."

"Yes, I do. I'm desperate."

"Kieran…"

"I have two bottles of Rosé in the fridge."

"I'll be there in ten minutes."

My last circuit around the room landed me in front of the barnwood-framed mirror beside the couch. I was just filling out a profile tonight, but it kinda felt like I was going on a date. I went through my usual full inspection. Honestly, I was looking pretty cute. I always had an extra few pounds hanging around, but it was currently hanging around in places that filled out my ruffled babydoll top and tightened my artfully torn jeans in all the right places. My hair was growing long and it fell past my shoulders. The dark brown curls played well against the navy-blue top. The happy cataloguing stopped when I got to my face. Not my best feature. The nerves returned, so I bolted away from the mirror.

While I waited for Pen, I cleaned. That's how I always dealt with stress. And anger. And particularly loneliness. There was nothing like scrubbing a toilet to make the rest of life seem manageable. The problem was I'd been dealing with loneliness for so long that my house was already spotless. Not even a dirty dish in the sink. Time for drastic measures. I pulled out my cotton swabs and canned air to clean the keyboard of my laptop.

I was so engrossed I didn't hear Pen let herself in.

"I take it back," she said from right behind me, making me jump and squawk like a frightened bird. "If you've resorted to buffing your keyboard, you definitely need to get laid."

"Funny, smartass," I replied.

While I cracked open the wine, Pen leaned against the back of the couch. She was perfectly put together like it was another workday. Better than that. She looked like she was trying to make someone jealous. When I took a day off, I usually didn't shower and I definitely didn't get out of my pajamas.

She wore her brown hair short and choppy in one of those styles that looked like she'd just rolled out of bed. It suited her round face and big green eyes. She had a baby face, looking a decade younger than her thirty-five, and her skin was soft as a toddler's. Not for the first time I bemoaned my crow's feet, a fate she'd never share. I was only two years older, but it looked like ten which was distinctly unfair. I couldn't fault her for her lean form, however. Her gym had an indoor pool and she swam an hour a day, five days a week, year-round.

It seemed like one of those nights, so I brought the bottle with me to the living room. No sense in running back and forth when we were sure to empty it soon. We dropped into our normal spots on the couch and I wiggled back into my biggest throw pillow.

With a skeptical eye, Pen inspected her glass. She swirled the wine and gave it a sniff. "Is this the good stuff?"

I turned the bottle to show her the simple white label bearing the name of our favorite local winery. "Early Mountain Vineyards. Only the best for my Pen."

She took a sip and sighed. "You're buttering me up and it's working."

"You deserve it."

"More butter," she laughed her reply.

I shrugged and sipped my wine. If only she knew how long I'd been planning this. Worrying about it. Losing sleep over the whole idea.

"How long's this dry spell lasted anyway?" Pen asked, pulling her knees up to her chest. She'd already half-emptied her glass and I hurried to catch up.

"Since Alex left," I said. "Honestly? Since a while before Alex left. Things were bad with them for a long time."

Talking to Pen about my ex wasn't easy. She didn't like them at all, particularly after they lost interest in our relationship and pulled away. Pen blamed Alex for falling out of love first, but that wasn't their fault. The way they'd picked fights that left me crying on the bathroom floor certainly was, and it was that which Pen would never forgive.

She scowled as usual and avoided even using their name. "They would have me swearing off relationships, too." She ended with a muttered, "Asshole."

"Well, I'm ready to put it behind me," I said, injecting as much positive energy as I could into the words. "Where do I start?"

Pen laughed and leaned over to retrieve the wine bottle. "Bars. Coffee shops. I hear you can meet people in the produce aisle at the grocery store."

"I've tried all that." I left out the details of squeezing tomatoes for forty-five minutes, waiting for someone to hit on me. No one had, but a bag boy had followed me around the rest of the store, looking suspicious. "I've been waiting for something else to come along but nothing has. Please help me with these websites, Pen. I don't know what I'm doing."

"Okay. Okay," she said, pulling my laptop toward her. "I'll help."

Relief flooded me so much I actually giggled and threw my arms around her neck. Her cry of disgust at the girly gesture was the cherry on top.

"Okay. I pulled up all the sites I could think of. Should I join them all? Increase my chances?"

"Definitely not," she said, tapping my password into the lock screen. She clicked browser windows shut as she spoke. "If you're on too many sites, you look like a slut. Or desperate. No Tinder. No one ever fell in love by swiping right."

"What does that mean?"

"Don't worry about it. I'll explain the swiping when we download the app."

"But you said…"

"No OkCupid. That's for straight people to cheat on their spouses."

I felt like I should be taking notes.

"You shouldn't be using any of these." Her fingers flew across the keyboard and I scooted closer to look over her shoulder. "You need to be on Swingle."

"Why? Are you on Swingle?"

"Not anymore."

"Then why should I use it?"

"I don't use it because it's where people go to look for a girlfriend, not a hookup."

The bottle was empty, so I struggled to my feet and grabbed the other. Maybe I should've bought three. "And you're always just looking for a hookup."

"Hey now," she said. "There is an art to casual dating. You're right, though. I don't want a girlfriend, which is why I stay away from Swingle."

"What if I'm not necessarily looking for a *girl*friend?"

Keys clicked and Pen swung the screen toward me. "No worries. You can choose your sexual orientation here. Hetero, homo, bi, or pansexual."

"Wow! They actually have an option for pansexual? There's never an option for me." But there it was, at the bottom of the list but definitely present. "That's progressive."

Pen selected pansexual and clicked next. "I thought you'd like that. Wait 'til you get to all the options for genders."

There were more than twenty options, including Kinner and Two Spirit along with all the terms I knew for cis, trans, and nonbinary people and a few I didn't. I picked cis woman for myself. Pen barely made fun of me for having to select every gender option when we got to the "people I'm interested in" section. My head was buzzing with the choices and the wine wasn't helping, so I slowed down. The progress bar showed we were only on page four of forty-two. I'd never make it if I kept up this pace.

The problem was, the more pages we went through, the more nerves were getting the better of me. I couldn't clean, so I reached for the next best thing. Sitting next to my phone on the coffee table was my *Goonies* floaty pen. I snatched it up, tilting it from side to side so the little fake doubloons tumbled around in their liquid chamber. The longer I watched the pirate ship and treasure moving around inside, the less I worried that this whole thing was a huge mistake. After a minute, I caught Pen's side eye and half-smile.

"What?" I asked.

She stopped typing and shook her head at me. "I can't believe you still have that thing."

"This is my favorite pen."

"I got it for you as a joke."

"Well, joke's on you. I love it."

"*The Goonies* isn't even that great a movie."

Now she'd gone too far. I pointed the pen into Pen's face, the water bubbling up at my aggressive movement. "Don't make me kick you out of my house, Penelope Chase. *The Goonies* is a classic and I won't hear anything against it. Plus, you love action films!"

"*The Goonies* is not an action film," she said, turning back to the screen.

"Um, excuse me." Going over our old argument was almost enough to make me forget about the terrifying new step in my dating life. "Car chases, gunshots, explosions. What more do you need for an action film?"

"In the '80s? Tits."

I rolled my eyes and spun my pen between my fingers. "You're such a horndog."

"A horndog who bought you a cool pen."

"Like five years ago."

"You're still playing with it, aren't you?" She turned her full smile on me and said, "And you aren't freaking out anymore 'cause I made you roll your eyes."

"You make me roll my eyes literally every day," I replied. She was right, though. My hands weren't shaking anymore.

We got through all the basics pretty quickly—name, date of birth, pronouns, and location. Penelope did all the typing while I sat back wavering between excited and terrified. Then came the more difficult questions.

Pen read aloud from the screen, "I'm open to non-monogamy. Yes or no?"

"No."

"That was quick. Not even willing to entertain the idea?"

"Nope. I know you're into that and I'm glad it works for you, but it's not for me."

"Not judging you, Kieran. Just checking in."

She didn't push and I was glad. She knew enough of my history to let it go, even if she didn't agree with my old-fashioned dating habits.

"Okay, let's move on to profile pictures!" Pen rubbed her hands together in anticipation, the ring splints she wore for typing clicking against each other. It was a new set, the metal flashing brightly in the warm light. They wrapped around her knuckles so tightly they nearly disappeared into her pale flesh, accentuating the delicacy of her hands. "What've you got?"

"Um…"

"Come on, you've got pictures of yourself." She blinked at my silence. "Don't you?"

I shrugged, trying to be cavalier about it. I didn't like my face. It was too long and too severe. My shockingly straight nose had a weird bulb on the end and it dominated every photograph. My smile was even worse—so wide it squeezed my eyes shut. My skin color was somewhere between too bronze for most foundations and too pale for darker shades. Penelope made fun of my resting bitch face, but neutral was the only look that worked for me. At least I had plump lips, but my mouth was too big for my jaw.

"I have my headshot from work," I said, snatching up my phone and scrolling through the albums. It was mostly random screenshots from on-line searches I'd forgotten about and pics of my favorite art from museum trips, but I'd grabbed the decent headshot off the company website. "I look pretty good in this one."

Pen took the phone and squinted at the screen. "Not bad. You're a little serious, but we can work with it."

HomeScape Settlement Services, the real estate title company where I worked, had hired a professional photographer two years ago. I'd worn my favorite suit that day, the one that fit just right everywhere, and I'd taken a lot of care with my makeup. Alex and I had broken up a few weeks earlier and I'd cut my hair for a fresh look. I'd grown it out since—the short curls thing never looked as good on me as I thought it would, but it wasn't too far off how I looked now.

Pen uploaded the headshot then examined it closely, deciding the best way to crop it for the website's limited dimensions. "Good call on this one. You look great in that suit and super professional. It'll keep the losers away."

I was giddy until she asked for more photos. I offered the other shots from the same day, even one where I was smiling more, but Pen said no.

"Not more headshots. Something different. Don't you have any selfies?"

She scrolled through my photo file. I could tell by the look on her face that she wasn't impressed. "I don't like selfies. They're weird. I always look terrible. I don't know how to do it right."

Pen tossed aside my phone and fished her own from her pocket. "No problem. We'll get some thirst traps of you later. In the meantime…Here. We'll use this one."

I didn't have a chance to ask what a "thirst trap" was because she showed me the picture on her phone.

"Pen," I breathed. "This is…actually good. Where did you take this?"

She grabbed the phone back and started typing into it. A moment later, my laptop dinged with an incoming email. "The Indigo Girls concert last summer at Wolftrap. I showed it to you. You don't remember?"

I didn't and I was sure that I would remember seeing a rare good picture of myself. Not good. It might be the best picture of me I'd ever seen. I swung the laptop screen around to look at it on a bigger screen. I was walking away from the camera in the warm light of sunset. I was looking back over my shoulder, my curls, slightly longer than in the headshot, flew out beside me like a cape, the setting sun picking up the copper tones in my normally dull brown hair.

It wasn't only my hair that looked good. My body was twisted, which hid the few extra pounds I've been meaning to take care of for the last fifteen years or so. I almost looked skinny. And my clothes flattered my rounded shoulders and bony hips. The image cut off below my butt, so my short legs and wide feet were out of the frame. Most surprising, however, was my smile. It was big and natural, no doubt laughing at whatever ridiculous thing Pen had said to make me turn around, but my eyes weren't squinty and my mouth wasn't crooked. I looked like a model for some miracle drug, cured of depression and out living their best life.

"Now it's time for the juicy stuff," Pen said, settling into the couch with my laptop on her knees. "Introduce yourself. How would your best friend describe you? Hmm…how would I describe you?"

She took too long thinking about it, so I blurted out over the rim of my wineglass, "Come on, how would you?"

"Calm down," she drawled. "I'm trying to come up with a few different ways to say 'hot.' How about 'Sexy single with killer jugs'?"

"Why are we even friends?"

Pen laughed and I couldn't help but join in. She was ridiculous, but she was always on my side. "Yeah, okay. Maybe something else."

She typed for a minute and then clicked away without reading what she'd written. "Hey! What'd you say?"

"Don't worry. I didn't talk about your boobs."

"What did you say?"

But she'd already moved on to the next question, "Which describes you better: happy-go-lucky or impassioned?"

"Can I pick neither?"

"Nope. Have to pick one. I'm going with impassioned."

"Why? I'm not impassioned."

"Yesterday you lectured me for our entire lunch break about the importance of a comingled materials recycling program for the office because asking people who brush off recycling to separate their paper, plastic, and aluminum is a losing battle."

I had done that. I even used most of those words. Maybe I was impassioned.

"See? I know you better than you know yourself. That's why I'm writing your profile for you. Refill my glass so I can get to work."

CHAPTER TWO

I would've been fine if I'd gotten to the intersection before the light turned red. Preferably twenty minutes before, but it was definitely the red light's fault that I'd be late to work. Traffic in Woodbridge was the worst in Northern Virginia, and the traffic in Northern Virginia was the worst in the country. My sister sent me an article all the way from Brussels about how DC metro traffic beat out both New York City and Los Angeles as the most congested. It listed traffic as the largest factor in the overall unhappiness of the population. It wasn't a surprise to me, considering I sat in it every day. She kindly explained that traffic was the reason I was single and sad at thirty-seven years old. Moving to Brussels was the best thing my sister ever did for me.

I left skid marks in the parking lot as I whipped into my spot. There was a similar pair behind Penelope's fire-engine red SUV, but it was indicative of how late I was that Pen beat me into work. Her company's office was next door to mine in the world's most nondescript strip mall. Three Keys Real Estate had the office space on the end of the row, so they had more natural light. Penelope, being their most successful Realtor, had three windows in her office alone. My company's office, connected by a dimly lit hall and our shared clientele to Three Keys, was far less glamorous. My boss, Randy Clune, started HomeScape Settlement Services when he was young and hopeful. That had been a long time ago. He made a decent living, to be sure, but in comparison, Three Keys was the popular jock to our dorky high school band member.

I was so late that I didn't have to use my keycard to get into the building. I slipped past Randy's office without being noticed and hurried into my own. When I tossed my purse on the desk, the floppy top opened and my cell phone skidded across the worn wooden surface. I caught it right before it slipped off the edge.

"Nice save," came a baritone voice from the door. I should've known I wouldn't be able to slip in undetected.

I turned my best smile on Arthur, refusing even in my head to call him "Arty the Party" as he'd recently asked us to do. I may have issues, but at least I wasn't sufficiently into my midlife crisis to match Arthur. He looked a little better today than usual. His face, normally scruffy enough to mistake him for a disreputable sailor, was clean-shaven, though there wasn't much that could be done about the uneven tan lines around his watery eyes. His suit wasn't too wrinkled and his silver hair, thinning everywhere, particularly in a softball-sized coin at the back, was neatly combed. His wife must've dressed him this morning. Or maybe one of his two teenaged daughters who lived in mortal fear of his mismatched socks ruining their reputations.

"Morning, Art. How's Susie?"

"Gorgeous and perfect in every way." His wife was an executive for a nonprofit in the city and she was, I had to admit, gorgeous. Way out of his league. He could be sweet, but I'd never understand how a relatively plain fifty-year-old man with absolutely no panache and a challenging sense of humor could hold on to a bombshell ten years his junior. "You're late. I'm pretty sure my uncle didn't notice because he wouldn't notice an alien invasion if it happened in his front yard, but it's not like you."

Beautiful wife, new BMW in his driveway and the boss's nephew. Arthur was everything I usually hate in men, but he was actually a nice guy. If Randy had spotted me coming in late, I'm sure Arthur would've played interference until Randy forgot.

"I'm not late," I said, hiding my phone behind my back as it rattled with yet another notification. "I have five minutes until the staff meeting."

"It's a good thing," Art replied, turning to leave. "You might be able to do something about those bags under your eyes."

The minute he left, I shut the door and leaned heavily against it. It wasn't just the bags. My eyes were bloodshot. I looked like hell and it was all Penelope's fault. After she'd finished writing my profile we'd sat around chatting while she sobered up enough to drive. She could tell I was still nervous, so she entertained me with stories of her coworkers until I started giggling. Once I start laughing with Pen, it's tough to stop and she didn't leave until after midnight. When my alarm went off this morning, it was the victim of some intense profanity.

My phone buzzed with another alert. I put the screen close to my stinging eyes.

Someone's into you! Check your Swingle app for the details of your new admirer!

The notification was stacked on top of at least five others. It had been like this all morning. I'd been in too much of a hurry to check them before leaving the house, but I had a few minutes until the meeting. I listened at the door for Randy's heavy footsteps on their way to the conference room. There was only silence.

With a nervous excitement I hadn't felt in years, I logged in to the Swingle app. The little red heart over the mailbox icon had the number ten inside. Not bad for a few hours of a live profile. The first message I clicked on was from MarkH429, but there must have been something wrong with his profile. The contents of the message were greyed out and all that came up on my screen was a form letter from Swingle. That was okay. If he liked me, he'd try again. The fifth time I got the same message, I started to worry it was my profile that was messed up. I'd paid the nineteen-dollar monthly fee, but maybe this was an attempt to get more money from me?

Before I could check into the problem, the telltale shuffle of Randy's footsteps neared my door. I shoved the phone into my pocket and rushed out of my office, making it to the staff meeting just behind my boss.

CHAPTER THREE

Penelope and I had a long-standing tradition of meeting for lunch on Wednesdays at Layla's Lebanese Restaurant. Pen swore they had the fluffiest hummus in the United States, but I went for their trademarked Garlic Whip. Somewhere between the consistency of mayonnaise and whipped cream but with the soft bite of raw garlic, the spread was a delight to put on anything. I made the mistake once of asking what was in it and the owner ranted at me in Lebanese for a solid five minutes, assuming I was some kind of culinary spy sent to steal his prized recipe. Penelope said if I got us banned, she'd never speak to me again and I've been silently polite to all the employees since that day. The owner still glared at me from the kitchen every time I came to lunch. Every Wednesday for three years. He really knew how to hold a grudge.

Pen was already at our corner table, flirting with Rebecca, our usual waitress. Rebecca gave one last good-natured laugh before leaving to get my unsweet tea. Pen's sparkling water with lime was already sweating on the table.

"Is there a single woman alive you don't flirt with?" I asked, sliding onto the bench seat.

Leaning forward in her chair, her eyes sparkling, Pen crooned, "I never flirt with you."

"You've flirted with me." I decided to give her a taste of her own medicine and leaned in close, drawing a fingernail across her wrist and down her pointer finger. Her fingers were all wrapped in the fine filigree of her silver ring splints. The delicate bands, thinner than a normal ring, wrapped above and below her knuckle to prevent her fingers hyperextending when she typed. I tapped one and said, "You're doing it right now."

"I flirt with you for the same reason I flirt with Rebecca."

"Because she knows we're immune to her charms," Rebecca said, returning with my drink.

"If that's true," Pen said, turning her dazzling smile on Rebecca. "Then why are you so...*extra* attentive to us?"

Rebecca bent over, her palm flat on the table so close to Pen's chest that a deep breath would have her rubbing against Pen's boobs. "Don't be flattered. I like you for the big tip you're gonna leave me."

"Just the tip?" Pen drawled, enunciating each word with teeth and tongue.

Rebecca threw her head back and barked out a laugh. The movement exposed a lot of skin around the low scoop neck of her T-shirt. I'll admit I stared, but just for a minute. I looked away quickly, feeling like a perv for checking out the waitress. Pen's gaze lingered much longer than mine.

"Just the tip, sweetie."

She patted Pen's shoulder as she walked away, but I noticed how her fingertips lingered. She also put a little extra sway in her hips as she crossed to the kitchen. Pen didn't turn to watch her go, but I might have. Just a little bit. I mean it had been a long time since I'd been with anyone.

A really long time.

I expected Pen to tease me for the lingering gaze, but she was busy with her phone. Her smile was still in place, her teeth on full display, but the wolfish glint had gone. She slid her thumb across the screen, preferring the dragging method of texting to the repeated taps that weren't good for her joints. Somehow she always managed perfect messages without typos. Every time I'd tried it came out as alphabet soup. Her grin only widened as she finished her message and dropped the phone onto the table.

"Why are you in such a good mood?" I asked. She looked like a kid with her first kitten.

"You know that gorgeous row house in Georgetown I've been talking about? The rich divorcee who's financially gutting her husband?"

"Of course." I waited, but she just grinned at me with that little-kid smile of hers, so I knew. "You got it!"

"I got it!"

If Penelope had been the type to scream with joy and wave her hands in the air, this would've been the time to do it. She'd been after the house for months, ever since she heard the owners would be listing it soon. The historic brick row house in the old-money section of DC was the sort of listing that could earn Pen a quarter-million-dollar commission. A career-changing listing. The fact that she landed it was amazing, considering those listings usually went to better established firms, but she'd worked her ass off to win it.

"Five bed, six bath, five thousand square feet." She was almost singing. She talked about houses how other people talked about lovers. "Built in 1800. Can you believe it, Kieran? Built before the White House but it has heated floors and a Wi-Fi-linked hot tub."

"Why would you want your hot tub linked to your Wi-Fi?"

I never found out because Rebecca came back with my falafel platter and Pen's fattoush. With a fork full of lettuce and spiced pita hanging forgotten in the air, Pen went back to fawning over her new project. "It's on 28th Street. Really great location."

I'd done a title search for a nearby property last year. Twenty-eighth put it in Georgetown's East Village, the neighborhood with the grandest homes, and it butted up against Rock Creek Park. My property had been smaller and had still sold for over two million. Pen's could easily go for two or three times that.

"Anyway, who cares about houses," Pen said, a sly smile making her cheeks glow. "Have you gotten laid yet?"

"Pen!" I looked around and, sure enough, Rebecca was wandering closer to us, studiously nonchalant. "My profile's only been up since midnight. I'm not that good."

"You're not that bad either." She winked at me and I couldn't help laughing into my falafel.

"I wanted to ask you something actually." I pulled my phone out with one hand while I scraped the last of my Garlic Whip out of the cup with my other. Rebecca put another at my elbow and I snatched it up greedily. Let her eavesdrop as long as the Garlic Whip kept coming.

"What's that?" Rebecca asked, peering over at my glowing phone. "Swingle? Kieran are you dating?"

"I...uh..."

I stared at the Garlic Whip like the blob of yumminess had asked me an important question. Pen filled in the awkward blanks of my stammering non-answer. "Kieran's jumping back into the dating pool."

"Oooh. Do tell. How's it working out?"

Again, Pen answered Rebecca's question, "She joined last night. It's a new thing for her. All her previous relationships started the old-fashioned way."

"Sex in the backseat of a Camaro?"

"Oh god," I mumbled to the Garlic Whip. My face was so hot the stuff should be boiling.

"In person," Pen clarified. She didn't laugh, which was sweet and a little unexpected. "She hasn't used any of the apps before."

"Oh sweetie," Rebecca said, dropping her tray on an empty table and looking at me like I'd announced that I had one week to live. "Those apps are trash. All the people on them are trash."

"Rebecca!" Pen gave her a wide-eyed, pleading look.

"What? They are. Well, the men are. You might find some decent women on there, but if they're decent why do they have to descend to using a dating app?" She patted me on the shoulder far less provocatively than she'd done with Pen earlier. "No offense, darling."

"None taken," I replied automatically. Then I mentally kicked myself. Why had I said that? I was definitely offended.

"It's all married men looking to hook up. You be careful on those apps. No one tells the truth anymore."

"I'm keeping an eye out for her," Pen jumped in. She gave me one of those soothing looks she used when her clients had to admit they didn't have the money for the houses they wanted to view. "She'll be fine. She isn't only looking for men."

"Good for you," Rebecca said, grabbing her tray. "But try going out, too. You're much more likely to find someone good in the real world."

Sure, like I hadn't already tried that. She scampered off and Pen scowled after her. For a minute I thought she might follow Rebecca to scold her. I wouldn't have minded. I could've used the time alone to gather my dignity. I knew she wouldn't budge though. Pen never let me wallow alone. She said it was the worst thing best friends could do to each other. It was pretty sweet of her. I had a tendency to wallow.

"What was your question?"

I shook off Rebecca's words and pointed at the phone. "How do I use this thing?"

"You hold it to your ear and talk."

"You know what? I'm gonna go ask Rebecca how to use this app. She's way nicer."

I pretended to stand up, but Pen popped over onto the bench beside me before I could move. Taking the phone from my hand, she tapped on the Swingle app. "Your home screen will show you potential matches nearby."

I leaned over her shoulder as the loading screen faded away, dissolving into a pretty androgynous face with an equally androgynous name beneath it. Pen scrolled up casually and half dozen faces flashed by in a smear of color. "Wait a minute. Slow down."

"It's easier if you tweak the interface a little. Hang on." Her tongue poked between her lips as she tapped her thumb onto the gear icon at the bottom of the page.

While she messed around in my settings, I asked, "I thought you said you didn't use Swingle. How do you know how to change the settings?"

"I said I don't use Swingle *anymore*. Some uptight lesbians got mad I was doing the casual thing and reported me. It was easier to just bail rather than deal with all the haters."

I opened my mouth to ask more about what sounded like a fun story, but she handed my phone back. I had to admit, it was a lot easier to see the profile pictures now. Rather than a list of thumbnail photos, I saw just one person at a time.

"Swipe right if you like them, left if you don't. It's as easy as that."

She'd grabbed her own phone, but I took her arm before she could get distracted. "Wait. What does that mean? Like swipe *to* the right or swipe *from* the right?"

"What? How are you so bad at technology?"

"It's not clear!"

Rebecca shot us a curious look and the kitchen door swayed ominously. Pen scooted closer. "Okay. Don't get us kicked out." She placed my finger on the center of the screen, which had locked in the time we were chatting. "Now watch me."

It felt so ridiculous, sitting here in the corner of a bustling restaurant, Pen holding my finger against my phone screen. I looked over at her and grinned, barely controlling my giggle. I could tell from the twitch of her lips that she was holding back laughter as well.

Pen glanced up at me and rolled her eyes, jerking her chin toward our joined hands. "No, I mean watch what I'm doing." I gave an exaggerated sigh and turned back to the blank screen. "If you see someone you like…"

"Wait a minute," I said, nudging her with my elbow. "Now you're looking at me. I thought you said to look at the phone?"

"Kieran," she growled. When I giggled she took a deep, long-suffering breath. I loved making her do that. "Okay. I'm looking at the phone, too. So imagine you see someone you like on the screen."

"That's gonna be hard," I said, stretching my neck to look around our fingers. "All I see is my reflection."

Pen twisted the phone, angling it so it showed a reflection of her profile. She jutted out her chin and raised a provocative eyebrow. "Better?"

I finally released my laugh and nudged her again. "Perfect."

"You're such a tease." She scooted closer and adjusted her grip on my hand. "Okay. You see someone you like on the screen. You swipe your finger from the center of the screen *to the* right. Like this."

Her movement was as exaggerated as her speech, guiding my finger slowly across the screen until it slid off the right side. It was condescending, but also helpful, so I didn't give her too hard a time.

"All the way off the screen like that? Or should I stop at the edge?"

"Oh no. All the way off." She scrunched her eyebrows together and said in a serious tone, "The further you swipe right, the sooner they respond."

"You're a jerk."

"I'm also hot. That's how I make the jerk part work."

"You think so, huh?"

"I know so." She put my finger back on the center of the screen. "So now imagine you see someone you don't like."

"I can't." I tapped her reflection. "You're still there."

Pen shook her head and her mouth lifted in a half smile. She tilted the phone until it showed a reflection of the ceiling tiles. "There. All that blank whiteness. It's like Arty the Party's forehead. Picture him."

"I like Arthur."

"Then ask him out."

"Not like that. He's, like, your dad's age."

"Exactly. Someone you'd never date." She slid my finger the opposite way, forcing it off the left side of the screen. "Then you swipe your finger *to the* left. Get it?"

"Yeah, that makes sense."

Pen released my hand and leaned back into the booth, spreading her arms out over the top. It had been nice to have her hold my hand like that, and I almost asked her to show me again, just to annoy her, when my phone buzzed. It was the same notification I'd been getting all morning, but when I opened the app again, I saw another one of those weird messages.

"I have another question about Swingle."

Pen had let her head roll onto the padded back rest and she murmured, "Okay. Shoot."

"Is there something wrong with my app? Look at all these error messages."

I didn't even finish the sentence before she doubled over laughing.

"What?"

Pen hooted so loud the owner stuck his head out of the kitchen to glare at us.

"Why is that funny?"

"Maybe Rebecca wasn't entirely wrong."

"What do you mean?"

"Didn't you read any of the Swingle guidelines?"

"What guidelines?"

"The ones regulating the messages users can send to each other."

I shrugged as Rebecca collected our empty plates, leaving the checks behind.

"These are all blocked messages from others who didn't read the guidelines." When I didn't respond, she rolled her eyes. "Unsolicited dick pics, Kieran."

"Ew! What? I like men and I still don't want to see that! Why would ten guys," My phone buzzed with another, familiar message. "Eleven guys send me that?"

"Don't ask me. I don't get down with that nonsense." She took my phone back and tapped around. "You can turn off the blocked message notifications so they go straight to trash. There. Now you'll never know how many gross guys are out there."

"Why don't they do that automatically?" I asked, grabbing my purse and following her out into the sweltering afternoon.

"So you know how many gross guys are out there, duh." She leaned against her car but jumped back again as the hot metal scalded her skin. "You sure you're up for going back to that?"

I was pretty sure I wanted to date a woman right now, but I wasn't going to give her the satisfaction of knowing that. "It's not every man's fault that Nick cheated on me."

It wasn't. I knew it wasn't, but that didn't mean my heart believed it.

"No," Pen replied in a hard voice. "That was all his fault."

The drive back to the office through Woodbridge's stop-and-go traffic was deflating. It gave me that much longer to think. And to cry. It wasn't only what Rebecca had said. The mention of Nick after lunch and Alex the night before reminded me of my terrifically bad romantic history. I was thirty-seven years old and I had been divorced once and recently dumped by someone I'd lived with for five years. I'd only ever had sex with two people. No wonder all I was getting was cheap solicitation from disgusting guys. What did I have to offer in a relationship anyway?

What with the worse-than-usual traffic and the diminishing romantic prospects, I wasn't in the best mood when I pulled into the lot to start the second half of my workday. I sat in my car for a few minutes, trying to pump myself up with the two good things I had going for me. First, I hadn't cried enough to ruin my makeup. More importantly, Pen had gone straight from lunch to show a client a rental unit, so she wasn't here to see me sad.

I had known it would be like this. Trying to date at my age wasn't easy. Trying to use a dating app wasn't easy. I'd heard the horror stories of being ghosted or never finding anyone after years of trying. Why was I putting myself through this?

I picked up my phone to delete the app but saw that I had a missed text message. I must've been crying more loudly than I thought. It was from Penelope and the moment I read it, I knew I wouldn't be deleting the app.

Don't get discouraged—the right person will find you. You had a message from a cute redhead in there. Maybe give her a shot? xxx

CHAPTER FOUR

She wasn't a cute redhead. She was a drop-dead gorgeous, make-you-drool-onto-your-keyboard bombshell. Her pic was a full-body shot in a bikini she filled out indecently well, so I waited to look at her profile until I was home alone.

With the curtains drawn.

It wasn't just the pics that got my motor running. Her message was flirty and funny at the same time. After cooking dinner and washing up, I settled into the couch and read the message again.

I'm sure you've heard this a dozen times today, but you look amazing in that suit. So amazing I'll let you buy me dinner.

I guess the headshot was a good decision for my profile pic after all. I'd have to admit that to Pen eventually. If I didn't give her the chance to gloat over her knowledge of women at least once a month she got surly. Still, the redhead's compliments and the joke about buying her dinner were enough to make me look deeper.

I hadn't been poking around her interests for more than a minute or so when she sent a chat request. Considering that her sun-kissed body was filling my tablet screen and making my palms sweat, I leapt at the chance to chat with her. Between messages, I checked out the dozen photos on her page. There was only one picture where her midriff wasn't visible. That one showed her painted into a little black dress that left nothing more to the imagination than her bikini did. Not that I was complaining. She had a killer body.

Still, there wasn't much there. Our chat was surface to say the least. There was a lot of flirting from her end and a lot of awkward attempts to keep my cool from my end. Her profile said she wanted a long-term relationship, but she wasn't building one with this chat. She hadn't asked me any questions beyond the superficial. I tried to listen to the alarm bells going off in my head, but they were drowned out by a ticking clock counting down the long years of my celibacy.

So what if she was interested in me for my body? I was really interested in hers. Also I didn't know any of the clothing designers she gushed about in her interests list. I kept trying to find something to build a relationship on, but there would be time for that.

My phone rang while Redhead was describing her perfect trip to Paris. That was a little past first date material, so I felt fine splitting my focus with Pen's call. There was a lot of crowd noise and the heavy thump of a bass line in the background. It was Wednesday, Pen's hookup night, and she was obviously already on the prowl.

"Hey sexy," Pen shouted into the phone. "You message the redhead yet?"

"As a matter of fact, I'm chatting with her now. And her name is…" I had to look it up. "Carla."

"It only took you five minutes to find her name. I can see you've formed a strong connection."

"Screw you, Pen."

"Nah," she said with a confident sigh. "I'll let one of these lovely ladies swilling top-shelf vodka take care of that for me."

Carla had stopped her monologue about her favorite hotels in Paris and asked when we could meet up. I hedged a little in my response, and while I was typing I said to Pen, "Try not to break any hearts tonight."

There was the clink of glasses from her end of the line and I heard her order a martini. Pen always drank martinis when she was after the more sophisticated, professional lesbian. She used to prefer younger women, but said she got tired of the twentysomethings. They were apparently too loud and enthusiastic. Now she usually went for the slightly older women she called "cougar adjacent."

"You know I'm always very clear with my intentions."

"Have you practiced your line?"

"It isn't a line, it's a disclaimer." She sipped her drink noisily, knowing how much it annoyed me when people ate or drank while on the phone. "By the time I try to warn them off they're already on the hook."

"Fine, have you practiced your disclaimer?"

Pen took on a faux-serious tone, like an overeager actor in a dramatic scene. "I'm not going to fall in love with you. I'm not going to call you tomorrow. I probably won't remember your name. I'm not saying this to hurt you, I'm saying it to make my intentions clear. I can give you the night of your life, but I can't give you anything more than that. If that doesn't work for you, let's stop this now with no one hurt."

Every time I heard her say it, I put myself in the shoes of the listener. I could see the intensity in those emerald-green eyes. The heat and the sorrow there. I could feel the mingled sting and thrill the speech would evoke. Pen was like a jaguar, a beautiful hunter whose prey came willingly. As far as I knew, no one had any objections to what she had to offer. It wasn't my thing, but, if they were looking for no strings attached, they hit the jackpot with Pen.

"You're such a romantic." My tablet pinged with Carla repeating her request for a date. I chewed on my bottom lip, told myself not to be so nervous, and told her I'd love to. "Have fun. Can't wait to hear about your conquest at work tomorrow."

"Not at work. I'm doing showings tomorrow. Drinks after?"

Carla's next message was full of heart-eye emojis. I couldn't help but beam. "I might have a date tomorrow night."

I expected a gasp of surprise, but I guess Pen wasn't as shocked as I was that I could get a date with this ridiculously beautiful woman. "Even better. Meet me for drinks after and tell me all about it."

"You're assuming I won't go home with her."

"Please! You aren't a first-date lay. That's why I respect you so much."

Carla suggested dinner rather than the coffee or drinks options I'd thrown out.

I told you I'd let you take me to dinner, remember? The Source. Seven o'clock. Make us a reservation.

Pen and I said our goodbyes more quickly than usual. Someone was winking at her from the other side of the bar and Carla's suggestion left me choking for air. While The Source wasn't the most expensive restaurant in Washington DC by far, it was well outside my price range, especially for a first date. Divorce is an expensive process and I'd only managed to keep my house by moving Alex in to help with the bills. Once they were gone it was a struggle to keep up. I was only recently getting back on my feet. I made a decent living, but not The-Source-for-a-first-date decent.

I almost made up some excuse to cancel, but there was her profile picture staring at me with its suggestive grin and ample cleavage. It wasn't like I was broke. I could afford a meal at a fancy restaurant for a date with that woman. I wasn't unattractive exactly, but I'd never dated anyone who was so obviously out of my league. I could live the fantasy for one night and then steer her toward other options in the future. This was probably an attempt to make good on her opening line. And she seemed to like me. We'd been chatting for over an hour.

I took a deep, calming breath and spoke aloud as I typed, "Sounds perfect. Can't wait to see you there."

CHAPTER FIVE

The Source was owned by Wolfgang Puck and had all the glitz and glamour that came with a celebrity chef. It was located inside the Newseum, a sprawling, modern structure of concrete and glass dedicated to the freedom of the press and the First Amendment. I'd been to the museum once with Pen to see *Rise Up*, an exhibit on the media coverage of the LGBTQ-rights movement. We'd had a drink in The Source's ultra-trendy bar but hadn't stayed to eat. I'd been impressed by the restaurant. Or perhaps intimidated was a better word.

That first visit had been on a cold Sunday afternoon and tourists dominated the clientele. This time couldn't have been more different. I strolled through crowds of businessmen in expensive suits, their ties loosened despite the early hour. They laughed in that throaty, carefree way that only rich men can and I tried my best to act like I fit in. I'd changed from my business suit to a low-slung dress in a rich purple that made my grey eyes glow almost blue. I knew my clothes looked the part, but my nerves were totally showing.

Traffic into DC can be difficult to judge, so I'd taken my dress to work and changed in the back-hall bathroom. I'd waited until everyone else had left so I wouldn't catch any flak from Art. Only Penelope knew about my date and I'd sworn her to secrecy. If it went terribly, no one else needed to know. If it went well, no one else needed to know that either. The upshot to staying at work rather than taking the time to go home, was that I was really early to the restaurant.

I rounded the corner from Sixth Street to C Street NW right at six thirty. I liked to be early, but a half hour was a little excessive. I pushed through the heavy glass door and glanced over at the bar. I could chip away at the time by sipping a glass of wine and fiddling with my phone, but I didn't want to be tipsy when Carla arrived.

"Welcome," the bubbly host said. "Do you have a reservation?"

"I do," I replied, faking the confidence I wished I felt. "But I'm pretty early."

"That's not a problem. What's the name?"

"Kieran Hall. Table for two."

"Good evening, Ms. Hall. It's a pleasure to have you dine with us tonight." He seemed really nice, even when he was looking at his computer screen rather than me. "Oh. It looks like your other party has already arrived. Would you like to join them?"

Panic filled my chest. What was she doing here already? I checked the clock over his shoulder and it definitely said six thirty. Was I late? Were we supposed to be here at six, not seven? Was Carla sitting at the table, thinking I'd stood her up? She was probably starving and embarrassed. I pulled up our last conversation as I jogged up the floating metal staircase behind the host. I'd order the first thing I saw on the menu so we didn't have to wait too long.

The main dining room was on the second floor, completely open with the entire exterior wall glass, looking out on the summer sun, just beginning to lower in the sky. The surrounding buildings reflected the sun back at me, throwing sparkling shadows into my vision. Carla sat at a table at the far end near the kitchen. To my immense relief, she didn't look angry at all. In fact, she was smiling and laughing with the server, who had just brought her a plate of food.

My relief changed to confusion in a heartbeat. As we got closer I could see that she also had a full glass of wine, with a bottle sitting near her. Apparently she hadn't waited to order until I arrived. I scrolled through the chat as we walked and saw that yes, we had agreed on seven o'clock. It had, in fact, been her suggestion.

"Kieran!" She chirped as the host deposited me at the table. She didn't stand, but held out her hand, knuckles up, to me. "You're just as stunning in person as your profile."

I wasn't exactly the type to kiss the back of a woman's hand, so I took her fingers in mine for a moment. I held on longer than I had intended. Her skin was like silk and the pale white of heavy cream. She slid her fingertips across my palm, locking me with those doe eyes.

"I'm sorry," I said, the waiter pushing in my chair as I sat. "I didn't realize I was late."

"Nope," she said, popping a dumpling into her mouth. "You're early."

I bit my tongue to keep my annoyance from showing. If I was early, why was she already eating? I wouldn't necessarily call myself old-fashioned, but I did expect my date to wait for me before starting dinner. The waiter asked me what I'd like to start with, noting that my date had the lobster and golden beet dumplings. Not only had she already ordered, but she'd selected the most expensive appetizer on the menu. I chose the first thing I saw and he poured me a glass of wine from the bottle at Carla's elbow. I didn't miss the sour look she threw at him for pouring without asking her. I was still too nervous to start drinking, so I ignored it in favor of water.

Soon enough we fell into normal first date conversation sprinkled liberally, from her end, with flirting. It actually seemed to be going well. The edge of annoyance at her rudeness melted away in the glow of her killer smile. My excellent Taiwanese beef noodle soup helped, as did the wine. I took a hesitant sip and could tell by the smooth finish that it was far more expensive than what I normally chose.

"He's not good at refilling the wine, is he?" Carla said, her lush lips twisting into a frown.

It was an odd complaint, given that she'd just put down her empty glass. I forced a smile, noticing for the first time how dull her hair was, like she'd torched it with too much hair color and cheap shampoo.

"Ugh! It was such a terrible week at work," she bellowed, slumping forward and plopping her elbows onto the table. "You'd think if they'd ride me as hard as they do, they'd pay me better."

"What do you do again?"

Our entrees arrived as she answered. "Human Resources at this worthless financial company downtown. Maybe if they were better at their jobs, they could pay me what I'm worth."

Her dinner was an entire roasted duckling on a plate of drunken noodles. She tore into it before the waiter had set my chili-roasted cod in front of me. She continued through a mouth full of noodles, affording me occasional glimpses of her meal in the process of its destruction. "I'm sure you make twice what I make."

"Oh, I doubt it. We aren't that..."

"Don't be so coy," she said, propping her chin on her wrist as she chewed. "You're a lawyer."

"What?" I said, choking on my water. "No, I'm not. I'm a real estate title agent."

Carla waved her hand dismissively. Most people didn't understand what I did, but it was rare they thought I was a real estate attorney. "Whatever. I'm sure you make a killing with suits like that one in your profile picture."

An inkling of what was going on started to form in my mind, but the wattage of her smile made me give her the benefit of the doubt for now. I took a second sip of my wine and decided it wasn't as good as the first impression. The excellent fish smoothed over a great deal of awkwardness. I rarely cooked fish because it was so difficult to get right. This fillet was perfect, flaky and silky smooth with just enough oil in the sauce to compliment the lean fish and bite of chili. We ate in silence that wasn't comfortable per se but wasn't awkward either. Not until she emptied her wine glass again.

"Jesus, is that idiot ever going to come back to the table?" she asked after scouring the room with her gaze. Her eyes were less luscious in person. They were almost beady, in fact. "Is it too much to ask to have a refilled wine glass?"

I'd had enough. I reached across the table and snatched up the bottle, emptying it into her glass. It had been sitting right there next to her the whole time. If she was so insistent on having her glass full, why didn't she pour it herself? She glared at me as though I'd done something unforgivable when the waiter arrived to ask if we wanted another bottle.

"We'd like it if you were attentive to your customers, but I suppose that's too much to ask," Carla said. She sniffed and turned haughtily away from him, showing me a razor-sharp line where her makeup stopped at the edge of her jaw. Her own skin tone was several shades off from her foundation. "But yes, we'll have another bottle. Kieran is paying, after all."

"Am I?" I asked in disbelief, but Carla was back to attacking her duck, picking it down to the bone. The waiter and I shared a look of disgust. "We don't need another bottle. I won't be drinking any."

She looked like she would have argued, but he hurried away. I slid my barely touched glass toward her. At this point I could only hope she'd make it home safely, more for everyone else's sake than for hers.

"So tell me, Kieran. Where did you go to school? Georgetown? American? Or did you move here after college?"

It was clear from her tone and how she clicked her teeth after the question that she wouldn't like my answer. I rather relished her revulsion. I didn't want her to approve of anything about me since I didn't approve of anything about her.

"I moved here with my ex-husband before college," I said, waving off the dessert menu as politely as possible. "I have an associate degree in finance from Northern Virginia Community College."

She laughed, throwing her head back to reveal the beginnings of crepey, weathered skin around her neck. She tossed the menu back at our waiter without looking at him. "Crème brûlée and a decaf cappuccino. You're so funny, Kieran."

"How is that funny?"

"A community college. What a lovely joke."

"It isn't a joke. I couldn't afford a four-year college and I don't need a bachelor's degree for my job."

Carla ignored me in favor of her dessert. I suppose my educational defects made me no better than a piece of furniture to her. I finished my water and the waiter appeared to refill it. He pasted on a smile and asked Carla about the dessert.

"I suppose it's the best I can expect from Wolfgang." She turned to me with a smirk that made me want to slap the teeth out of her mouth. "Savory chefs always try but they're helpless. Crème brûlée is such a pedestrian dessert."

"I'll be sure to pass along your impressions to our James Beard Award-winning pastry chef," our waiter replied as he set down two checks, one in front of each of us. Carla's was so long it hung over the end of its bamboo tray. I could've kissed him.

"Kieran will pay both of these," she said, sliding the tray back to him with the tip of two fingers.

"No, she won't." I stood, slapping some cash down on my tray. "The change is for you. She can pay for herself."

He gave me a wink and an apologetic smile as I spun and marched out. Carla's indignant spluttering followed me all the way to the stairs.

CHAPTER SIX

I was so mad after dinner that I started walking north to clear my head. It didn't work. I wasn't crazy enough to walk alone all the way to Adams Morgan at night. I caught an Uber outside the National Portrait Gallery and rage texted Pen until we got to Ninth Street.

Until a few years ago, Washington DC didn't have any lesbian bars. Then two opened within a few months of each other and the whole world rejoiced. Or maybe that was just Pen, thrilled that she didn't have to wait for the weekly ladies' nights at the innumerable gay bars in Logan Circle to find a hookup. I've never been sporty like Pen who, until a series of knee and ankle surgeries over the last four years, played on a lesbian softball team in the city. Her favorite bar was A League of Her Own, but I wasn't into the sports-bar theme or a wall of video games. Riveter's, on the other hand, was high-class chic with all the velvet trimmings I adored. The crowd there was more refined and less white than League and the drinks were fancier.

I was still steaming as I pushed my way into the crowd and the roaring bass. As late as it was, the plush entryway to Riveter's was darker than the street. The walls were painted royal purple and the décor was a blend of steampunk and vampire-chic—heavy on dark accents and flickering light. Hidden speakers pumped a synth beat and Banks's sultry voice. Pen was sitting at the quiet, secluded far end of the bar. She was on the phone, an untouched glass of Rosé in front of her.

"Hey Kieran! Long time, no see."

Abby, Riveter's sultry and sweet bartender, leaned on the rail in front of me and flashed a smile. Abby was the embodiment of joy in so many ways. She carried weight with an undeniable sexiness I could never quite pull off. She always had some quirky fashion accessory to draw the eye and her wigs were works of art. Today's was cobalt-blue and swirled into a perfect beehive. The frames of her horn-rimmed glasses were the exact same blue, as was the splash of paint on her rose-pale wrist. Obviously, she'd been in a rush after leaving her studio and hadn't removed all traces of her latest work in progress. Her earrings were a pair of twenty-sided dice she'd made herself. She would be an absolute fantasy if I was remotely close to her type, but she liked her women butch.

"Hey Abby," I said, settling in beside Pen. "Two dry martinis please."

"Comin' right up!"

Pen ended her call as Abby stirred the drinks in a chilled shaker. "Sorry about that. You know, I'm not sure I'm going to like working for a Georgetown snob."

"All your clients are snobs. Everyone in DC is a snob."

"I'll choose not to take that personally since I live in Woodbridge now," Pen replied as Abby set the drinks down between us, smoke coming off the frosted glasses in the warm air. "Martinis? Your date went that well, did it? Thanks for buying me a drink."

I plucked the skewer of olives out of both glasses and tossed them onto a cocktail napkin. Then I grabbed one drink and tipped it back like a shot. I could almost hear the hiss of the anger steaming out of me as the ice-cold alcohol tempered it.

Handing the empty glass back to Abby, I snatched the one Pen had been reaching for and gave it the same treatment. "You're welcome. These are delicious, Abby. I'll take another."

For a minute or two Abby and Pen were frozen in place, open-mouthed and staring at me. My anger started to crack through the martinis' ice crust. Sure, it wasn't like me to down two martinis like water, but everyone's allowed a bad day. As I opened my mouth to argue, they both snapped into action. Pen took an impressive sip from her wine and Abby started rinsing the shaker.

"It was like that, huh?" Pen asked as another martini landed on the bar in front of me. She glanced at Abby and said, "How about a club soda to go with that?"

Abby had already made one, complete with a twist of lemon, and put it down next to my growing collection of olives. As soon as she left to serve a couple at the other end of the bar, I started ranting about my disaster date.

Yes, it was a rant and it was extremely undignified, but if anyone had reason to rant, it was me. Luckily for me, I had the best friend in the world and she listened intently, peppering my monologue with indignant grunts at all the right places. When I mentioned Carla's comments about my degree her face got so red I thought she was having a heart attack. When I told her about storming out after only paying for my part of the meal, she hooted and clapped her approval. Abby shot us a smile and that anger I'd been carrying melted another inch.

My martini was empty again and I wanted another, but Pen stopped me, taking the hand I'd raised to summon Abby in hers and sliding the club soda in front of me. "I want to make sure you make it home tonight."

I held the soda water but didn't drink. I was still more inclined to chew the glass. Then Pen ran her thumb over my other hand and some of my anger leaked away in the repetitive pressure.

"She's barking up the wrong tree if she thinks title agents are rich. I can't even get you to buy me lunch," Pen said, pushing her empty glass away and reaching over the bar to grab a bottle of water. Abby shot her a warning glare that changed into a smile with Penelope's wink. "Maybe we should ask where she went to college. She's not real bright."

I grunted, finally sipping my soda water. It was surprisingly refreshing and I was so thirsty.

"And look at her pictures," Pen continued. "She's way too skinny. Bet this was her only meal this week."

"Not funny."

Okay, that was kind of funny. Not enough to make me laugh, which probably wouldn't happen for another five years, but I smiled.

"Was the food good?" Pen asked, her eyes following a middle-aged woman in a midriff shirt.

"It was excellent." I waited until she looked at me again and raised an eyebrow. "That one's dressed like she raided her daughter's closet."

"She probably did." With a half-smile, Pen replied, "I took her home a couple weeks ago."

"Did it go better than my date?"

"I can't remember." She emptied her water bottle and took both my hands. Her palms were so soft and her grip was light but sure. "Tonight was terrible and I'm sorry, Kieran. But hey, you got the bad date out of the way, so it can only go up from here, right?"

"Why would you jinx me like that?"

Pen laughed, but her face sobered quickly. She looked into my eyes and, as always when she held my gaze like this, I felt safe. She'd looked at me like that when Nick left. And when Alex left. Pen was always the one who made me feel better. Tears sprung to my eyes, but I didn't want to cry in public, so I looked away.

"You're going to find someone amazing, Kieran." Her gentle, throaty tone and warm hands weren't going to help with the crying problem. "I promise. We just need to keep the losers at bay."

"What if…"

"Nope."

I'm the loser. I finished the sentence in my head since she wouldn't let me say it out loud.

"So she got the wrong impression from your profile pic," Pen continued, refusing to let me wallow in my negative thoughts. "We need to change that impression."

"How?"

"New pics, dummy." She accompanied the teasing with a squeeze of my hands.

The tactile reminder that she was leading me through this helped, so I squeezed back. "You're always the smart one, Pen."

CHAPTER SEVEN

I felt better the next day, at least emotionally. Physically was questionable after three martinis, but it wasn't as bad as it could've been. I got up on time and went for a run before work, a thing I rarely did and always regretted the moment it started. I had a healthy breakfast, washed all my dishes and made my bed before leaving the house. My mom would've been so proud. The traffic even cooperated and I was the first into the office. There was something incredibly rewarding about brewing the initial pot of coffee, especially after drinking half a bottle of gin at Riveter's.

The first half-hour of my workday went by in a blissful solitude. Randy arrived fifteen minutes after me, but he locked himself in his office with little more than a wave of appreciation for his full coffee mug. I wouldn't see him for the rest of the day, and that was fine with me.

Carol arrived next, at nine o'clock on the dot, and unlocked the front door on her way in. She was much friendlier than Randy, asking about my plans for the weekend, but her back, aching in her seventh month of pregnancy, quickly forced her to her desk's ergonomic chair. Carol was our receptionist/office manager/group therapist and I dreaded the months we would be without her when the baby was born.

The rest of the office trudged in behind Carol, Arthur bringing up the rear. I had cleared out both my electronic and paper inboxes and was settling into an extensive review of closing documents for next week when Arthur's grinning face interrupted my work.

"You had a date last night."

It wasn't a question and I immediately suspected Pen of blabbing. That was ridiculous, of course, because Pen hated Arthur and also hated gossip. "Why would you think that?"

He ticked off his answers on his fingers as he spoke. "You lingered around last night, waiting for us to leave. You had a dress hanging from the back of your door. You were nervous and excited all day. You didn't go out with Penelope after work. And there was a smear of foundation in your shade on the bathroom counter this morning."

"Why were you in the women's bathroom and how do you know my foundation shade?"

"I wasn't and I don't, but the rest was true and you confirmed my suspicions. Don't change the subject. How was your date?"

At least I didn't have to worry about my only work friend being a creep, hanging around the women's bathroom. I shrugged and answered, "It was awful, but I learned a lot."

I picked up my file and walked out of the room, hoping he would take the hint. He didn't. Art followed, wearing a fatherly grin. "What'd you learn?"

"Not to date someone because they're hot," I answered, making my way through the back hallway that connected to the real estate offices next door. "Pick someone I'm compatible with instead."

"It is possible to find both. Or so I've heard."

I knocked on a door and pushed inside. "I'll believe it when I see it."

Arthur hung back while I talked to the Realtor about his clients' closing. The appraisal had come back lower than expected and I worried the mortgage company might get cold feet. Any other title agent would be interested, but Arthur ignored the entire exchange, picking at his fingernails to show his boredom.

The conversation finished, I left, Arthur at my heels, continuing to press me for details of my date. Most of his questions were a thinly veiled attempt to discover my date's gender, so I spent a lot of time avoiding pronouns to mess with him.

"So how did you meet this mysterious hot date of yours anyway?"

I stopped to let a Realtor and her client pass. We exchanged pleasantries with the pair and I stumbled through introductions while wracking my brain for a way to get rid of Arthur. Unfortunately, I'm terrible at thinking on my feet and they left without saving me. Arthur crossed his arms and raised an eyebrow at me.

"Ugh. Fine." I dropped my voice and mumbled, "A dating app."

"Couldn't hear you."

His smile said he'd heard me fine so I growled a little louder, "A dating app, okay? I'm on a dating app."

"Online dating?" He said the words as though they were in a foreign language. "Our little Kieran has finally joined the twenty-first century and discovered the Internet?"

"Screw you, Art."

"I'm teasing you, kid," he said like a doting uncle rather than an annoying coworker.

"Well, don't." I wasn't in the mood for his condescension. Not from a happily married guy with the perfect life.

"Be careful, okay? I've heard a lot of horror stories about the people on dating apps."

"From who?"

"From whom."

Yep, that was it. I was gonna punch him. Right there in the middle of the Three Keys Realty office.

"It's all the same people, no matter which app you're on, and nothing ever comes of it," Art said, rocking back on his heels.

"You've never used a dating app, Art." My look of disdain warped into shock as I realized he might be confessing to cheating on his wife. "Have you?"

His face went deathly pale, quite the sight since he hated going outside and his skin was so fair. "God no! Not me. Other people. I know other people who've used them."

The squeak in his voice confirmed his words and I had a really hard time holding back my laughter. As always, Pen saved me. She came out of her office accompanied by a leggy brunette wearing blue jeans and a positively radiant smile. Arthur excused himself with the dubious explanation of pressing work matters and scurried away. He didn't hate Pen as much as she hated him, but there was no love lost between them. Eventually, Pen peeled her eyes from her guest and turned her smile on me.

"So you're alive," Pen said. "And you look much better than I expected after last night."

"Someone made me drink a lot of water," I replied before turning to the brunette. "Hello, I'm Kieran Hall."

She had a stronger grip than I expected, but her hand was soft and warm. "I've heard a lot about you, Kieran."

Since the stranger didn't seem inclined to introduce herself, I turned to Pen for an explanation. She was probably a client and a wealthy one at that if she expected me to know who she was without a greeting, so I should be nice even though she came off as arrogant.

"Kieran, this is Ashley Britt." Pen flashed me a toothy grin as soon as she said the name, turning back to Ashley. "The photographer."

The photographer. I could feel my face heat up and tried desperately to stop the reaction. Pen had a lot of friends, but she lived a very compartmentalized life and most of us hadn't met each other. Even without having met Ashley, I knew far more about her than I wanted to. While Pen tended to favor romantic entanglements with a life span measured in hours, she also had a few friends with benefits. Ashley was one of those friends. In fact, Ashley and her wife were both Pen's *friends*, sometimes together, sometimes separately.

In addition to their regular meetings of a less professional nature, Ashley photographed Pen's listings and she was super talented. Nothing sold a home faster than perfectly staged photos.

"Nice to finally meet you." I somehow managed a smile to match the comment. She was a friend of Pen's and any friend of Pen's was a friend of mine. "Your photographs are incredible."

"Thank you," she replied. "That's so sweet."

Pen pulled her office door shut as she turned to me. "Speaking of photographs, want me to come over tonight so we can get some new ones of you?"

"That would be great," I said, leading them down the hall. "Unless you have other plans."

"We should be done by the time you're off work."

A look that definitely included a wink passed between them and I hoped they were professional enough to get a hotel room rather than hooking up while photographing a client's house.

Ashley looked fun enough, so I tested her with a joke. "Sorry to hear that."

As I hoped, instead of being offended, she laughed, rolling back her ridiculously long neck and elbowing Pen in the ribs. "So am I. For her sake. Trust me, I'll get what I need."

I was starting to like Ashley. Pen scowled at us, but there was a twinkle in her eye. "Don't make me sorry I introduced the two of you."

"If only her ego was as solid as her abs," Ashley said, leaning close.

"I wouldn't know."

Pen's growing indignation was enough to set me laughing.

"What do you need pictures for anyway, Kieran?" Ashley asked. "If you need a headshot, I'd be happy to help."

"Her headshot's what got her in trouble in the first place," Pen said, stopping in the lobby, which was significantly busier than mine. "Her profile pic on Swingle is her headshot and she snared a gold-digger. We need some tasty selfies so she can catch someone less superficial."

I cut Pen a warning look. Ashley seemed nice, but I barely knew her and I didn't need a stranger, particularly my best friend's booty call, judging my romantic and sexual shortcomings.

Ashley gave me an appraising look. "Men or women?"

"Both," I said. "Or neither. I'm open to everyone."

"Hmmm. Usually men like to see tits and women like to see lips. Lucky for you, neither will be a problem. I don't know what nonbinary folks are into. Maybe a little of both? Help her with the best angles, Penelope?"

"That's my plan."

She was a photographer so I suppose it wasn't as gross as it felt that she could talk so clinically about which of my body parts I should show off, but it felt weird. I doubt I'd have felt that way if Pen had said it. Chances were she'd just help me with the shot, not spell out why I should aim a camera at my cleavage. Subtlety didn't appear to be one of Ashley's strengths.

"Swingle, huh?" Ashley's smile was mostly a leer.

I looked around, but everyone nearby was engrossed in conversation. Even with their distractions, I wasn't sure I wanted to talk about this in such a public place. Pen leaned in, bringing the three of us closer and pitching her voice low. "Kieran's jumping back in the dating world after a brief absence."

"How's it working out for you?"

"One disaster date," I replied, but I didn't want to sound like a sad loser in front of Ashley. I put on an upbeat tone and continued, "But I'm talking to someone new and it's going well."

"Really?" Pen looked at me with such a warm, sweet smile that I almost felt bad about the lie. "That's great! I can't wait to hear all about it."

Yep. I was a jerk.

"My wife and I used to use Swingle," Ashley said, shoving her hands into the back pockets of her skinny jeans. The posture was flattering to literally every inch of her body. Most of those conversations that had been distracting folks earlier became far less interesting than Ashley's killer body.

I was about to ask for the sweet story of how she and her wife met on the app, but then she and Pen made eye contact and the pieces clicked into place. Ashley and her wife didn't meet each other on Swingle. The two of them met Pen there. I remembered that Ashley wasn't just using her hall pass with Pen, she was their third. I'd always wondered where Pen found Ashley and now I knew. It would have been incredibly fortuitous in a professional setting for Pen to just happen to find a photographer looking for a third. Not even Pen had luck that good.

"Time for us to head over to Georgetown," Pen said, holding an arm out for Ashley. Pen gave me a wink as she pushed open the door. "See you around five thirty?"

Ashley waved over her shoulder to me. "It'll probably be more like six."

They swept out into the muggy day, taking all my energy with them. I checked my watch to find it was noon. Guess I would be eating lunch at my desk today. That was probably for the best. I could use the time finding someone to message on Swingle. Maybe by the time Pen came over tonight, I really would have someone new.

CHAPTER EIGHT

Ashley had been right. Pen didn't get to my place until quarter past six. She made up for it by bringing pizza. She was in a great mood, and that made two of us. We laughed through dinner even though the pizza was veggies on cauliflower crust. I'd accepted long ago that Pen's dietary needs, along with her enforced days of rest, were sacrosanct, so I didn't complain too much about the lack of pepperoni.

"Tell me about this new person you're messaging," Pen said as I washed our dishes.

I handed her a plate to dry, letting my smile grow. "Chloe. She's a nurse who lives here in Woodbridge. Forty-two, divorced, two dogs, and owns her own place."

"Wow," Pen said, stacking the dry plates into the cupboard. "Really? I thought you were lying this afternoon when you said you'd found someone new."

My voice was super shrill when I shouted, "What? Of course not!"

"Oh thank goodness. You were lying." Pen stacked the last plate in the cupboard. "I was worried I couldn't read you anymore."

"I said I wasn't lying."

"Yeah, but as bad as you are at lying, you're even worse at denying it when you do. It's okay. I would've lied to Ashley, too. She can be intimidating."

"I wasn't intimidated," I grumbled, but I knew this lie was no more convincing than the others. "She's just…"

"Exactly," Pen said, flopping down on the couch beside me. She looked tired. "She's just…"

"Why do you…Never mind. None of my business."

"You're my best friend. Everything is your business. But no, I'm not going to explain my relationship with Ashley to you." She grinned that wicked cat grin of hers. "And I'm definitely not going to explain my relationship with Ashley and her wife to you."

"Fair enough."

"It isn't because I don't trust you or because I'm ashamed, because I'm not." She reached across me to grab my phone from the arm of the couch. "I can't really explain it to myself. I don't examine the things I do. I just do them."

I didn't want to examine them either. My stomach squirmed at the thought of her and Ashley together. I know Pen was a welcome addition to their marriage, but my ex-husband's infidelity still stung too much for me to understand open relationships.

"Let's get to this, shall we?" Pen handed the phone back to me, the camera app open and in selfie mode. The awkward angle of my chin and nostrils made me flip the screen over. "That's not how you take a selfie, Kieran."

"I know. I just…I hate this."

Pen wrapped an arm around me, pulling me close. It felt so good to be held by someone—anyone—that I melted into the feeling. I dropped my cheek onto Pen's shoulder, the soft cotton of her T-shirt as welcoming as an embrace. Why couldn't I find this in someone who loved me? Was it too much to ask to date someone who knew me as well as my best friend? I didn't think I'd ever dated anyone like that. Someone I loved and trusted at the same time. I'd trusted Nick and he'd shown me I was wrong. I loved Alex and they hadn't loved me back. It had never been easy with my lovers, but everything with Pen was easy.

As much as I wanted to wallow, I knew I couldn't. If I stayed like this, thinking too much, I'd start crying, and I'd already done too much of that over the years. I sat up, clearing my throat and flipping my phone back over.

"You okay?" Pen asked, her voice soft and almost husky. She must've been really tired. We should make this quick so she could get back home to bed.

"Yep. Let's do this."

I threw my arm up and snapped a quick shot. It actually wasn't that bad. My hair was down and wavy from a full day in a ponytail. It fell to my shoulders, highlighting the length of my neck and broadening my chest. My brunette curls almost looked bouncy. I hadn't worn much makeup to work and what I had worn had faded to a natural look. I'd swapped my slacks for yoga pants and my spaghetti-strap tank showed off the cleavage Ashley had deemed so crucial. Most importantly, my smile looked genuine. Probably because it was genuine for once.

"Not bad," Pen said, peering over my shoulder. "Except the eyesore in the background."

I squinted at the screen, sure I'd see a pile of forgotten laundry. "What eyesore?"

"Me. You can't put up a thirst trap with someone else in the background."

"Thirst trap?"

Pen reached over and scooped the phone out of my hand. "A sexy selfie. You catch someone's eye and make them salivate over how hot you are."

She tapped a button on the phone, adding a filter to the camera and aiming it at me. While she fiddled, I teased, "You've probably broken half these women's hearts anyway. I don't want them hating me on your account."

Pen swiped across the screen, her tongue wedged between her teeth as she tested different filters. "I assure you, I don't break hearts. That's what the disclaimer is for, remember?"

She was so adorable, with the tip of her tongue poking out like a kitten falling asleep, that I seriously doubted none of her conquests caught feelings.

It ended up being pretty fun taking pictures. Having someone else present while I took selfies seemed counterintuitive, but apparently there is a specific appeal to a selfie that can't be achieved with someone else taking the picture. Pen explained it, but I didn't really get it. I just trusted her judgement. Good thing that I did, too. We got some cute pics, very flattering thanks to Pen. How had I never noticed how nice my lips were before?

Pen left after we uploaded the best one to Swingle. She looked dead on her feet, but she promised to be careful on the drive home. I didn't press her because she hated people being overly protective, but I prowled my living room until she texted to say she was home safely.

Chloe messaged while I was crawling into bed.

I like the new pic. Did you take that tonight?
Yeah. I was feeling cute.
You're looking cute, too. Are you going to bed? Is it too late to talk?

I checked the time, biting my lower lip. It was late, but tomorrow was Saturday. I could be tired for one day.

Not too late for me. What about you?
I have tomorrow off. I'm all yours.

I liked the sound of that. We'd only chatted a little that afternoon and there was so much more I wanted to know. I asked about her dogs and confessed I was pet-free at the moment.

My ex took our cat and I can't bring myself to get another yet.

You don't get to see the kitty? No joint custody agreement?
Things didn't end on the best terms. I miss Max, but I don't want to see Alex ever again.

I knew I shouldn't be talking about my exes this early, but Chloe made me feel comfortable enough to share. Besides, if I was going to scare her off with my baggage, might as well do it now.

I know what that feels like.
I found out more about Blair during our divorce than in all our years of marriage.
Fortunately I got the boys after they left.

I noted the gender-neutral pronoun and my heart rate picked up. My hands shook a little when I sent the next message, I was so excited to get the words out.

Your partner was nonbinary?
Yeah. Does that freak you out?
Not at all. Alex was nonbinary, too.
So you understand how hard it can be for the partner of a person struggling with their gender.
Absolutely.

No need to go into anything more than that this early.

And here I thought you couldn't be any more perfect.

That made my racing heart skip a beat. This was my kind of flirting. I pulled over the extra pillow and propped it behind me. I wouldn't be going to sleep any time soon.

CHAPTER NINE

I've always loved a dull Friday night. Even when I was a teenager, I went out on Thursdays instead. Of course, I missed the wild partying times I was supposed to have in my twenties because I got married at eighteen. When you don't have a frame of reference for something it's tough to miss it, even if all your friends say it's great.

My idea of the perfect Friday night is getting home early, making breakfast for dinner and curling up in my pajamas with a trashy '80s movie and a cup of herbal tea. I was spreading a fistful of cheddar cheese over my Denver omelet when my phone buzzed. Chloe's message flashed into view long enough to make me grin, but I decided to wait until after dinner to read and respond.

We'd been up far too late last Friday and Saturday had been a complete loss to exhaustion. She'd had several long workdays, keeping us from talking much, but I'd spent most of Thursday dead on my feet from another late-night conversation. The more I thought about our conversations, the more I realized I'd made myself a little too available. Work was important to me and I'm never at my best when I'm exhausted. I should have set firm boundaries with Chloe from the start, for myself as much as for her, so tonight I'd eat my dinner and at least let Molly Ringwald's entire family forget her sixteenth birthday before I started the conversation again.

The omelet was really good, but I had a hard time appreciating it. I sat at my two-seater dinette in the open-plan living room and mechanically moved egg from plate to mouth, my mind fixed on the cell phone I'd left on the kitchen counter. I blamed the dinner choice. If I'd gone with my first instinct—blueberry pancakes with tons of butter and no syrup—I wouldn't be replaying every sentence from our two conversations in my head. I was thinking about how she'd called me perfect when my fork smashed into bare porcelain. Looking down, I saw that I'd cleaned my plate like a good girl.

"I guess that means you get dessert," I mumbled through my smile.

I paused the movie and took my lemon verbena tea to the couch along with my phone. Chloe's message was a simple question about what I was doing on a Friday night and I grinned at the television before answering.

Checking out Molly Ringwald's polka dotted underpants.

It took so long for Chloe to answer I thought I'd scared her off. My humor could sometimes be unnecessarily provocative. Maybe I took a step too far this time. Or maybe it was a stupid joke. I was grabbing my phone to apologize and explain when she responded.

I hope you paid your dollar like everyone else.
It was worth it.
I haven't watched Sixteen Candles in ages.
Does it hold up?
It's problematic to say the least.
Racism, misogyny, homophobia and the threat of sexual assault.

Sounds like the 80s to me. Or are you too young to remember them?

I'm only five years younger than you!

Answer the question Clarice.

Silence of the Lambs was the 90s.

An era I'll admit I remember better than the 80s.

Same for me. Blair was a few years older and they always teased me for being a 90s kid rather than an 80s kid.

How long were you two together?

Shit. Why'd I ask that question? No more talk about exes, remember?

Twelve years. What about you and Alex?

Five. I was married once before them.

When did they reject the binary?

About a year before we split.

Blair came out as genderqueer on our anniversary four years ago. The idea of being nonbinary was new then.

At least it was new to me and we didn't know anyone else who went through that.

It was sorta us against the world for a long time.

This was exactly what I was worried about. I wanted to know more about Chloe, not her ex. It was hard to think of a happy future when we were talking so much about our sad pasts. I waited so long, chewing my lip and thinking about how to steer the conversation away from this topic, that Chloe continued before I could respond.

The timing stung. Blair basically said "Happy Anniversary! You aren't a lesbian anymore!"

I hadn't thought of that. I'm pan, so it didn't affect me in that way.

But you know that your sexuality doesn't change with your partner's gender, right?

Yeah, I know.

It was selfish of me to feel that way.

But being a lesbian is one of my favorite things about me.
I love Blair but I didn't want to lose myself in loving them.
In the end it wasn't right for either of us to be together.
I'm selfish, too, because I like you and I'm excited to get to know you
I'm excited, too.

Finally I thought of a way to steer this conversation in a new direction. It would be so much easier to do this in person, so it was time for me to make a move. This wasn't how I normally worked. I liked partners to ask me out, but desperate times called for desperate measures. Besides, what I'd done in the past hadn't worked out for me, so it was time to try something new.

Excited enough to meet me for a drink?

I shuffled around the living room, waiting for a reply. After exactly one second, I decided I'd made a terrible mistake. The people I dated usually liked to be in charge and I was totally fine with that. After three seconds, I wished I could take my message back. Maybe I'd turned Chloe off by asking her out? Had I blown any chance with her by being too forward? My mind was going a million miles a minute and it had only been five seconds since I'd sent my message. Was this what it felt like for people who did the asking? This was terrible.

Absolutely. When are you free?

All that pent-up fear and embarrassment ripped out of me in a burst of laughter. I'd asked a woman out and she'd said yes! It felt good. Really, really good. Now I know why they like doing this so much. The rush of a yes was well worth the fear of a no.

Tomorrow night?

That was too soon. Why had I said that? I sounded desperate. I sounded pathetic. She was going to say no. This was awful.

This was the last time I ever asked anyone out.

I can't.

I knew it.

I work late this weekend. How about Monday? I get off at seven.

I was on cloud nine. I took a screenshot and fired it off to Pen with a promise she didn't have to respond, but I wanted her to be the first to know I had a date.

Perfect. Meet at eight?
Can't wait.

We signed off for the night right as Pen's response came back. It was a crude joke about when Chloe would really be getting off. If only she'd been there to see my epic eye roll. She followed it up with a congratulations for successfully asking someone out for the first time. I hadn't even mentioned that. She just knew. Between Chloe and Pen, I was feeling great about the people in my life.

CHAPTER TEN

Monday night didn't work out after all. Chloe texted me after lunch to say she couldn't get away from the hospital on time and didn't want to make me wait. She was super sweet about cancelling, but I worried it was more about me than work. We'd only chatted three times and then I went straight into asking her out. In the real world that wouldn't be fast, but online dating seemed to have a whole different rule book. One that I had trouble translating.

When she asked to reschedule for Tuesday, I lied and said I was busy. It was silly and petty, but I had two very good reasons for doing it. Mostly I didn't want to be too available, which was ridiculous for a thirty-seven-year-old woman, but there it was. There was also the fear it would be another disaster à la Carla and I wanted to have Pen on standby in case it imploded. I had already selfishly taken her out of her house for one Tuesday rest day, I wouldn't do it again. When I suggested Wednesday instead, Chloe agreed so quickly I felt guilty for the lie.

We made plans to meet at eight at a bar in Woodbridge and I frantically texted Pen. My first date with someone new in five years had been a disaster and my second had been cancelled. I wasn't exactly feeling good about this. I liked Chloe, but now I was so afraid it wouldn't go well that I couldn't stomach the idea of seeing her. I shot off a second text to Pen, announcing that I was going to cancel with Chloe.

"Absolutely not." She came storming into my office instead of texting me back. "You're going on that date."

"I don't know," I said, but I couldn't help feeling better with her in the room. "It's too embarrassing. She cancelled."

"And immediately rescheduled. She's a nurse, isn't she? That sort of thing happens with medical people."

"That's just it! Do I want to get into something serious with a woman who's going to flake out on me all the time?"

Pen settled into her usual chair and dropped her loafer-clad feet onto my ink blotter. "Better she flake out on you than on her patients, don't you think?"

"No," I replied grumpily. "Yes. I don't know. I don't think I can go through with it."

"You can and you will."

"What if it's a train wreck?"

"What if it's the best date you've ever been on?"

"It won't be."

"How do you know?"

Pen did this to me all the time. She spent so much time issuing logical rebuttals that I forgot to freak out. It wasn't working this time. "Because I would know if she was *the one*, wouldn't I? Isn't that how it happens? You meet them and something clicks."

"You haven't met Chloe." She laughed low and warm when I stuck my tongue out at her. "Besides, you're kinda oblivious, Kieran. The perfect person probably served you coffee this morning and you were too busy freaking out to notice."

I tossed a balled-up sheet of paper at her but missed by a mile. "You brought me my first cup of coffee this morning. Why were you in the office so early anyway?"

"Had a lot of work to get through." She jumped up as her phone buzzed. "You're going to meet me at Riveter's before the date and I'll keep you focused."

It wasn't a request so much as a demand, and I'd never been good at denying Pen anything. So I showed up at Riveter's at seven on Wednesday night, nervous but looking pretty good. Pen was already there and already working. She had a woman in a neat business suit and flowing silver hair leaning in close. When Pen saw me, she tapped a finger to the woman's chin in a provocative gesture that nonetheless sent the woman back to the dance floor alone.

I slid into the newly empty seat and tucked my shaking hands under my thighs.

"Looking good, Kieran," Abby said, rose-pink wig skimming her jawline. "Martini?"

"Not tonight. I'm meeting someone for drinks later and I don't want to show up drunk."

"She's two-timing you, Penelope?"

"I'm not nearly good enough for her," Pen responded with a wink.

"I met someone on Swingle," I blurted out, wanting to get Abby's warning out of the way.

"Aw, that's sweet," Abby said as she made me a club soda. "I met my baby on Swingle."

"You did?" My voice only trembled a little.

"Yeah. I went on like a million dates before we met." Abby's smile was so genuine. I tried one of my own but my lips weren't cooperating. "It was fun, though. I met some great folks. You won't be compatible with everyone, but that's okay. Try to have fun."

"Okay." I almost managed that smile. "Yeah."

Once Abby had slid away, Pen turned the full force of her stare on me. "Stop fidgeting."

"I'm not fidgeting,"

My bracelet rattled against the bar and she reached over to still it with a hand over mine. Her fingers were cold from her drink, but her touch was firm and undemanding. "You're going to be fine. She's gonna love you."

"Yeah, you're right, but…"

"But what?"

I toyed with my bracelet, unsure how to frame my other big fear. "She's…really hot."

Pen laughed and squeezed my hand. "Is that a problem?"

"I mean if I want to maintain any sort of dignity it is." I leaned close to her and whispered, "I'm ready to explode over here. She wears men's clothes and that…like…really works for me. What if she wears a suit?"

Pen's eyebrows scrunched together. "That would be a problem?"

"You know how I feel about women wearing men's suits."

"Do I? You've never said anything."

"Sure I have."

"Nope. I would've remembered."

The bracelet was now in constant motion, swirling around my wrist. I couldn't keep my eyes or my hands off it and I knew my cheeks were getting hot. "Ugh. It's so hot. A woman in a man's suit is enough to melt my panties right off."

Pen was quiet long enough to make me wonder if she'd heard me, but then she said, "Didn't you say you were horny? Why would it be such a bad thing if your panties melted off?"

"It's a first date!"

"Don't be such a prude, Kieran."

I made a face and looked into the crowd because I couldn't hold still. Across the dance floor there was a group of women that looked like an office party. Some of them were obviously straight and obviously curious. Riveter's must've been deemed the "safe" place for them to let loose away from flirty men. Either that or one of the group swung our way and she'd convinced her buddies to choose her place for once. One of them kept staring over at us and looking away when anyone noticed.

"She likes you," Pen said, smiling at the woman whose head snapped back to her companions. "She's going to come up to the bar for another drink in a minute. Bet you anything she sidles up next to you."

"I already have a date tonight," I said, sneaking another peek. "And she's your type."

"Straight?"

"Curious."

We both laughed, leaning over the bar and snorting with the shared memories of Pen's many conquests. At least the laughter made my hands stop shaking.

"What're you so nervous about? I thought you two had, like, everything in common."

"We do," I said. I had to tell her. I needed to get it out. "Including all our baggage. Basically the only thing we talk about is our exes."

"That can't be the only thing."

"No, but...I don't know. I want to talk about other stuff, but her divorce and my breakup with Alex are very similar. It's normal that we started bonding there, but I kinda want to move on, you know?"

"Maybe you should look into other people then," Pen said, signaling Abby for another drink. "Like the curious hottie who keeps staring over here."

She was cute, but that wasn't what I wanted. "You go for it. I like Chloe."

Curious finally got up the nerve to head over, and Pen locked on to her like a shark scenting blood. She marched up to the bar right beside me, bringing a cloud of rich, musky perfume with her. She asked Abby for a Manhattan in a voice of leather and whiskey. Pen was nearly drooling and I couldn't help rolling my eyes.

Curious's eyes flicked to us once, but she looked away just as quickly. While she waited for her drink, she picked at the corner of a flyer for Abby's next art show. Pen nudged me and I nearly slipped off my stool into the stranger. I returned the nudge and the movement caught Curious's attention. She smiled at us and slipped one of the flyers into her jacket pocket.

"Your friends seem nice, but they're a little loud, don't you think?" Pen asked, leaning across me to smile at her mark. "You should stay here. I'm pretty good company."

I watched Curious's reaction in the mirror over the bar. She blushed and looked down, trying to hide her smile. So it had been Pen that she'd been checking out. Looked like Pen had snagged another one. Was any woman immune to her charm?

"I'm flattered, but I'm not gay."

"Are you sure?" Pen asked, her smile slipping from flirty to perplexed. "Because you walk pretty gay."

I cringed. That didn't sound much like a pickup line, but then what did I know?

"I what?" Her voice was a full octave higher than it had been and dripping with indignation. "That's not even…Yes, I'm sure. I'm straight."

The grin Pen turned on her was triumphant, which seemed an odd choice considering their exchange. "Okay, but you have a pretty gay walk."

Curious, who was acting significantly less so, huffed and turned away with her drink. I snuck a peek as she headed back to her table. Pen was right. It was a distinctly gay walk. All shoulders rather than hips and a wide, almost aggressive stance. I couldn't say that I'd ever defined a gay walk before, but I also knew for certain that she had one. Too bad Pen had pissed her off.

"That was fun."

"You struck out, Pen," I said. "How is that fun?"

She winked at me and pointed to her watch. "Never count me out. But you have a date to get to."

I swore and hopped off my stool, yanking down the short sides of my dress. "Wish me luck?"

"You don't need it, but I'll wish it to you anyway. Good luck. Have fun."

CHAPTER ELEVEN

The atmosphere at Hank's Bar and Grill couldn't have been more different than Riveter's. Where Riveter's was all polished mahogany and plush velvet, Hank's was scarred pine and vinyl. There were darts and pool tables in the back corner beside a jukebox full of classic rock. They had only four beer taps and two house wines on the menu. Most everyone drank from brown bottles or cans. I loved it. If there was anywhere I'd find the uncomplicated soft butch I craved, it was Hank's.

Chloe certainly looked the part. She'd secured a high top for us near the dart game in progress and stood when she saw me. Her smile slipped a fraction as her eyes slid over my clinging mid-thigh dress and three-inch heels. It was exactly the reaction I'd been looking for. What was the point of a sexy little dress if it didn't make your date forget her name?

She kissed my cheek by way of greeting and apologized for the bar.

"I realize now it isn't exactly the classiest place in the world." Her wallet chain rattled against the barstool as she slid back onto her seat. "I should've picked somewhere else."

"No way," I replied, greeting the waitress and ordering a Bud Light. "It's perfect."

Chloe already had a Guinness, but she took a moment to chat with the waitress whom she knew by name. It gave me a chance to look her over and I liked what I saw. Most of her pictures online were in hospital scrubs but these worn jeans and navy-blue button-up suited her better. She was powerfully built with a fair amount of muscle but enough extra weight to soften her form. Her hands were delicate, wrapped around her glass and sporting a single wide band on her right thumb. I loved the butch-femme dynamic and we embodied it well. We drew a fair amount of attention from the mostly straight crowd, but I couldn't tell if it was because Chloe was a regular or because we looked good as a couple.

"How was your day?" Chloe asked as her phone buzzed. She didn't even look at the screen, keeping her eyes locked on mine as she flipped it over.

I couldn't help but smile at the perfect reaction. "Getting better every minute."

It was unforgivably cheesy, but she ate it up. I couldn't imagine what I'd been worried about. She clearly wanted to be here and so did I. Time flew by as we talked and laughed. Chloe told some hilarious hospital stories, never mentioning anyone's particulars but painting a vivid picture of unbelievable antics. She inspired me to drag up funny stories from my job, many of them prominently featuring Pen.

Chloe's phone buzzed for the third time as our second round of beers was delivered.

"Okay, I have to know more about Penelope," she said, wiping foam from her stout off her upper lip.

"She's my best friend."

"She sounds like a character."

"Definitely."

"You never dated?"

"God no," I said. Chloe's phone buzzed again. "She doesn't date anyone."

She finally cracked and glanced at the messages but turned her phone right back over. "Nun?"

I laughed so hard I choked on my beer. "Literally the opposite. She doesn't believe in relationships that last more than twenty-four hours. And she isn't my type."

Chloe leaned in, the corner of her mouth curling up. "And what is your type?"

I reached out to where her hand rested on the tabletop. Running one fingertip along her knuckles and down her thumb, I slowly twisted the band on her thumb. "Well, I like a butch who knows who she is but doesn't take herself too seriously. A woman with...experience that can dedicate herself to one woman. Namely me."

Chloe swallowed before she answered. I could see her throat contract and release in slow motion. Two beers and no dinner gave me an unfamiliar confidence that left me sounding pretty smooth. "Good to know."

She leaned in. Not enough to be forward, but enough to let me know she would be forward if she didn't respect me as much as she did. I leaned in the same amount, letting her know that I appreciated that she respected me, but didn't want her to respect me too much. If I was honest, and the third beer that landed in front of me at that moment wanted me to be honest, I really liked Chloe. Liked her enough to let my normal rules fly out the window.

Chloe's phone went off again and her veneer of patience finally cracked. She scowled and snatched the phone, typing aggressively before looking a little sheepish and deleting a few lines.

I waited until she finished to ask, "I know it isn't any of my business, but is everything okay?"

Chloe sighed and took a long sip of her beer before answering. I didn't even hide how closely I watched the length of her neck stretch as she drank. Even scowling she was hot as hell. "I'm sorry about that. It's...well, it's my ex."

Alarm bells. Loud ones.

"They aren't taking it well that I'm dating again."

"Oh."

"Please don't worry." She reached out and took my hand, her eyes big and round and full of compassion. "It's sort of a new breakup and we were together a long time."

"I understand."

Chloe looked around, her eyes narrowing. "Someone here must have told them. We used to come in here together and they sort of know us. I'm sorry. I should've taken you somewhere else. I just thought it was close to home for both of us and all."

She looked so worried, but I was relieved. It was finally clear what had been bothering me about all the ex talk we'd had. I was worried Chloe was still hung up on her ex, but it was clear now that it was her ex that was hung up on her. The more worried and disappointed she looked, the more I was sure I wanted to see more of her.

"I was so nervous about meeting you. You are seriously hot and I'm getting too old to date hot women and I wanted to feel comfortable because I was so nervous." The babbling was even more endearing. "But I should've known someone here would tell Blair."

When she tried to stand up, I held her hands tighter. "Chloe, please don't worry. I don't want you to go."

Now she looked relieved. "Really? This isn't ruining our date?"

"Not for me," I said, stroking her hands. They turned to putty in mine and she settled back onto her chair. "Breakups can be hard."

Chloe turned one hand over, twining her fingers through mine. It felt so good to have my hand held like that I bit my bottom lip. I missed this so much and Chloe was so warm and kind. When she looked at me, I felt like I was tipping forward into her eyes. There was a strength in her that I craved, but it was mixed with compassion. I heard it in the way she talked about her patients and her ex. I wanted someone to care about me like that and I wanted it to be Chloe. I rubbed the pad of my thumb across her palm, forcing myself to look away from the depths of her eyes. Heat rose in my neck and I knew she could see it. I wanted her to. I wanted her to know the effect she was having on me.

"Shit," Chloe said.

I looked back up, but she wasn't looking at me. She was looking over my shoulder toward the plate glass windows of the bar. I twisted in my chair and saw, standing on the sidewalk outside like something out of a sad movie, a person with their palm pressed against the window and tears streaming down their face.

"Blair?" I asked in a quiet voice.

"Yeah." Chloe ran a hand through her hair, her eyes danced around the room, not wanting to settle on anything. No one else was looking at her. Whoever told her ex that Chloe was here on a date wasn't about to fess up now. Chloe looked like she wanted to crawl into a hole and never come out.

"Well, this is a new one on me," I said, forcing a laugh. Chloe didn't laugh. She just looked sad.

"I should talk to them," she said, staring at the tabletop, her ears glowing red. "I understand if you want to go."

Minutes before, I'd wanted nothing more than to stay here with her all night. Now I wanted to stay here with her forever. Anyone who was this kind to an ex crashing her first date was a saint in my book.

"I'll leave if you want me to, but I'd rather stay and finish our date." The desperate hope in her eyes melted my heart. "You're kind and thoughtful even to someone who you aren't married to anymore. That's exactly the person I want to spend more time with."

"Really?"

I leaned in, but not too far with Blair watching. I didn't want to hurt their feelings any more than they already were. "Compassion is sexy, Nurse Chloe."

She smiled so widely and so sweetly it was like looking at a little kid. She got up and hurried out of the bar. I didn't watch her go. I turned a little on my stool so that the mirror over the pool table showed me what was happening outside. I liked her compassion, but I wasn't a fool. Sometimes exes have a power over people. History can make them forget the present. I wanted to be sure Chloe wasn't diving too deeply into her past.

True to her word, Chloe was kind to Blair, who was obviously shattered. They cried so much it was painful to watch, but Chloe's body language was the perfect mix of kindness and distance. When Blair tried to step closer, Chloe took a step back, but she reached out a hand to Blair's shoulder. That seemed to help, but it was also a subtle way for her to keep Blair literally at arm's reach. I wondered if she'd learned the technique in her nurse training or if it was innate.

They talked for a while and I tried to ignore the other patrons shooting glances at me. Their looks were neither interested nor mean—they were pitying. As the conversation continued, I started to feel a little sorry for myself, too. I waved off the waitress's offer of another round and tried not to watch the mirror too closely.

Blair nodded in a final sort of way and wiped their nose with their sleeve. Chloe gave their shoulder a squeeze and then came back in the door. Blair lingered for a moment before leaving, looking not exactly happier, but at least no sadder. Chloe stopped next to a middle-aged woman with hair so bleached it was frizzy and fried. They had a conversation that was distinctly more heated and brief than Chloe's conversation outside.

"I'm sorry." She sat back down, her eyes suspiciously shiny. There was no trace of tears on her cheeks, but she looked tired. "They're having a hard time. And I had a word with the person who called them. It won't happen again."

"Are they going to be okay? They seemed pretty upset."

"Yeah," Chloe ran a hand through her hair again and the rumpled look was really working for me. My mind formed a picture of that hair, even more rumpled, resting on my pillowcase. "They don't really have anyone to talk to anymore so they're lonely."

"I understand that." I took a deep breath and decided to broach the subject I hadn't wanted to talk about tonight. "Alex had a hard time with their transition. We had a lot of queer friends, but they didn't all like how Alex came out."

"What do you mean?" Chloe asked, taking a long drink from her beer.

"There's this narrative in the queer community about how you're supposed to feel when you're trans or nonbinary. Basically that your entire life before the moment of your transition was torture and you have to reject that and embrace your transness or nonbinaryness completely. Alex didn't want to do that."

"They weren't tortured about their gender?"

"Not at all. They felt different and wrong most of their life, but they also loved their time as a butch dyke and embraced it. They were someone else after their transition, but they still embraced the woman of their past. Not all our friends were supportive of that."

"I imagine it was confusing."

"For everyone. Alex knew they didn't want to embrace a story that didn't fit them any more than they wanted to embrace a gender that no longer fit them. Some of our queer friends thought Alex wasn't really nonbinary if they didn't completely change their narrative. One trans friend stopped talking to them because he said they were invalidating his experience. It was a confusing time."

"You said things didn't end well," Chloe said, taking my hand in hers again and speaking in that low, smooth voice that made my heart race. "Did things...escalate?"

"They didn't hit me, but they definitely took their anger and feelings of betrayal out on me. It didn't help that they'd fallen out of love. Eventually all we had left was their anger. I tried to be everything they needed, but I could never fix what other people had broken." I waited for Chloe to look at me before I said, "Some things, people need to come to on their own."

She held my eyes in hers so tightly I could almost feel her embrace. I let my fingers slide from hers, stroking her hand down to her wrist. Her arm shivered under mine and the muscles of her forearm tensed.

"Do you want to get out of here?" she whispered.

CHAPTER TWELVE

I was barely through the front door when it slammed behind me and Chloe pressed her body against mine. Her lips flew all over my neck and cheek, landing on mine with a force that drove the breath out of me. With desperate fingers I pulled her close, crushing into the heavy wooden door with her full weight. The press of her was intoxicating. Warm and strong with that perfect hint of softness I'd seen from across the table and wanted to feel now. I wanted to feel every inch of her.

Her frantic lips slowed and she pulled away. A whimper of loss started in my gut and flew up out of my body in a breath. A coil of desire ripped through me, fed by the separation. It was so cold without the heat of her. She pulled back to cup my face in her hands, looking hard into my eyes. The passion glowed even in the dark room, stealing my breath away.

"You're so fucking beautiful," she whispered, her lips brushing against mine. "So fucking beautiful."

I didn't even have to beg. She was on me again, her hands sliding against my skin where they could and clawing at fabric where they couldn't. I gripped her face this time, holding her close to kiss her on the lips. They were amazing lips, plumper than I thought they would be. The bittersweet burn of Guinness clung to them, making our kisses sticky. Her tongue carried the pungent ripeness of alcohol into my mouth. She was amazing with her tongue, teasing and licking as she explored my mouth. Another groan exploded past my lips, swallowed in the depths of her mouth. When she would have taken her tongue away I sucked it gently, drawing her back inside me. I felt her knees buckle and chuckled into her mouth, adding the hint of vibration to the already delicious kiss.

"Damn," Chloe panted as I released her. I looked up at her through my lashes and she stumbled. I held on, my hands gripping her butt tightly. "Damn."

I took advantage of her distraction to rip open her belt. She looked down at my hands, watching in a daze as I slipped the button free and unzipped her jeans one tooth at a time. Her throat bobbed as she swallowed hard. Stopping there, I leaned back against the door, hooking my fingers in her belt loops and smiling. What she returned was less a smile than a snarl, all teeth and hunger.

She dove back in, her mouth landing on my neck rather than my lips. The straps of my dress slid down as she slathered my shoulders in kisses and gentle bites. Doubt gripped me as the fabric fell away. This was the moment I had craved and feared. She would take my clothes off, but would she like what she saw? Would my extra weight or my thick thighs turn her off? What if she didn't like the shape of my breasts? I slammed my eyelids closed and forced the thoughts from my mind. Taking a deep breath, I tried to focus on what my body was feeling, not what it looked like.

I dropped my head back, running my hands through her thick hair. It had been so long. Too long since I closed my eyes and relaxed into a lover's touch. As she pulled the top of my dress down, revealing my naked breasts to the chill night air, my doubts flared and melted beneath her touch.

Her hands wandered across my skin, lighting me up inside with each touch, each caress. Her kisses moved from my chest to my belly and I felt the impact of her knees on the floor as she explored me. She had a delicate touch for such a powerful woman and the dichotomy was intoxicating. Gentleness and strength. Tenderness and resolve. Her mouth followed in her fingers' wake, soothing the fire of her touch with hot, wet kisses.

Too wet.

My eyes flew open, showing me the dark corners of my ceiling. I listened as hard as I could and there it was. A quiet, almost imperceptible sob. I didn't want to look down. I didn't want it to be happening, but I knew it was. Chloe wasn't kissing me anymore. She was crying, her head pressed hard against my belly.

"Are you…"

Before I could get the question out, she shot up and away, turning her back to me. She held her head in her hands and her back heaved as she cried.

"Chloe, are you okay?"

She cried even harder, quiet sobs swallowed up by her hands pressed against her face. I took an awkward step forward, reaching out for her. What was I supposed to do? Pat her on the back? Hold her while she cried? I didn't have to decide because she whipped around, still keeping her face averted from mine like a vampire crouching away from the morning sun.

"I'm sorry!" she screamed, snatching her jacket off the floor and fighting with the door handle. She finally managed to get it open and was through it in a flash, her loose belt buckle smacking hard against the wood. "I'm so sorry!"

The door slammed hard in my face. There was a single, muffled sob that filtered through the door and then I was standing, naked to the waist, alone in my dark foyer. After a few minutes I heard the sound of an engine roaring to life and then squealing tires. I stayed perfectly still, hoping against hope that it was a bad dream and I'd wake up passed out in my office or something. Was a brain tumor-induced hallucination really so much to ask?

The cold air on my exposed skin finally made me move. I pulled my dress back into place and slumped against the door.

"Stupid. Stupid. Stupid." I grabbed fistfuls of my hair and banged the back of my head into the door in rhythm with my words.

How could this have happened? It was so clear in retrospect. The scene at the bar had made it seem like the lingering feelings were Blair's, but there'd been so many red flags long before tonight. They'd been apparent since the first night we talked. The signs were all there but I was too lonely and too horny to notice them. Now I was even lonelier and definitely hornier, but I had humiliation to add on top of it. Sure, I didn't have the best relationship history before this, but at least I'd never had anyone start crying about their ex while going down on me. Life just kept getting better and better.

I pressed my palms into my eyes until little stars popped in the darkness. It didn't help the ache between my legs, but it definitely helped fuel the anger burning in my guts. If she didn't want me, why had she driven across town to sleep with me?

"Women!"

My shout echoed in the hollow rooms, reminding me, as though I needed the reminder, how very alone I was.

"Stop feeling sorry for yourself, Kieran," I growled into the darkness. "It's pathetic."

Grabbing my purse from the floor, I headed into the living room, flipping on lights as I went. I finally managed to pry the phone from inside and checked the time. It was late. Much later than I usually stayed up and way too late to call Pen, especially on a hookup night. I sent her a text instead, informing her that I was picking her up for work in the morning.

We needed to talk.

CHAPTER THIRTEEN

Pen lived in a Woodbridge townhouse community not far from me. I say it wasn't far and that was true geographically. Price range was a whole different story. Pen had expensive tastes but she wasn't born rich. She had to work for the finer things in life, so she worked damn hard. Unlike me, she hadn't been through an expensive divorce that left her barely clinging to her plush digs. Maybe she was on the right track with the whole not-settling-down thing. The Belmont Bay neighborhood, hugging the waterfront and a national wildlife refuge, was a prime location Pen had paid out the nose for.

There wasn't much parking, but I managed a spot close to her front door. The sun was kissing Pen's postage stamp lawn when I climbed the steps to her front porch. The grass was so deeply green, an unusual color in this exclusive commuter suburb, and the porch so bright white it reminded me again the joys of having an effective homeowners' association. Mine ensured residents didn't have too much trash in their front yards and left it at that.

Pen's phone was in her hand when she answered the door. "Just got your text. Come on in." She stepped aside to let me pass. "Let me grab some food and my meds."

"Sure," I said, admiring her house as always.

Like mine, it had an open floor plan. Unlike mine, it had twelve-foot ceilings, gleaming hardwood floors and a couch that made me sleepy just looking at it. We'd shared innumerable bottles of wine on those deep cushions. I'd slept off a few of them there, too. While sitting on that very couch I'd cried in her arms when I found out about Nick's affair.

"Want a smoothie?" Pen asked, pulling a second travel mug down from her cabinet.

"Definitely," I responded, slipping onto a barstool. "But I'd rather have coffee."

The kitchen was even more gorgeous than the living room. The counter was bright white quartz with a butcher's-block island in the center of the room. The cabinets were dark chestnut with gleaming chrome hardware. I loved this kitchen so much. If only I could afford to redo mine with some of those features. Of course, the low countertops, rounded corners, and soft-close cabinets and drawers weren't vanity in this case, they were a necessity. A fact I was reminded of when Pen snagged her bag of meds from a cabinet.

"We'll have to stop somewhere for coffee," she replied, her head buried in the cabinet.

Normally her morning meds included five pills and a supplement shake. The shake was already made, waiting next to her breakfast smoothie, but she grabbed an extra bottle this morning. I recognized the shape and size of the pill as her more powerful pain killer.

"Everything okay, Pen?"

Her voice was flat when she replied with a simple, "Yep."

That was about all I could expect from her and it was enough. She didn't talk about her health much, but she was always honest when she did. It had taken her more than a year to tell me she had hypermobile Ehlers-Danlos syndrome.

I'd never heard of Ehlers-Danlos syndrome before I'd met Pen, but I'd learned a lot in the years since. To the outside world, EDS can look negligible at best and a cool party trick at worst. In reality it was a gene mutation that affected the body's collagen production. Since collagen is the building block of connective tissue, the main symptom is hypermobile joints. When Pen was a kid, she used to show off to her classmates by contorting her elbows and shoulders into crazy positions. It was also the reason she had that baby-soft skin that made me super jealous.

In life there is always a downside and the downside to EDS was pretty massive. That hypermobility led to joints that would dislocate at will. I'd seen her ankle go out just walking down a carpeted hall. Once a tendon stretched to its limit, collagen wasn't there to pull it back into shape. Constantly dislocating joints led to extreme and chronic pain.

She kept it quiet and I had to admit, it was probably the right thing to do. Like so many other people in her life, as soon as I'd found out, I started treating Pen differently. Not something I'm proud of.

I would reach to pick things up for her and recommend hanging out at home rather than going out. Worse, I asked her about her health a dozen times a day. I'd thought I was being kind, but I was really being patronizing, as she told me in great detail when we finally had a fight about it. She wanted me to treat her like I had before rather than something fragile that might break at any moment. It took us a long time to get there, but it meant a lot that she cared enough about our friendship to let me screw up and still take me back.

I was about to ask about the lack of coffee when Pen's bedroom door burst open. I recognized the woman who tumbled out into the living room, her hair a mess and only one shoe on. It was the one whose walk Pen had called gay the night before. I shot an amazed look at Pen and caught sight of her sliding the bag of pills behind her back, hiding it from the view of the woman who'd spent the night in her bed. The woman stopped short, looking back and forth between Pen and me. I could tell the moment she recognized me, because red shot up her neck and onto her cheeks. She looked like she might have a heart attack if she didn't take a deep breath.

"Uh...good morning," I said, breaking the awkward silence.

The woman looked at me in horror. Her mouth dropped open and she mouthed something, though no sound came out. Apparently she wasn't ready to examine what last night had meant, at least not with me. She transferred her stare to Pen but must have known better than to expect too much support from that source. Pen gave her a long, appraising look from head to toe and winked. She gurgled a laugh that made it all too clear she was still under Pen's thrall. Without a word, she slipped on her second shoe and bolted for the door.

Once the door slammed behind her, I turned back to Pen. She knew damn well that I wanted an explanation, but she shrugged and tossed her pills back, washing them down with a long gulp of her shake.

She handed me my smoothie, a sickly green color but smelling like strawberries, and headed for the door. I knew I wasn't likely to get details out of her about the night. Pen wasn't the type to kiss and tell, but I couldn't help teasing her a little about this one.

"Well," I said as I walked past her out the front door. "She certainly walks gay now."

Pen snorted, nearly spraying shake everywhere, and locked her door. The woman was pulling away, and she kept her eyes on Pen the whole time. Pen watched her, a crease of worry forming between her eyebrows.

"I don't think this one took the disclaimer to heart."

CHAPTER FOURTEEN

It wasn't Pen's laughter that got to me—I was expecting that. If she'd had a woman half-strip her and then start weeping onto her stomach, I'd have ruthlessly teased her. She would never hear the end of it. No, it was the fact that, while she was laughing, she groaned and clutched her side. That, mixed with the extra pain pill she'd taken, sent me right back into mother-hen protectiveness. Before I could make an ass of myself by asking about it, we pulled into the parking lot and she turned her sweet, serious scowl on me.

"How about I take you to lunch with me and the Rainbow Zebras?" We got out of the car and she slid her arm around my shoulders. "I promise it'll cheer you up."

The last thing I wanted to do was spend my lunch break with a bunch of strangers, but Pen was usually so opposed to any of her groups of friends meeting each other. The invitation was such a surprise, and she looked at me with this soft expression I couldn't figure out. If she'd been my girlfriend, I'd have expected her to kiss my forehead or something equally squishy. No way

Pen was gonna do that, but it felt good to be looked at that way. Plus her arm around me felt nice so I let my head drop on her shoulder.

"That's sweet."

"It's also self-serving," she said, giving me a little shove, the soft expression gone. "I don't have a car today thanks to you, so if you say no you're keeping me from my friends."

It was a fair argument, and I was always going to give in anyway. In eleven years, I had never denied Pen anything. We agreed to meet in her office at eleven thirty and then went our separate ways. I accomplished exactly nothing for the next three and a half hours. Unless occasionally recalling the previous night and curling into a quivering ball of embarrassment counted. If it did I had enough billable hours to take the rest of the week off.

On the drive to lunch I ran through everything I knew about the folks we were meeting. It wasn't much. All I knew was they all had EDS. She'd mentioned one of them, Vanessa, had started using a wheelchair the year before, but the rest of them were a complete mystery. Their shared diagnosis had brought them together, and that seemed to be enough.

Most of the drive I fretted about Pen and her new pain, but when we pulled into the restaurant parking lot, she looked fine. On days like these it was easy to forget that she had a chronic illness. She teased me as we walked in for checking my phone for messages from Chloe.

"Do you really want her to call?" Pen asked, letting me open the door. "After that scene last night?"

"No," I said. *Yes.*

She wasn't fooled. "Come on, Kieran. Have a little self-respect."

"You didn't see how hot she was."

"No, I did not. Tell me, was she an ugly crier or a sexy crier? Is there a way to sexy-cry about your ex while scoring with another woman?"

I didn't answer but I could feel my face heating up. Even I wasn't sure if it was embarrassment or anger.

"Where do you think she went after she left your place last night?"

"Okay, Penelope," I said, holding my voice as steady as possible. "I get it."

"Do you? 'Cause it doesn't sound like you do." She reached over and grabbed my hand. It always amazed me how strong her hands were when their skin was so soft. "I don't want to see you hurt again, Kieran. You deserve better."

"Penny!" someone shouted from across the room.

I stared at the floor so no one could see me cry. Pen squeezed my hand and I felt a little better, but not much. Mainly I felt awful because I wasn't sure I believed that last part of her speech.

"Come on," she said as she steered me between tables. "Let's get some grub."

I didn't look up until we reached the table. By then I was sure I had control over the grief that had gripped me.

I pulled up short. "Oh."

A pair of tables had been pushed together and a dozen women, all unmistakably queer, sat around them.

"What did you think the rainbow part meant?" Pen whispered in my ear.

"How colorful you all are?"

Pen laughed and dragged me forward. "We are colorful as hell."

A woman with dark, spiky hair spun her wheelchair toward us. "My language is colorful, does that count?"

"Sure as fuck does," shouted another woman, this one wearing a broad leather collar.

"Zebras, this is Kieran," Pen said, her wide smile returned by everyone. "Kieran, these are the Rainbow Zebras."

"Pleasure," I said. My West Virginia twang, always more prominent when I was super drunk or super nervous, drew out the word into something almost risqué.

"Come sit next to me," Vanessa said as someone called Pen over.

I was happy to drop into the seat beside her. I'd worn taller heels than usual today. A hint of vanity I allowed myself after the previous night's humiliation. If I had one quality feature, it was my calves.

"So you're the famous Kieran," Vanessa said, leaning on the arm of her chair and looking me over. "I thought you'd be taller."

I snorted into my water glass. "And you're the famous Vanessa."

"You thought I'd be shorter, didn't you? I did lose an inch or two. Five ankle surgeries before thirty will do that to you. That's a benefit of the chair. No one knows I'm tiny."

A waitress came by to take everyone's order, and I used the distraction to wrack my brain for all the details Pen had shared about Vanessa. As with everything else in her life, she hadn't said much. I knew Vanessa had thrown a big party the previous summer right after she was fitted for her chair. She'd called it her Walking Retirement Party and had lit a ceremonial pyre for her forearm crutches. The fire department had been called.

I'd been amazed at the time that anyone would celebrate the loss of her mobility, but seeing her teasing smile now, it made perfect sense. When joint degeneration was inevitable, acceptance seemed the most reasonable choice.

"Can I ask you something?" I leaned closer to Vanessa so she could hear me over the lunchtime crowd.

Vanessa's suggestive drawl rivaled Pen's when she answered, "Libra, but on the cusp so I'm wild as a Scorpio."

I laughed and she winked back. "Why do you call yourselves The Rainbow Zebras?"

"Cause we're all queer, sweetie."

"I picked up on that." There were more tattoos and pompadours at the table than Riveter's saw in a week. "Since you're all women. I actually meant the zebra part."

"Actually that's not because we're queer, that's 'cause of Ehlers-Danlos." When I gave her a quizzical look, she continued, "EDS is more common in women than men. Helpful for those of us who like to cruise the message boards looking for dates."

Every woman within earshot rolled her eyes. More than one made snide comments about having to chase both Vanessa and Pen off. Pen looked our way with a predatory gleam in her eye, but she immediately turned back to her conversation with the only member who looked unhappy.

"So," I nudged Vanessa back on topic. "The zebra thing?"

"Zebras are the mascot of the EDS community. Ever heard the saying 'when you hear hoofbeats, look for a horse, not a zebra'?"

"Sure. I grew up in the country, there's an old adage for everything."

"Most medical students in America have it burned into their minds. To look for the mundane. The easiest explanation is usually the correct one."

"Makes sense."

"Except sometimes it really is a zebra." While she explained I looked around the table. The group included the full spectrum of women. Femme and butch and everything between. Tall, short, thin, heavy, and several races. This group was a rainbow in more ways than one. "EDS is rare and difficult to diagnose, most of us have a hard time getting a doctor to even believe us. When I complained of pain to my first doctor, he told me I had fibromyalgia."

"I've been accused of drug seeking by two doctors," said a willowy Black woman across the table. "The rest say I'm flexible and I should be glad."

"I've had it lucky," Vanessa said. "At least fibromyalgia is real. A lot of doctors think we're making it up."

"They refuse to see our stripes and call us wild horses," drawled a pale blonde with a mountain twang that rivalled mine.

The whole table laughed along with her. The sentiment had the practiced ring of a group motto. Pen looked up at the laughter and caught my eye, but then she turned her grin on Vanessa who held her hands up in mock innocence. If there were ever a pair of wild horses, it was these two.

"I'm surprised Penny didn't tell you about the zebra thing," Vanessa said as the waitress deposited a hummus platter in front of her.

"Oh, I try not to be too nosy." I thanked the waitress for my club sandwich and explained, "Didn't want her to feel like she was some interesting museum exhibit."

That's how I'd felt when I came out. Everyone I told started in with the twenty questions and it was exhausting. I'd gone through it again when I explained Alex's pronoun change. I shoved a fry in my mouth and chewed as Vanessa watched me.

"What brings you to our little group today?"

"Pen's trying to cheer me up." Grilled sourdough bread hugging a huge stack of deli meat was improving my mood, so I decided I could be honest. "I had a horrible date last night."

Vanessa nodded and dropped the remnants of her pita triangle back onto the plate. "I have some horror stories myself. Being in the chair doesn't help, although I kept myself busy for a while with folks who liked the kink."

I choked on my fry and she chuckled.

"Speaking of, you'll have to forgive me for not flirting. Penny would kill me."

My forehead crinkled, but I noticed that Pen was keeping a close eye on us. She was always watchful, but this felt more protective. It actually felt kind of nice for her to look out for me. "Why? Are you a player?"

"Of course. Just like her." Vanessa continued, "Penny's very protective of her friends and she talks about you enough to make me run the other way."

Before I could ask what she meant by that, Pen leaned over us, a hand on both our shoulders. "And what are you two lovely ladies talking about?"

"Me dating," I said.

"You," Vanessa said at the same time.

Pen's face went so pale I thought she might pass out. She didn't look at me, but rather at the remains of my lunch when she asked, "You and me dating?"

Vanessa roared with laughter and smacked the table. I could see her wrist bend back farther than should have been possible, but the movement didn't seem to hurt her at all. Color came back into Pen's cheeks and she finally met my gaze, rolling her eyes as she jerked her chin at her friend.

"Funny," Vanessa spluttered. "As if you would ever date anyone."

I could feel Pen's hand relax against my skin. Her whole body slumped beside me, in fact. I laughed along with them, but I couldn't help the ripple of annoyance that spread through me. Was the idea of dating me so awful? It's fine that she didn't commit, but she didn't have to freak out quite so much at the mere thought of being my girlfriend.

"So how are things going with that cougar of yours?" Pen asked Vanessa.

"Claire is hardly a cougar. She's only fifty."

"Yeah and you're thirty." Pen shot me toothy grin. "I do love an age-gap romance."

The two of them fell into a banter that had the ring of familiarity to it. The longer they chatted, the more I relaxed. There was something intimate about this moment that I hadn't seen in Pen's banter with Ashley or any of her colleagues. It wasn't like what she had with me, either. She was teasing like usual, but she was flirting, too. Pen never flirted with me, even after Nick and Alex were gone, but she was relaxed when we talked. I could see the walls she put up with Vanessa. Or maybe they were different walls when it was just Pen and me. Either way, I was quickly forgetting all about the previous night's disaster.

The reprieve only lasted as long as the meal.

Back at work later, I couldn't settle to anything. I stared at my computer screen without blinking for so long my eyes dried out. I checked Swingle in case Chloe had messaged, but she had disappeared from my app. That meant one of two things. She had either blocked me or deleted her profile. I dug my *Goonies* pen out of my purse and spent approximately thirty minutes agonizing over which one it was and what it meant. If she'd blocked me, she had no intention of dating me. If she'd deleted her profile, she had no intention of dating anyone because she was back with Blair. That realization took two minutes. The other twenty-eight minutes of my ruminations were spent sloshing the pen back and forth while realizing that it didn't matter either way. I wouldn't be hearing from her again.

I couldn't figure out what had gone wrong. Why would she have messaged me in the first place if she wasn't over her ex? Was there something about me that drew her in when she was clearly still rebounding? It was impossible. All she knew about me was in my profile. There couldn't be anything there that would say I would be a good person to hook up with while she was still into someone else. Was there? I wasn't sure because Pen had written the whole thing.

I went back to my profile, but there wasn't a lot I could see on my phone. I needed to use a real computer to get the dirt on myself. Biting my bottom lip, I shot a glance over at the idling monitor on my desk. Randy didn't pay for an updated monitoring program for the computer network. Unfortunately I knew that because I had once walked in on Art looking at some websites that would definitely fall under the "not suitable for work" category. No one should have a Thursday like that one. Still, I wasn't like Art. It felt wrong to use my work computer to fine-tune my online dating profile.

My desk phone rang and I snatched up the receiver. "Uh… Kieran Hall, HomeScape Settlement Services."

"Hello uh…Kieran Hall," Penelope said, laughter swallowing her words. "Did I catch you at a bad time?"

"Nope. You're just the person I wanted to talk to."

"If I had a nickel for every time a woman said that to me."

"You'd have one nickel," I teased. "Listen, Pen, what did you put in my profile about Alex?"

"Alex? In your dating profile? Nothing." I knew she was thinking because I could hear her clicking her fingernail against her teeth, so I waited. "Yeah. Nothing."

"You didn't say anything in there about me breaking up with someone recently?"

"Well, yeah. Under relationship status there was an option for 'recently separated' or something like that. I didn't mention Alex though."

While she spoke, I made the decision to misuse the company computer this one time. There it was, showing I was recently separated, but there was a comment section that Pen had filled in.

"I was divorced seven years ago from my high school sweetheart," I read aloud. "After my divorce I had a serious relationship that recently ended and I'm ready to start looking for my next serious relationship."

"Yeah," Pen said.

"Alex and I broke up almost two years ago."

"And you haven't been ready to date until now."

Indignation crept into my voice as I clicked the edit button. "I was enjoying some time to get to know myself. It's not that I wasn't ready."

"That's literally what you said to me when you asked for my help. You said you were ready to get out there again. Meaning you weren't ready before."

"I know what I said." I sounded like a bratty teenager, but I couldn't help it. "You didn't have to tell the whole world."

"Then change it, sweetie," Pen said, her tone softening. "I'm sorry. I was only trying to help."

"I know," I said, feeling like a jerk for being so grumpy. "I appreciate everything you do for me. I just…"

"I know," she said quietly when I couldn't find words to complete the sentence. "It's tough."

I bit the inside of my cheek to keep from crying and saved the changes to my profile. After some thought I went back in and changed my relationship status from "recently separated" to "divorced" which wasn't quite as accurate but it had more finality without the "recently" part.

"I'm sorry I'm such a bitch, Pen."

"You're not a bitch."

"Debatable. Anyway, why'd you call me?"

"I'm heading out early to hit the pool. I'm going to catch an Uber so you don't have to worry about taking me home."

"Are you sure that's a good idea?" I asked, thinking about the pain pill again. "Aren't you in pain?"

"Girl, if I skipped swimming every time I slipped a rib laughing at your hookup attempts, I'd never get a lap in."

"Very funny. Have you talked to your doctor?"

There was a long silence from Pen's end of the phone and I realized I'd overstepped again. "Kieran, I've had EDS my whole life. I know how to manage my symptoms."

"I know. I'm sorry," I rushed out. Conversations were not going well for me today. "I'm being pushy."

"It's okay. I love that you care. Just don't care too much, okay?"

"I think I can handle that." I knew I couldn't. Pen was the most important person in my life. She was more than a friend, she was the only family I had. I couldn't stop caring, but I could at least keep it to myself. "Have fun at the pool."

"Oh I will. There's a very cute lifeguard there. Maybe I can convince her to help me with my breaststroke."

I rolled my eyes as we said our goodbyes. As rigid as she was about her schedule, there weren't a lot of times when Pen stopped chasing skirts. I turned back to my computer, ready to close out the Swingle webpage and pretend I'd never stepped a toe across the line of professionalism. Problem was, when I looked back I had a little red heart over the mailbox icon. It wouldn't hurt to spend another few minutes on the site. After all, I thought as I pushed a stack of paperwork away, the job would still be there after I checked that one message.

CHAPTER FIFTEEN

The next few people I swiped right on turned out to be a waste of my time. There were two men who each seemed nice enough, but one got weirdly angry when I wouldn't meet in person the same day and the other just vanished from the site. Pen said I got ghosted, but I thought that required actually knowing someone's name first. We never even got to that point before he ran off. Then there was a woman that I didn't click with. At least she and I were able to admit it wouldn't work. A week after the disaster with Chloe, I was ready to give up and get a cat.

Thursday morning I was scheduled for a loan closing with a young couple buying their first home. I'd emailed the husband several times to set the appointment. Unfortunately, he neglected to mention he and his wife were bringing their four-month-old baby to the closing. At least they said it was a baby. It may have been a demon released from the pits of hell. I heard the wailing from the parking lot and hoped the parents were going to meet Pen. She hated kids even more than I did but she would never turn down a commission, even if there was an infant involved. The screaming grew louder and louder, then finally burst through the front door of our offices.

It was inevitable, of course. I was in some loop of misery that wasn't destined to end any time soon. Carol came to collect me wearing that teary, sweaty look pregnant women had around cute babies. She was practically hopping. I groaned inwardly and pretended to be thrilled. I really didn't want to explain for the millionth time how I was that apparently defective brand of woman who never wanted one of those smelly, screaming beasts of my own.

The baby, who was most unfortunately named Chester, howled through introductions as we settled into the conference room. I barely knew their accompanying Realtor, a wispy older woman who wore a business suit well enough to be labelled a mommi but lacking the attitude to pull it off. This was going to be a very long closing. I tried to shout over the baby for a little while, but it was a losing battle. The husband smiled sheepishly and apologized for his offspring.

"Teething," he said as if I was supposed to know what that meant.

The wife got up and carried Chester around the room, bouncing him up and down and cooing in an annoyed rather than soothing way. The husband watched her, smiling absently. When their eyes met, they shared a look so sweet it made my teeth ache, but then Chester shrieked and they both cringed.

The baby quieted enough that I could hear myself think, but then all I could think about was whether junior was going to barf. Mom was shaking him pretty vigorously and I pictured a can of soda exploding after the same sort of jiggling.

"Is this your first?" I asked as I notarized the first of many signatures.

The husband laughed and it was a pleasant sound. That, mixed with the attractive set of his jaw, was almost enough to smooth over my current low opinion of men. "How can you tell? We'll get used to it once we get settled."

When he glanced over his shoulder, his wife gave him a weak smile. I remembered smiles like those too well. They were two people who truly loved each other but worried every single day if the stress of what they were doing would shatter them. It had with Nick and me, I hoped it wouldn't with them. Marriage was so hard. It took very special people to make it work. And very special love, too.

"It'll help so much when we get our new place," the wife whispered, sitting back down. The baby seemed to be asleep, but none of us were interested in testing it. "I'm sorry about Ches."

"It's fine," I said, spinning the next page toward them on the desk. "He's adorable."

I followed the little white lie with an explanation of the Virginia Land Record. It wasn't too complicated, but I was happy to see that both husband and wife gave the documents their full attention. The Realtor was texting. I'd never seen a Realtor less interested in a closing. This was, after all, the part where they got paid.

As I slid the signed document back into the stack, the wife and I snuck a peek at Chester. He was definitely asleep. His head lolled off her shoulder and his mouth was open in a perfect O. Drool liberally spiked with milk trickled onto his chubby cheek.

"Do you have any kids?" she asked.

I checked her name from the document in front of me. Kristin Spencer. She was kind of cute, too, behind the exhausted eyes and frazzled hair. "No, Mrs. Spencer. I married young and divorced young. No kids for me."

"Please, call me Kristin. And it's not too late."

I chose to believe she meant to find someone else to marry, not to have kids. "I've actually just gotten back into the dating scene."

"Good for you," Mr. Spencer said. "Found anyone special yet?

After explaining the next document to them, I admitted, "I keep thinking maybe so, but it's not as easy on this side of thirty. I…well, I'm using one of those dating apps. It's embarrassing, but nothing else worked."

Her husband held the paper for Kristin so she could sign one-handed while juggling their baby. It was sweet how he stepped right in to help without her having to ask. A moment of appreciation passed between them. It was the briefest touch of their eyes, but there was an affection there that I craved. I wanted to have those simple moments with someone.

"That's not embarrassing at all," Kristin said, pushing the page back to me. "Everyone uses dating apps."

"Maybe in your generation," I said, feeling every one of the ten years' age difference between this couple and myself. "But last time I was dating it wasn't exactly seen in the best light."

"Well, it's seen very differently now," she replied, the warmth in her tone making this feel like a friendly chat rather than a lecture on modern society. "Matthew and I met on a dating site and look at us now."

She slid her hand across her husband's arm and he smiled down at her. It was such a sweet moment that I didn't ruin it by mentioning the milky spit bubble forming on Chester's lips as he slept. Or the distinctly unromantic smell coming from his diaper. It was great to know real people found love on dating sites. Not hookups like Pen or disasters like me.

The rest of the closing went like clockwork and, when they shook my hand with tears in their eyes, I was sad to say goodbye. That was until Chester woke up and started singing the song of his people again, but you can't have everything. Their Realtor came to not long after Chester, ripping herself away from her phone and scurrying from the room.

I took the paperwork back to my office to sort for filing at the courthouse. My phone pinged. The Swingle app opened straight to the new message. The sender was a man and I was close to deleting it, but his profile picture caught my eye. I took the plunge and swiped right to see more. Instead of squinting, I pulled up the site on my work computer, looking guiltily toward Randy's office as I did. The guy was cute, with a square jaw and a light growth of beard. If I had a type when it came to men, he fit it almost as well as Chloe had fit my type for women.

What the hell, I needed to put myself out there, didn't I? With a deep breath and another guilty look around the office, I started my reply.

CHAPTER SIXTEEN

He didn't turn out to be as charming as Chloe, but he wasn't as flirty as Carla, so I decided to give Kevin a chance. When we chatted online he was less talkative than I would like, but I chalked it up to being a guy. I'd never met one of the species who shared as much as I wanted him to, though I'd heard tales that such a creature did exist.

Within the first few days of chatting, I'd learned that we shared a love of Early Mountain Vineyards and a dislike of team sports. Everything else was pretty much surface-level discussion of our days. I didn't hate chatting with him, but I wasn't exactly yearning to get my hands on him. Maybe that was a good thing? Yearning hadn't worked out for me yet. Maybe ambivalence was the key to lasting love.

After a week, he asked me out. I'd started messaging someone else too, but that wasn't going anywhere. It was all making me a little sad, so I accepted the date with Kevin. Not the best reason to agree, but Pen kept encouraging me to give everyone a try. This date couldn't be worse than the last two. That thought was the best proof yet how naïve I was being about this whole dating thing.

Kevin seemed excited, the first time he'd shown any real emotion in our interactions.

Excellent. I have the perfect date planned. How about next Monday?
Perfect date? That's a lot of pressure for a first date.
Trust me.

He followed it with a winking emoji but wouldn't give me any more details. I should've been nervous, but he was so excited that it rubbed off on me. I looked at his profile picture again and felt the familiar butterflies of physical attraction. He could not have looked more different from Nick and that was absolutely a good thing.

I'd met Nick my sophomore year of high school. I'd gone to a tiny school outside Morgantown, West Virginia and there weren't exactly a lot of newcomers to the area, so when he showed up my hormone-riddled heart turned to mush. At the time I mistook my interest in butch women, of which there were many straight versions in West Virginia, for an attraction to feminine men. Nick fit that bill. He was tall and thin with delicate features, pouty lips, and long eyelashes. He also paid me a lot more attention than I was used to.

I didn't exactly fit into Appalachian culture with my dislike of the outdoors, hippie intellectual parents, and undefinable otherness. It took a long time to realize that my otherness was queerness, but by then I was in love with Nick so it didn't seem to matter much. When we were married and settled in the DC suburbs, I decided I could trust him with my truth. The revelation didn't go over well. I'd fallen for him because he wasn't like the closeminded rednecks I grew up with. In the end he wasn't as openminded as I thought.

Nick stretched far enough to agree to couple's counseling, but he never committed to the process and I was too bitter about his rejection of my sexuality to be understanding. I still loved him though. I wanted to make it work. That's why it hurt so much when I found out about his affair. It hurt even more when he told me he wanted a divorce so he could marry her. I should've been the bigger person, happy for him finding love again and having the children I never wanted. Even after all these years, I couldn't bring myself to forgive him for breaking my heart. Kevin may not score points for charm, but at least he didn't remind me of Nick.

On Sunday night, Kevin texted me the address of a bar in Alexandria and told me to meet him there at seven o'clock the following evening. The timing worked out well and I made plans to meet Pen at nine, leaving it to her to find a place to ogle women that wasn't in the heart of DC. I thought it would be a big ask considering Alexandria is mostly Department of Defense contractors and rich, white professionals, but apparently Pen had a spot there anyway. To make my intentions clear with Kevin, I told him I had an early start Tuesday and he readily accepted my need to leave early. Another point in his favor.

Since I wasn't going into the city, I had time to go home and change beforehand. Kevin had been texting me since late morning, each message better than the last. I teased and he flirted, I flirted and he teased. It was clear he was excited about his surprise date and that made me excited, too. I spent the drive trying to guess what he'd planned. We'd talked a little about our interests, but nothing in our favorite food, movies, and TV shows pointed to an obvious perfect date. But I didn't know what my perfect date looked like. It would be really exciting if Kevin knew.

The address he'd given me was for a bar in Old Town. I'd looked it up online, but there didn't seem to be anything special about it. It seemed likely that this was somewhere to meet to grab a drink before our perfect date began. I had noticed that their wine list included a few bottles from Early Mountain. Maybe that explained why he'd chosen this place to start our date.

I wore a conservative sun dress in a shade of blue that complimented my eyes but wasn't too flashy. This was nothing like my date with Chloe. I was not going to go home with him tonight and this outfit was designed to be cute but not give anyone the wrong impression. Unfortunately, this turned out to be one of those rare chilly summer nights. I hurried down the sidewalk to get out of the brisk air.

The bar was thumping and Kevin was pacing the sidewalk.

"Hey!" he yelled, waving me over.

Kevin was even better looking in person than his profile picture. He hadn't shaved in a few days, sporting a thin growth of neck beard. He looked great in a tight-fitting T-shirt under his sports jacket and an even tighter pair of dark-washed jeans. He bent down to kiss me on the cheek, which I thought was a little forward for our first meeting, but at least he didn't try to look down my dress.

"Perfect timing," he said, with a hand on my shoulder leading me toward the bar. "The show just started."

"Show?"

My question was swallowed in a blast of sound as he opened the front door. It bore little resemblance to music and was so loud I cringed. I thought it might sound better once my mind had time to adjust to its new surroundings.

It did not.

Kevin kept his hand on my shoulder as we wove between people and furniture. I was about to shake him off when he stopped and pulled out a barstool stuck under a high-top table near the side wall. Unfortunately, it was also near a massive speaker, which probably explained it being the only unoccupied table in sight.

Kevin shouted something at me but I couldn't make out his words over the roar of music. I shrugged and he mimed tipping back a drink before scurrying off. He hadn't asked what I wanted, but I assumed he'd bring me one of the wines we'd discussed. I assumed wrong. Seemingly hours later, as the band was winding down a song that sounded like mumbled Mandarin accompanied by toddlers banging on pots, he pushed his way back through the crowd with two cans of beer.

"Whew," he said, plopping down across from me and shouting over the banter of the lead singer. He pushed one of the cans toward me. "Gansey."

"Beg pardon?" My ears were still ringing.

He waggled his beer can. "Narragansett. You like it?"

I took an experimental sip. No. No, I did not like it. It tasted like a shittier version of PBR, something I did not think was possible. I tried diplomatic noncommittal in my answer, "Mmm. I've never had this before."

"You've never had a Gansey?" He said it like I'd confessed to never noticing the sun. "It was my favorite back in my school days. We never had anything else at the frat house."

That little nugget was the only thing I learned about him because the band started up again with a bass line that rattled the fillings in my teeth. This song was worse than the last, though Kevin was transfixed. That song bled into the next and the next. Kevin kept his eyes glued on the stage apart from the occasional glance my way. The smile I returned grew weaker with each song. Had he really thought the perfect first date included an activity that kept us from speaking to each other for an hour? My boredom led me to look up the band on my phone.

According to the sticker on the drum kit, they were The C-18s, an experimental punk band made up of laboratory chemists from Quantico. Nothing on the band's religiously updated Facebook page told me why Kevin would be a fan or why he thought I might be. The only other break in their hour-long set came while Kevin was waiting in line for another beer. That first sip had been all I'd needed and hadn't touched mine since. He sang along to the encore song before turning his sweaty grin on me.

"Cool, right?"

I gave a half-hearted nod and he grabbed my hand, dragging me back through the crowd toward the exit. Since another band was about to set up and they looked to be in the same vein as The C-18s, I saw this as a blessing. Yet again, I was quite mistaken.

He hurried me through the streets, giving me little time to wonder where we were headed. Preferably somewhere quiet and quaint with a dessert menu and craft cocktails. We zipped past the bar where I would soon meet Pen, and I considered yanking my hand free and darting inside. I didn't have the chance. He was practically running.

"Where's the fire?" I gasped as we waited to cross the street.

"I know you have to be home early," he said, jogging between cars and throwing up a friendly wave to a sedan blaring its horn at us. "I want to make sure we make it for the main event."

Great. Another event. Not a quiet place where we could get to know each other.

He skidded to a stop outside the one place that was my worst nightmare. Okay, not my worst nightmare. My worst nightmare would be a karaoke bar packed with creepy clowns and drunk coeds. This place didn't have a single clown in sight.

There was a ten-dollar cover to attend this travesty of musical incompetence, but Kevin was gentlemanly enough to pay for both of us. He was also gentlemanly enough to buy us drinks, though he neglected yet again to ask me what I wanted and returned with a pair of cans suspiciously similar to the one I'd left behind half-full. This beer was actually worse because it was lukewarm, so I didn't even taste it. Truth be told, it would've been better to get blackout drunk so I didn't have to be on this date anymore.

"Are you gonna sing it?" Kevin asked, leaning in uncomfortably close to me as he started on his second beer.

"Sing what?" I asked, pressing my untouched can to my lips to avoid any attempt at kissing.

"Come on!" He dragged out the last word, giving it the tone of an inside joke. "Your song."

It was at this point in the evening that I began to wonder if he had asked me out by mistake, intending this date for some other woman he was chatting with. Someone for whom this may actually be fun. He smiled and shook his head, returning his attention to the blonde singing so vigorously she tumbled off the stage.

When she was done and her friends serenaded her with hoots and whistles, Kevin turned his grin back on me. "Are you ready to sing it?"

"Kevin," I said, checking my watch. "I don't know what you're talking about and I have to..."

"Country Roads!" he shouted. "Come on, I told the emcee to keep it on hold for us. I thought we could do it as a duet."

I stared at him and silently counted to ten in my head. When I was finished, I set my full can on the table, grabbed my purse, and headed for the door. He caught up with me on the sidewalk.

"What the hell, Kieran? I went through a lot of trouble to set this all up."

"Had you put any time into actually asking me what I wanted to do, you would have known I think this is ridiculous." I could see the bar where I wanted to be—the bar where Pen was—directly over his shoulder. The sooner I got rid of Kevin, the sooner I could go over there. "Why would you think this is a date I would want to go on?"

"Is this some sort of joke? You talked about music nonstop in your profile."

"Did I?"

"Country Roads is your favorite song!"

"I'm from West Virginia. It's practically a requirement for us to like that song. It reminds me of home and my parents." The bouncer slipped off his stool and through the door as I started to shout. I wasn't that angry, but I was deaf from sitting next to a speaker all night. "If you'd asked me about it, I would have told you I love that song, but I hate when it's covered by crappy bands, sung at karaoke, or wailed at weddings."

"What? Why?"

"Because there's nothing worse than listening to a scream-pile version of a sentimental song. I would never sing it at karaoke."

"I mean you could've said that part in your profile." He spat the words at me with such bitterness I took a step back.

"And how are we supposed to get to know each other when we can't even talk because the band is so loud? Why would you think I'd love that band?"

"You love live music."

"Since when?" I shrieked, running clawed fingers through my perfectly styled hair. I noticed then how much it stank of stale beer and vape smoke.

He threw his hands into the air like a spoiled child having a tantrum. "Whatever."

I didn't have to walk away from him because he left of his own accord, slinging the door to the karaoke bar back open and storming inside. I growled in frustration and stomped my foot on the sidewalk. Another wasted evening. I'm not proud to admit I stomped every step of the two-block walk back to the bar where Pen was waiting.

CHAPTER SEVENTEEN

I found Pen in the back corner of the bar, a martini in one hand and a forty-something redhead in the other. I found an unoccupied barstool nearby and ordered a glass of wine. While I waited for Pen, I pulled out my phone to check my profile.

There was a section for musical interests and Pen had written that my favorite song was "Country Roads." Kevin had been right that she hadn't added anything about my aversion to karaoke, but even I could see there was no way to share that nuance in the limited space given. I stood by my assertion that he could've found out through a conversation with me.

"Hey gorgeous," Pen drawled over my shoulder. "Can I buy you a drink?"

The bartender chose that moment to drop off my wineglass. I took a long swallow, grateful for my first drink tonight that didn't taste like recycled rainwater. "You can buy the next round, I'll need it. That is if your friend doesn't mind."

I looked around for the woman who'd been draped over Pen moments before, but she was nowhere to be seen. Pen sat next to me, wearing a wide smile. Even in my foul mood, that smile was infectious. No wonder she got all the women.

"My friend decided to try her luck elsewhere after she heard the disclaimer." If this turn in fortunes bothered Pen, I couldn't detect it in her voice or her manner. "It's for the best. She wouldn't have waited while we talk about your date."

"You'd rather hear my pathetic attempts at dating than hook up with a hot redhead?"

"She wasn't that hot and she was vapid as hell," Pen said, signaling for another drink. "I'll pick your company over anyone's."

"You're the only one who does." I couldn't help but sulk. It had been a tough month and I had nothing to show for it.

Pen put all her attention back on me, a little crease forming between her eyebrows. "It didn't go well with Kevin?"

"What did you put in my profile?" I didn't want to blame Pen, but after the third misunderstanding of my personality and interests, I was getting annoyed.

"Haven't you read it?"

"Why would I read my own dating profile?"

"Well, one would generally want to know if it matches them. Then again, one would normally write their own."

The crease between her eyebrows deepened and her eyes flashed with anger. It wasn't misplaced, I knew that, but I wasn't feeling charitable at the moment.

"As my best friend, aren't you supposed to know me better than anyone?"

"No."

"Who should then?" I threw my arms in the air and barked, "Are they available to write my profile?"

"Yes, they are." Pen glared at me. "They're *you*. You should know you better than anyone. Why did you ask for my help if you were just gonna bitch about what I did for you?"

She stood so abruptly her stool banged against the wall. She tried to brush past me and I made a wild grab for her, my hand wrapping around her wrist. Her skin was so warm and so soft, touching her brought the cruelty of my words home to me.

"Please don't leave." She looked down at my hand. In my panic I was gripping her too hard, so I slid my fingers between hers and held on to our entwined fingers with my other hand. I tried my best to cradle her hand rather than squeeze, but I was really, truly scared for the first time in a long while. "I don't know what came over me."

She continued to stare at my hands, but she wouldn't meet my eye or say a word.

"I'm being a bitch. I didn't mean to."

She extracted her hand from mine but didn't leave. To my immense relief, she dropped back onto her stool and grabbed her drink. She still wouldn't look at me.

"There's no excuse for my behavior. I'm sorry." When she still didn't say anything, I decided drastic measures were necessary. I slid out of my own stool and bent down on one knee beside her chair. "I'll beg for your forgiveness. Is that what you want? Because I'll totally do it."

She finally cracked, a grin splitting her lips. "Get up, nerd."

"Not until you say you forgive me." I was getting louder, and I struggled to hide my smile. "I'll stay on my knees in front of you until you say it."

Pen giggled and I knew I had my best friend on my side again, no matter how awful I was being. People were starting to stare though.

"Dearest Penelope…" I started.

"Get off your knees, you idiot," she said, pulling me up by my clasped hands. I was waving them in front of me like I was praying. "I forgive you."

I hopped up and threw my arms around her. She hated to be hugged, especially in public, so I made sure to squeeze her extra tightly. She held on for a few seconds before swatting my arms away. I didn't particularly want to let her go, but I finally gave in.

Once I was back in my stool, I lowered my voice and shame wiped away my smile. "I really am sorry. I don't know what came over me."

"I do. You haven't been laid in years. Tell me what happened with that dumb guy."

She listened politely while I told the story. It sounded even worse in the recounting. The terrible band would have been bad enough, but Pen knew how much I hated karaoke, so she truly understood the depths of my pain. It wasn't only that it was so ill-suited for me. It wouldn't have been a good first date for anyone, even if they liked music as much as he seemed to think I did. First dates were supposed to be about getting to know someone. If you couldn't talk, how could it be a good date, let alone a perfect one?

"That's…" Laughter spurted out and she pressed her fingers to her mouth to stop it. "That's really bad, sweetie. What was he thinking?"

"God only knows."

"Seriously, would you please stop dating men? They're stupid and they smell bad. I don't want to have to grin across the table at another dumb dude you date."

"I haven't dated a man since Nick!"

"He was bad enough to cure me of the breed if nature hadn't taken care of that for me." Pen's jaw flexed, making it clear she was swallowing the lecture she longed to give. I deserved it, but it was sweet of her to refrain, especially given my behavior tonight.

"Why would Kevin think I'm so into music?"

"Sometimes people see what they want to see."

"Do you think…" I was careful to phrase the question without any hint of blame. "We could take a look at my profile and try to figure out why he thought I loved music so much?"

"Sure," Pen said, snatching my phone.

She kept one eye on the crowd, and I noticed how many women in the bar were eyeing her. Pen chewed on her bottom lip as she scrolled through the questions.

"I deleted 'Country Roads' as my favorite song, but that couldn't have been the only thing he saw."

She murmured agreement and I leaned in to read over her shoulder. As always, working through a problem with Pen made me feel better about everything. If anyone could fix it, Pen could and it didn't hurt that she smelled wonderful tonight.

"New perfume?" I asked. She smelled like lavender and sandalwood with an undercurrent of fresh linen and her usual eucalyptus soap.

"Hmmm?" She didn't look away from my phone, her intricately woven ring splints tapping on the screen as she scrolled.

"Is that a new perfume?" I asked again. "I like it."

"Essential oil mix. Butches don't wear perfume."

"Do you count as a butch? You don't dress super butch."

"I wear women's suits because they highlight the goods," she said, waving a distracted hand around her cleavage. It was nice cleavage, accentuated by the high collar and many open buttons of her blouse. "I have some very nice, tailored men's suits for special occasions."

"You do?" My voice got squeaky and I coughed to clear my throat. "I've never seen you in one."

"Work is not a special occasion." She handed over my phone, "How about this?"

She clicked on the photo she provided for my profile, the one she'd taken of me the summer before. She'd added a caption beneath.

Always love the outdoors, especially when there's a concert involved!

"Why'd you write that?" I asked, genuinely perplexed. "Do I like concerts?"

"You loved this one. It's from Wolf Trap."

"It was an Indigo Girls concert. Of course I loved it."

"That's why I wrote it."

"I loved it 'cause I love the Indigo Girls and hanging out with you, not because I love concerts."

"You should've been more specific."

I was about to argue, when I saw Pen's grin. "You're making fun of me, aren't you?"

"Me?" she asked in mock horror. "Never!"

"I take back my apology from earlier."

She started typing. "Too late."

"Take out the outdoors part, too. You know that's bullshit."

"Chicks dig outdoorsy ladies."

"Chicks dig ladies who tell the truth."

Pen huffed and I bet she thought I didn't notice her eye roll. "Fine. You win."

After she was done, she handed over my phone and flagged down the bartender. While she ordered a club soda I noticed a woman across the bar sizing Pen up. She was pretty, but younger than Pen's normal targets, maybe early thirties with a thick blond braid. Pen didn't notice, her attention on her club soda and my phone.

"You're a jerk." I read her new comment aloud, "I was only having fun in this picture because I'm a sucker for old dyke bands and my best friend. I'll never smile like this on a date with you and I hate music."

"Sounds perfect."

I erased what she'd written and thought for a few minutes while I sipped my wine. Pen turned her attention to a busty Latinx woman with short, spiky hair and a graphic tee. I felt her eyes return to me a half dozen times, but she didn't push. When the bartender circled by, I refused a refill.

"What if I leave it without a caption?" I asked, but Pen didn't seem to hear me. She was busy splitting her time between the straining graphic tee and the blond braid. Both seemed intent on wooing Pen from across the room, but she seemed strangely distracted tonight.

"All these women are different," I said, indicating the two women. The redhead from earlier was back at the end of the bar, too, trying to catch Pen's eye. "Do you even have a type?"

"Women."

"That's a gender, not a type." She shrugged and I asked, "You would sleep with any woman you met, wouldn't you?"

"Hell no." Pen didn't seem to be giving any of them enough attention, but Graphic Tee was still making a bid while the other two wandered off. "I would never sleep with my doctor and she's super-hot."

"I'm surprised you haven't slept with her already."

That caught Pen's attention and she scowled at me. "You know how long it took me to find a doctor who didn't think

I was faking or drug seeking? I would never mess up that relationship."

She said it lightly, but I knew how serious she was. It was close to what the Rainbow Zebras had described.

"Let's get out of here," Pen said, draining her club soda. "I'll take you home, okay?"

Graphic Tee had apparently decided the time for sexy glances had passed, because she slid away from the bar and pushed her way through the crowd toward us.

"You don't have to do that." I slid my empty wine glass away.

"I know I don't have to, but I want to. I don't like the idea of you driving home alone when you're sad. I'll bring you back after work tomorrow to get your car."

The crease had formed between Pen's eyebrows and she reached out for my hand. If only Pen's hookups got to see this side of her—the woman who was sweet and thoughtful and gentle exactly when I needed it most—they'd fall into her bed even faster. It wasn't fair how much she hid from them. I was about to tell her so when Graphic Tee finally made it through the crush and leaned against the bar on Pen's other side.

She was nice enough to shoot me an apologetic smile and ask if we were together. When I said we weren't, she turned Pen's chin toward her in a surprisingly hot request for attention. When I tried to pay my tab, Pen waved me off and handed the bartender her credit card. She insisted again that I let her drive me home, but I wasn't going to spoil this one for her. I slipped out of the bar before she could protest again.

CHAPTER EIGHTEEN

Pen and I met before dawn for our annual drive out to Lucketts Spring Market in Berryville. She'd borrowed a pickup truck from a friend in case we got carried away and bought too much stuff. It was a wise move since we always got carried away and bought too much stuff. I supplied the donuts and coffee for the hour-long drive.

The day was perfect. The sort of blue skies that people wrote songs about and tall, cotton-puff clouds offering an occasional break from the blazing summer sun. Perhaps it was the conversation we'd had after the disastrous date with Kevin two weeks before, but Pen showed up in the butchest outfit I'd ever seen on her. Her jeans were well-worn and hung low around her hips. She broke out the Doc Marten boots she wore rarely and her Indigo Girls concert tee had seen so many washes it was almost see-through. She even wore a wallet chain. I felt a little plain in my knee-length pink skirt and white tank top, but we'd met at Pen's house so I couldn't change.

The drive was relaxing in that way only best friends can be in each other's company. We didn't have to talk to fill the empty space between us. I spent most of the ride nursing my coffee and watching the mountains get closer and closer. Woodbridge was just south of DC and it was all concrete and chain restaurants. This side of DC, its southwestern border, turned instantly rural. One minute you were in the bustle of the nation's capital, the next you were surrounded by empty woodland and farms as far as the eye could see. It made me think of home.

I'd lost most of my family when my parents passed away. My sister had spent a college semester abroad where she fell in love with both Belgium and an older man with a lot of money. No one was surprised when she stayed. We talked on the phone occasionally, but I hadn't seen her in five years. It was for the best. She and I had never connected. It wasn't either of our faults—our personalities didn't even mesh well enough to cause hate.

Our father had been a professor of physical chemistry, devastated that his daughters had no interest in science. We'd both gone into business, an area he thought had no soul. My mother had been a stay-at-home mom when we were little. She had been taking courses in nursing to start a new, empty-nester career when they were involved in a six-car pile-up on an icy mountain road. Everyone else suffered minor injuries, but my father's attempt to swerve had turned the car sideways in the middle of the accident and I was an orphan before the ambulances arrived.

Nick and I were living in Virginia at the time, but he was out of town for work. He half-heartedly offered to come home early, but I heard the reluctance in his voice so said he didn't have to. In retrospect, I should've been pissed that my husband couldn't bother to attend his in-laws' joint funeral, but I was so numb I accepted his excuses. Pen had been new at Three Keys and found me crying in the bathroom. When I told her I had to make the long drive back to West Virginia alone, she immediately offered to take me. We became friends on that drive and she'd been the most important member of my family ever since.

"Who are you chatting with these days?" Pen asked, pulling me back into the present.

"Um…no one. I'm taking a break."

She looked over at me for a heartbeat and then turned her eyes back to the road. "What are you thinking about?"

"When you took me home for my parents' funeral."

Pen nodded, her face grim at the shared memory. I hadn't been the best driving companion for the first hour or so that day, but she'd gotten me to open up and even to laugh once or twice. "Despite the reason, the drive back was fun."

"Car concert and Tim Hortons Timbits." I laughed, thinking of how many donut holes we'd packed away and how happy I'd been to have a new friend to make me smile in my darkest days. "No one makes a donut like Tim. Wish they had 'em in Virginia."

"I don't know," Pen said, grabbing a powdered donut from the box and chomping down. She spoke through a mouthful of pastry and raspberry jam. "Dunkin' isn't awful."

A shower of powdered sugar landed on her chest, dusting the Indigo Girls' screen-printed faces. She swiped at it, spreading the sugar rather than cleaning it off.

"Nice look. I didn't think Amy's face could get any whiter."

"I'd take it off, but you couldn't handle how amazing my rack is."

I balled up a napkin and tossed it at her face, but she snatched it out of midair and used it to clean up her mess. "And what do you mean you're taking a break?"

Crap. I was really hoping she'd missed that part. "I don't know. I…needed some time."

She squinted over at me as she checked for oncoming traffic before turning onto Route 29. "Some time for what? Haven't you had enough single time? I thought that's what this whole thing was about."

"It was about finding someone and I'm not having much luck." I didn't tell her I'd tried to delete my profile but opted to suspend it for a month instead. "I need some time to let my dignity grow back."

"None of those bad dates were your fault. Your dignity is intact."

"Sure doesn't feel that way."

Pen reached over and squeezed my knee, leaving her hand there after releasing the pressure. I'd had enough practice holding back my embarrassment and my tears by now, but that little sign of solidarity nearly cracked my resolve. Even better than the comforting weight of her hand was her refusal to push. She didn't say a word, just showed with her touch that she cared.

The market was always a big draw and, despite our early arrival, there was a sizable crowd milling around the fairground gates. Lucketts Spring Market was one of the largest congregations of antique dealers on the East Coast. This year they boasted over two hundred vendors, all lined up under tents between food trucks, beer gardens, and stages for live music. We'd been loyal attendees for years, always springing the extra cash for VIP tickets so we could arrive early and come back again on Sunday if we ran out of room in the truck. The first time we came was to furnish Pen's new place, bought with the proceeds of a particularly fine home sale. Every time after that had been self-indulgence and if there was one thing Pen and I could bond over, besides donuts and hot women, it was self-indulgence.

Pen was a remarkable shopper. Like so many butch women, she hated shopping for clothes and jewelry—the things I loved buying. But she was unashamedly obsessed with furniture, and she would prowl antique stores all day. A casually classy chair or a table she could fix up in her spare time would make her giddy. Lucky for her, Lucketts was the best place in Northern Virginia for casual classy.

We approached the day like it was a job. First, we got the lay of the land, scoping out our favorite sellers and noting those who'd done us wrong in the past. Shopping for antiques was a lot like fishing at the local bar. It was tempting to let the flashy one catch your eye, so one needed a wing-woman to remind one of past heartaches. The one that nearly roped me in again was a potter from Richmond. She had this way of describing her work as though you had to have it. There was also a fair amount of magic in her smoky eye and skinny jeans. Pen pulled me away just in time.

I was browsing another cera_icist's table, this one an obviously queer lady who was enticing me with a beautifully glazed sake set, when I realized Pen had left my side. That wasn't entirely unusual. She was an active woman and would wander away if I took too long oohing and ahhing. Normally she'd hover nearby, however, in case she needed to save me from myself. This time I had to step out into the crowd to look for her.

"No friggin' way." I looked down the main drag and laughed.

Pen had found someone to work her magic on, even here in this suburban hellscape. The next booth had a makeshift wall composed of heavier furniture lining their allotted space. Pen propped one forearm against an entryway bench that looked like it had begun life as a heavy bookshelf and a church pew before being brought together. Pen's body leaned toward a heavy-set woman with olive skin and rich, dark hair cascading to her waist.

I shook my head and looked on, wavering between impressed and annoyed. Lucketts was *our* thing. The place where Pen and I indulged our deepest décor desires. Now she was out here, trying to score with some random woman while I was being seduced by handmade pottery. Was she going to scuttle off to the parking lot with this woman? It's not like the bed of her truck offered the necessary privacy, but I knew Pen would never abandon me here, even though the woman was admittedly gorgeous.

As I watched, Pen turned her head and spotted me. When she waved, the raven-haired woman followed her gaze and spoke, but they were too far away for me to hear. After a moment of conversation, the stranger reached up on tip-toe and kissed Pen's cheek. As the woman walked away, heading in my direction, Pen shuffled her feet and I could've sworn I saw a blush dust her cheeks.

"Have fun," the stranger said as she drew level with me. She jerked her head toward Pen and smiled. "I know you will."

"Oh, no, I'm not…"

Before I could correct her misapprehension, the woman laughed. It was a sweet sound, with no hint at bitterness for my interruption. She put a hand on my forearm and leaned in to murmur, "Don't worry. She's sweet and amazing and has no expectations. You can change your mind and she won't hold it against you, trust me." Pen started in our direction and the woman shot her a wistful glance. "I'll give you some advice. Just let yourself have a great time. You will *not* regret it."

She gave me a wink and sauntered away just as Pen arrived at my side.

"Sorry to abandon you." She looked after the woman disappearing into the crowd. "What'd she say to you?"

"That you're sweet and amazing and I should let myself have fun with you."

"Sorry about that." She rubbed her neck and continued, "I tried to tell her it wasn't like that with us."

This close, I could see that she was definitely blushing. I decided to forgive her for abandoning me in favor of relentlessly teasing her. "Is this the unflappable Penelope Chase *blushing*?" She laughed, but still wouldn't meet my eye. I put my hand on her arm and felt her tense beneath me. "It's okay that your conquests think so much of you."

"They aren't conquests. They're…"

"Friends for a night? I know. It's okay, Pen. She obviously feels comfortable with your night together."

Pen laughed and finally looked up. The sparkle in her eye was the one I was used to, and it made my heart soar. She shrugged and said, "She should. That one took a year off my life."

"Okay, too much information!" I laughed, but there was a strange wriggle of discomfort in my belly at the thought of Pen's enthusiastic partners.

"You started it," she said, her arm relaxing beneath me. "Okay. Back to your pottery. Come on."

By lunchtime we were exhausted and well over our individual budgets for the day. We took a break for food and strategizing. That led us to the gourmet grilled cheese food truck and a complete abandonment of thrift. The sourdough toast was as bad an influence as the pretty potter. We ended up slumped back in folding chairs, sweating and wishing we'd chosen something other than cheese for our midday meal.

"What if someone amazing messages you?" Pen asked out of the blue, hitting me with that interrogative stare I couldn't ignore.

"Huh?"

"On the dating app you've abandoned for the moment," she clarified. "What if the person of your dreams messages you while you're on a break?"

"I won't know about it." I realized my mistake a moment too late and then had to confess, "I put my account on hold."

"Kieran…"

"I know. I know, don't lecture me. I need a little bit of time to forget everything before I give someone else a chance."

Pen leaned forward, sliding her hand across mine. Again I was struck by the gentle strength of her long fingers. I was also struck by her new fragrance. The lavender and sandalwood oil she'd rubbed into her neck and wrists. It caught me right beneath the sunshine and happiness in my blood and stuck.

"Kieran, you always find the person you're meant to be with when you stop looking."

The way she stared at me, I almost believed she meant it. I could've gotten lost in those eyes. Could've slipped into her embrace and let the world fly past. This must be what the women she seduced felt like. She was really, really good.

"Then it's a good thing I've stopped looking."

Pen scoffed, her throat flexing with her laughter. "Stop looking, sure, but you'll stop seeing if you put your account on hold. Turn it back on and wait for them to come to you."

Sure, it made sense, but then so had the pair of mismatched dining chairs painted a dreamy sage green that had torpedoed my budget. Things were weird that day. It seemed best to hedge my bets.

"Maybe."

"You are the most stubborn woman I've ever met."

"I'd have to be to spurn your advances."

She shook her head and looked away, a smile curving her thin lips. "I've never once hit on you."

"I won't hold that against you," I replied, standing up and holding out a hand to her. "Come on, we haven't even been to half the vendors."

Pen stood grudgingly. She clearly wasn't ready to give up the argument, but she was a sucker for distressed furniture. I had to keep her distracted so I could stay happily on the sidelines of the dating scene for a few more weeks.

CHAPTER NINETEEN

On Sunday morning I woke up without an alarm, an extravagance in which I rarely indulged. I'd changed my sheets Saturday as was my habit and now luxuriated in the feel of fresh, crisp linens across my skin. I slipped out of my pajamas so I could feel the uninterrupted caress of fresh cotton from the tips of my toes all the way up to my bare shoulders. I even rolled around a little before finally dragging myself into the shower.

Sundays usually meant spending the whole day in the house resting, and this Sunday would be no different. I'd actually never given myself a day off like this until I met Pen and she told me about her built-in days of rest. I had been the epitome of the weekend warrior, piling up activities and chores until I was so exhausted that going back to work Monday was a relief. I'd tried giving myself an actual day of rest and found that, while the need wasn't physical as it was for Pen, it was mentally necessary. If I didn't take time off, my anxiety always got the better of me.

After drying my hair enough to put it up in a messy bun, I dressed in clean pajamas and made a lavish breakfast. Sunday mornings were made for pancakes and no one could convince me otherwise. While I ate, I scrolled through the audiobook offerings from my local library, finally settling on an historical fiction novel set in early twentieth century Morocco and on a second helping of pancakes.

My earbuds in place and the story unfolding through the narrator's rich, throaty voice, I began to clean. For me, cleaning is never the frantic chore it seemed to others. My job rarely had visual progress markers, so I loved seeing the fruits of my labor while I cleaned my house. Watching the sink empty of dishes or the vacuum lines appear in my living room rug were fulfilling for me in a way that few other things in my life were.

None of my partners had ever liked cleaning as much as I did. My former mother-in-law was as meticulous as I, so Nick took neatness for granted. He never so much as picked up a sock in the ten years we were married. I hadn't minded until the relationship started to fall apart, but by then I resented everything about him. Alex was much the same, but their messiness was less indifference and more a product of the chaos of their mind. I'd been attracted to that chaos when we'd first met, especially after my neat, ordered married life. I craved chaos as much as I craved everything else about Alex.

We'd met in a bar six weeks after I'd kicked Nick out. I had been drinking heavily at the time, using alcohol to try to glue the pieces of my life together. I had the same success as everyone else who had tried it, which is to say none. Alex found me drunkenly crying on the dance floor with someone whose roaming hands were becoming annoying. They stepped in, sent the handsy person packing, and got me home safely. I begged them to stay and we talked all night, but never touched. I was floored to discover there was a human out there who wanted to get to know me when it would have been so easy to just take me to bed.

Alex had been my hero that night and they pulled me out of my darkness before my drinking could become a problem. They were so much kinder and gentler than Nick and I became lost in them almost immediately. They moved in two months later and saved me again, this time from an avalanche of bills and my crushing loneliness. In retrospect, I'd leaned too heavily on them and created a dynamic of my own helplessness that we could never shake. When things went bad, we had no foundation to fall back on, just codependence and unhealthy emotional habits. Still, I would always remember those early days fondly. The only other time I'd formed an attachment so quickly was with Pen. The difference was Pen didn't need me to be helpless to care.

The kitchen was the one place that was constantly dirty, so I started my cleaning there. As I polished my stainless-steel fridge, the female character in my audiobook ran into a former acquaintance, a handsome young officer. I should've picked another book, but I was invested now and let the story play. As I assumed, sparks flew the moment they spoke. My skin started to tingle, hearing how their eyes met. I visualized the scene, the images fed by countless romantic films and my overactive imagination. He stood tall in his uniform and she was demure in her Red Cross apron. I was swept into the story as I grabbed the vacuum cleaner from my closet, but there was a tinge of sadness to their charming reunion.

Things like that never happened in real life. Sparks didn't fly when gazes met. Eyes never lingered in that certain way. Hearts never beat together. No one walked into a room and saw someone they already knew and realized with a single look that their feelings had been love all along. It was a dream, distilled and distributed by Hollywood to hold people at the perfect mix of happy and sad so they'd keep buying tickets. Movies were nothing more than legal heroin and we were all junkies, desperate for another fix.

Rationalizing the ridiculousness of a meet-cute scene sustained me through vacuuming the floor and polishing the new dining chairs I'd bought at Lucketts the previous week. When the couple went through their first tribulation, his unit being relocated closer to the fighting and away from the woman he loved, I found myself lying on the couch. I lounged through the increasingly passionate letters back and forth between the lovers.

After a major battle that sent the main character into a torrent of anxiety, I found myself looking at my phone, my finger hovering over the Swingle app. There had been no little red hearts since I suspended my profile and that was fine. I was fine. It was okay that Juliana was alone and missing her love and I was alone wondering if I would ever find mine. My slipper chose that moment to slip off its precarious position dangling from my big toe. That dropped slipper saved me. The noise made me jump and I dragged my thumb away from my phone screen. I chastised myself as I sat up. I needed to stick to my decision to take some time away from Swingle.

I attacked the bathrooms next, scouring grout lines and even lying on my back to wipe away the accumulated dust behind the toilet tank. I was diluting bleach for the sinks and countertop when Rodrigo returned to Melilla and to Juliana. My phone chirped a low battery warning. I grabbed the glass cleaner while I plugged in my phone and retrieved my wireless earbuds. They had about three hours of battery life, so they could carry me through the guest bathroom and primary bedroom at least.

Losing myself in someone else's love story and the mindless joy of cleaning made me happier than I had been in weeks. It reminded me that I didn't need to find someone to love. The life I had built for myself was perfectly fulfilling. I didn't need to make room for someone new. I didn't need a passionate affair to ruin the perfect balance I had finally achieved. I already had everything I needed in life to be happy.

Then they kissed.

I've read a lot of sappy, heartwarming romances. There have been a lot of kisses that have made me gasp. There have been a few that have made me bite my bottom lip. This one made me cry on the bathroom floor.

Juliana professed her love, Rodrigo pulled her into his arms, and I sat down on the cold tile and howled as my tears fell. Then I howled even louder because I'd tried to wipe away the tears with my cloth soaked in ten percent bleach solution. Still, most of my tears were because of the kiss.

A perfect kiss. That moment of two hearts merging at the intersection of lips and then bodies and then souls. Wasn't that what living was all about? To find that moment in our own lives. To find that person who would hold us until we felt whole. The moment was beautiful and perfect in a way it had never been for me, and yet in that moment I truly believed that one day I would find it. I would move beyond a cheating husband, a codependent ex, and a series of pathetic first dates and I would find real happiness.

"I just have to move to Morocco to find it," I spluttered through my tears.

Once I could force myself to stand, I marched back into the kitchen and banged the pause button. I tossed the earbuds beside my phone and headed back to the bathroom, leaving a trail of discarded clothing across the newly vacuumed floor. A very long, very hot shower cleared both the ache from my heart and the lingering bleach from around my eyes. Since my cleaning pajamas were covered in sweat and snot, I traded them for yet another pair. Fortunately, my passion for sleepwear meant my closet did not disappoint. I picked a button-up cotton pajama set covered in little smiling Christmas trees. Pen and I had bought a matching pair for last year's annual viewing of *It's a Wonderful Life*, my favorite Christmas movie. We also owned a matching pink set with handguns for Pen's favorite Christmas movie, *Die Hard*, but she always refused to wear hers.

It was after two when I finished my second shower, which was eight o'clock in my sister's time zone and that gave me permission to have my first drink of the day. As long as it was a reasonable hour to drink for someone I knew, I was allowed to indulge. I hadn't expected to be emotionally attacked by an audiobook, so I hadn't had time to chill any wine. I dropped an ice cube in a Chardonnay I'd been saving for just such an emergency and settled back onto the couch.

I noticed in passing that my phone was charged but ignored it in favor of scouring my streaming services for a film that did not involve any romance. It was a tough call since I don't like horror films unless there are vampires and I detest sports films, but pretty much every other genre wove in a romantic storyline somewhere along the way. That left my options severely limited. I couldn't say when I picked up my phone and opened the Swingle app, but it was somewhere between switching from Netflix to Hulu and daydreaming about warm sunsets in Morocco. I noticed the open app and my empty glass at the same moment. It seemed more important to refill the glass than to stop the inevitable slide back into the dating world. Before I knew it, I was tipsy and checking out the profile of a new addition.

Skye was ridiculously cute, nonbinary, and had soulful eyes to match their perfect half-smile. Their profile was definitely new since my last log in. Had they been around before I would have taken notice, no doubt about it. While I spent my time digesting all the little, perfect details Skye's profile had to offer, several new messages appeared in my inbox. I discarded them each as they came, always returning to Skye. They had an originality and a wit that was completely absent in everyone else. Honestly, how hard was it to come up with a subtle, polite opening line? Something that didn't involve a crude sexual innuendo or faux disinterest? Apparently no one on Swingle could find that balance.

Honestly, though, I would totally have accepted any of those stupid pickup lines from Skye. Why hadn't they messaged me? They were perfect with skin tanned like desert rock with creamy undertones. Their robin's egg blue hair sat in a messy stack on top with the sides shaved down to the skin and there was not a single picture where they wore a full smile. They held back that last few inches of joy from their expression and it was so alluring. My heart beat faster thinking about what I had to do to earn a full, open smile, maybe even a laugh. I was smitten. They, clearly, were not since they hadn't messaged me.

I'd started a Marvel Universe movie but hadn't watched a single frame. Music swelled onscreen and so did my anxiety. It was one thing to suggest that first date with Chloe when I hadn't ever been the one to ask someone out before. It was another thing entirely to send out a message to someone who hadn't shown any interest in me. I suddenly felt cruel and judgmental for scoffing at others' pickup lines. What was I going to say if I ever got the nerve to message? I sighed, defeated, and typed out a quick text to Pen.

> **I need your help but you aren't allowed to judge me or say anything.**
> *I promise nothing.*
> **There's someone I think is really cute but I've never been the first one to send a message.**
> **Can a femme even do that?**
> *First—yes, a femme can make first contact. In fact it's hot when they do.*
> *Second- I thought you were taking a break from Swingle?*

I chose to ignore the second part. No need for Pen to know I'm too much of a sap to give up on love. The first part was both exciting and terrifying. Okay, I'm allowed to make contact, but how was I supposed to do that.

> **What should I say?**

Approximately one year passed while I watched the three little dots flash onscreen. It was in that moment I realized the utter cruelty of that particular addition to our electronic lives. Those three dots had turned into a twenty-first century equivalent of waiting for your home phone to ring. It was nerve-wracking to say the least. It felt like any chance of success I had with Skye hinged on surviving the dance of the three dots. Just as I was about to give up, Pen's response arrived.

> *I'm not usually the one who reaches out first, so I hope you can forgive me for not having a witty opening line. I've spent half my Sunday staring at your profile and it's starting to make me feel crazy. Maybe you could message me back so we could chat and both be crazy? If you're not interested, do me a favor and pretend this never happened? Thanks for a lovely distraction on this lovely day!*

I'll admit, I sat in shock reading it over and over. It was perfect. If someone had sent me that message, I would have been a giggling mess on the floor. There was humor and humbleness and vulnerability. Exactly what I'd have written if I had any idea how to write a message to someone I liked.

You're a goddess.
That's true. Good luck, Kieran. Tell me about the response at work tomorrow.
What if there isn't a response?
There will be. Good night!

I agreed with her. No one could turn away a message like that. I copied her entire text and pasted it into a fresh envelope icon on Swingle. The electronic whoosh as it flew out over the airwaves toward the alluring Skye felt like the whoosh of my heart as something big was starting. I sat for a little while, staring at the app, waiting for an immediate reply. After ten minutes, I realized it would take a while to formulate a response, so I popped my earbuds back in while I made myself dinner. Surely by the time Juliana and Rodrigo finally tumbled into bed and my frittata had set, Skye would have responded. I daydreamed about their present giddiness at receiving such a good message while I sliced asparagus and grated Gruyere cheese. Even if they were out of the house for the day or even the weekend, they'd be back and messaging me by late evening.

When I went to bed at ten o'clock Juliana was pregnant and Skye had not sent a response.

CHAPTER TWENTY

When I still hadn't received a response from Skye the next morning, I resigned myself to rejection. I had discovered through painful repetition that, in the world of online dating, a message which hadn't been returned within a few hours was being ignored.

The rejection made a dreadful Monday even more tedious. Our monthly staff meeting was worse than usual thanks to the conjunction of a rare Randy hangover and the dawn of corporate tax season. While HomeScape was in no danger of closing, each new tax season was a reminder that Randy's business was not particularly lucrative. He liked to yell when he was hungover, thus sharing his headache with the world, so the meeting was a lot of cringing and covering our ears.

Afterward most of us hid in our offices. On days like these we'd all learned to keep our heads down until the storm passed. If we were lucky, Randy would feel sufficiently guilty about his outburst to bring in bagels the next morning. The main drawback was that I hunkered down in my office without enough work to distract me from Skye's silence. It still stung, but my renewed hope, inspired by Juliana and Rodrigo, had me looking up other potential connections by lunchtime.

I'd made chicken salad with pecans and red grapes for lunch. Fresh tarragon and dill brightened both my sandwich and my mood while I read a Swingle message from a woman in Maryland. She seemed nice enough, but a quick Google-Maps search showed she lived two hours away, so I turned her down as gently as I could. I spent enough time in traffic as it was. Contemplating a relationship with such a hellish commute made me shiver from head to toe. Unfortunately, the DC Metro area was so spread out and the traffic so bad that a lot of my matches were like this one—out of my reach. My options were dwindling fast.

Even after a month off the site, there were depressingly few new potential matches. I'd seen the same faces so many times, I'd sorted them into three groups: for someone else, far away, and femmes. I knew there was little chance I'd find "the one" here, but I went through them again anyway. Pen had said this was the best site for me, but maybe it was time to start looking at the other options. The person I was looking for didn't seem to be on Swingle, but they could be somewhere else. The way Skye caught my attention had reminded me how good it felt to have a crush. I'd find that with someone, even if it wasn't with them.

That thought kept my hope alive, but my half-hour lunch break was up. I'd have to cast my broader net after work. The afternoon was far more interesting than my morning. Pen crashed into my office around one to inform me I was being kidnapped.

"Do I have any choice in the matter?"

"None whatsoever," she said as she grabbed my purse from the coatrack and thrust it at me. "Don't worry. It's work-related."

I was skeptical, but there was no way I'd miss out. "Does Randy know?"

"Hell no. Carol says he's cranky. I don't do cranky men."

"Come to think of it," I said, taking my purse and marching out the door. "Neither do I."

Once we were on I-95 heading north, Pen finally told me what we were up to.

"I need you for some role play."

"We're not that sort of friends, remember Pen?"

"Aren't you the comedian," she said, whipping around an RV from Arizona and gunning it until her engine whined.

"Just giving you a taste of your own medicine." She whipped around another car, nearly sending the bewildered driver into the median. "What's wrong? You only drive like a maniac when you're stressed."

"I'm not driving like a maniac," she said as she sped onto the exit ramp. She came within an eyelash of clipping a Mercedes. "Okay. Maybe I'm stressed."

"Wanna talk to me about it or just take out your feelings on that guy's bumper?"

Pen flew onto the 110 and we tore through Arlington, chewing up miles as she chewed on her lip. "I'm nervous," she said in a whisper.

I forced myself not to laugh. "You're what?"

"You heard me!" We weaved through traffic as we crossed the Potomac and Pen finally explained, "The Georgetown house is ready to show. I've got this massive commission headed my way but…Well, this property is different than I'm used to."

"A house is a house, right?" That's what she always said to me when I was flustered with a title search.

The SUV's engine purred as she coasted to a red light. She tapped the brakes and we both jerked in our seats.

"Not exactly," she murmured. She stared at her white knuckles on the steering wheel and took a long breath. "I don't know how to sell an eight-million-dollar property."

"*Eight* million?" My voice squeaked and Pen gave me a panicked stare like a wild animal. "I didn't realize it was that high."

"I didn't either. I did my comparisons last week and realized my initial assessment was too low. Met with the client over Zoom from her summer home in Cannes."

The light turned green, but we didn't move. I checked the rearview mirror, and the street was mercifully empty. Pen's eyebrow twitched as she repeated, "Her summer home in *Cannes*."

Granted, the usual Three Keys/HomeScape client didn't own a summer home in France. Most of them didn't even own a home yet. We did a lot more first-time homebuyer business than multi-million-dollar Georgetown properties. Still, Pen was outclassing us all even without rich clients. She was a born salesperson and an honest one at that. The combination was rare enough to be pure gold.

I reached out for her hand, but the light turned yellow and she smashed her foot on the gas, slipping through the intersection as the light overhead flipped to red. The momentum yanked my arm back and I let it fall.

Pen drove more carefully now that we were in a residential area, and her voice was equally calm. "The client barely listened to anything I had to say and that scares me even more."

"Why?"

"If she has no spoken expectations, that means she has rich-person expectations."

"Which are?"

"The moon at least. She'll expect I get a deal that's way over asking, but she'll accept anything even if I advise against it. That way she has her money and she can blame me if it doesn't live up. I'm screwed."

"A lowball offer on an eight-million-dollar property though. Even that would be a huge..."

"It isn't about the commission," she growled as she swung her SUV into a gated drive and punched in the code for the underground garage. "You know that."

I did know that. Pen took everything in life completely seriously. She played hard, she worked hard, and she was the best at everything. It was a compulsion and she knew it, but there were too many layers of psychology to tease apart to explain it. Instead, she dove into everything head first and made sure she excelled. It was why she'd earned this listing in the first place. No one Pen had ever represented could say anything bad about her, even if their home didn't sell as high as they wanted.

She threw the car into park and killed the engine, dropping her forehead against the steering wheel. It was so sweet and so strange to see her this vulnerable. I was such a sucker for butches with emotion.

"Hey," I said in a soothing voice. "You're going to be great." When she didn't respond, I put my hand on her shoulder. That made her tense even more, so I decided it was time for a grand gesture. I turned her shoulders to face me and cupped her round cheeks in my hands. Her eyes were big as saucers and full of so many emotions. It looked like a storm was raging inside her.

I put my face so close to hers our foreheads nearly touched. I waited for her eyes to settle on mine and whispered, "You are going to be great. We'll go through every detail and you'll sell this house and earn a dozen listings just like it for next year. Hear me?"

She nodded dumbly, her face bobbing in my hands. I smiled and she managed a barely perceptible twitch of her lips in return. Her eyes still swam, so I pulled her toward me, sliding my cheek along hers, and wrapped my arms around her.

In eleven years of friendship, I could count on one hand the number of times we'd hugged. She usually resisted and it always confused me because, when she gave in, she threw herself into the embrace. She hugged like she never wanted to let go, but it always started like this, with every muscle rigid as steel.

Finally, her body relaxed and she rested her chin on my shoulder. I held her loosely, not wanting to tweak any of her joints out of place but wanting her to feel the weight of my friendship. Sitting here in the low lighting of the garage, with the mingled smells of underground places, motor oil, and Pen's sandalwood and lavender scent, felt so right.

All I could think of was the scene where Juliana had held Rodrigo after his best friend was injured in battle. The only difference was those two were in love and the hug was a place holder for a more intimate encounter to come. This was as intimate as Pen got. Letting me into her fear was a step further than she'd ever allowed me. I knew Pen so well, but her emotions were as compartmentalized as her friend groups. Maybe there was someone out there—someone whose name she'd mentioned in passing over the years but I'd never met—who got to see Vulnerable Pen all the time, but that person definitely wasn't me. I held onto her now and hoped she understood that, if she ever trusted me enough to be that person for her, I was ready. When Pen pulled back, I realized I'd been holding her too long, but it had been so nice to have her arms around me.

We started our tour in the back yard. The landscaping was immaculate. A high privacy fence covered in climbing roses and bougainvillea circled the property. The yard was bricked over and boasted a lagoon-style pool off to one side that Pen labelled "quaint." I recommended a change to "intimate" because the setup reminded me viscerally of Shane's pool scene in the first episode of *The L Word*. On the other side of the yard, and in full view of the sunroom, was the famous Wi-Fi-connected hot tub. Behind the hot tub was a waterfall cascading down a rough stone wall. Pen used her phone to activate both the waterfall and the tub's jets.

"It's still ridiculous to connect your hot tub to Wi-Fi," I said as we moved inside. "But I'll admit it's super sexy."

Pen winked and replied, "I'm not going to spell it out during the tours, but that will be heavily implied."

The sunroom was the highlight of the house for me, but Pen focused more on the wired sound system than the spectacular backyard view. The interior wall had a pass-through fireplace to the living room, making it a four-season room, and the furniture invited long, leisurely Sunday mornings with coffee and newspapers. And pancakes.

The main-floor living room, one of three in the house if one counted the sitting area in the au-pair suite, was a bit stodgy for my taste. The opulence was distinctly masculine and old-world, with mahogany and dark leather predominating. I would have gone for something more welcoming for the first floor and saved the haunted-library motif for upstairs. Still, I didn't have eight million bucks, so it didn't matter what I thought.

What struck me the further our tour progressed was how passionate Pen was about the listing. It was clear Pen loved this house, but she didn't push her love onto me. She led me on the journey and compelled me to follow. Soon enough I stopped seeing myself as Pen's friend listening to her pitch and more as a potential buyer falling in love with an amazing home.

Pen wasn't simply describing modern amenities seamlessly incorporated into historic bones. She spoke about the house like a favorite niece. I tried to keep a critical eye, but part of me wanted to feel the same way about the house that she did. The critical eye dimmed with each new room and disappeared completely when we entered the primary suite's walk-in closet. Or rather the Hers side of the His-and-Hers walk-in closets. It was the size of my entire primary suite back home and featured a fainting couch at its center.

This was why Pen was so good at her job. She didn't just love her properties, she made potential buyers love them, too.

Our winding route had brought us back to the heart of the home, that beautiful sunroom. Pen asked me to sit and give my impression of the property. I told her my favorite bits and all the negatives I would confide in my Realtor if I was considering a purchase. She addressed some of my concerns with clever tricks to either fix or minimize them. It was a sly way to offer options without assuming my renovation budget was limitless.

"Okay," she said, sitting back and shedding the professional veneer. "How'd I do?"

"Perfect." When she rolled her eyes I continued, "Seriously. You had me planning new paint colors and fabric combinations like I actually have eight mill."

A wide smile spread across her lips as she seemed to finally believe me. "Okay. Thanks for your help. Come into the kitchen with me? I hate this room, it's too hot."

"Why'd we talk here then?"

"It was obviously your favorite room. Of course I would bring you here for the wrap up."

She tossed me a bottle of sparkling water from the refrigerator's open-house stash while I tried to remember if I'd said the sunroom was my favorite. I couldn't remember saying it out loud, but maybe she noticed how much my eyes lit up when we were in there. After all, she was excellent at reading women.

I was telling her the two or three little things from her tour I'd tweak when my phone buzzed. Assuming it was Randy demanding to know my whereabouts, I checked the message.

"Oh my god!"

"What?"

"It happened!"

"What?"

"They wrote back!"

"Kieran, you know how much I hate repeating myself. Please don't make me ask again?"

"Sorry," I shrieked, but I couldn't help giving a little hop in my high heels that nearly sent me sprawling to the subway-tiled floor. "Remember how you helped me write a message last night? That was to Skye and they finally wrote back."

Pen took a long sip from her water and drawled, "Took long enough. What were they waiting for?"

"I don't know and I don't care." Pulling up their super sexy profile pic, I turned the phone to Pen. "Skye. They're a nonbinary content creator from Fairfax."

"What's a content creator?"

"I don't know," I sighed. "I can't concentrate. Read this to me?"

Pen rolled her eyes, set her drink down in a long-suffering way, took my phone and scanned the message. After a couple of shrugs and nods of approval, she finally started reading out loud.

"Sorry it took me so long to answer your message. Inexcusable I know, but I hope to make it up to you in time. I hate making such a beautiful woman go crazy. And don't worry about not having a witty opening line. The whole charade is so artificial. Your message clearly came from the heart. There's nothing so sexy as a woman who allows herself to be vulnerable. Please write back and tell me you forgive me. Or better yet, tell me about the very first thing in life you were passionate about. It was dinosaurs for me. Specifically the stegosaurus. Alas my mother told me at the tender age of seven that I couldn't grow up to be a stegosaurus. I was crushed. Skye"

We stood together in stunned silence for a full minute, listening to the ticking of the grandfather clock in the living room.

"Damn," Pen finally said. "They're good."

"That was good right?"

"Really good. Can I help you write back?"

"Yes please! I could never follow that up."

CHAPTER TWENTY-ONE

I woke up the following Sunday morning to another message from Skye that made my heart flutter. They were super good at this charming me thing, even if it had taken them two days to respond. I lounged in bed, my back supported by every pillow I owned against my padded headboard. A cup of coffee steamed on my bedside table as I read and reread the paragraph of text.

After gushing for a solid half-hour, I tried my hand at a reply. It didn't go well. Charming and witty weren't my forte and, besides, it was much more fun to work these out with Pen's help. It had become our little ritual since Georgetown and I was enjoying responding almost more than receiving Skye's messages.

Pen and I had hung out in her gorgeous listing for an hour writing a response that made me swoon. Okay, really Pen wrote most of it. All of it. I was starstruck by Skye, but by the time Pen had finished a flirty but not-too-flirty response, I was a little starstruck by her, too. She was really good at this stuff. Unfortunately, Sunday was Pen's other rest day, though a negotiable one if she had insistent clients who wanted to do viewings. Either way, there would be no help for me today.

Sighing, I dragged myself out of bed and grumbled through a short run before breakfast. I was stepping out of the shower when my phone dinged with a new text from Pen.

Have you heard from your distracted partner who takes days to respond yet?
Ooooh someone's salty.

It took Pen so long to reply I was able to complete my entire moisturizer regimen before my phone dinged again.

Sorry—tired and cranky.
I'm sure Skye is suuuuuper dreamy and worth the wait.
I forgive you and I've shown you their pic.
I can't remember.
I'll show you again tomorrow ;).
Please don't.

I mulled that one over for a long time. I'd thought we were joking, but that message had a weird undertone. I tried to remind myself that it was impossible to determine tone through text, but the last thing I wanted to do was annoy my best friend. I didn't want to be that girl who had nothing to talk about apart from their partner of the moment. I stared at my phone screen, chewing on my bottom lip until a new message from Pen arrived.

LOL

My forehead scrunched at that response. Why had it taken her two minutes to laugh at her own joke? She must've been teasing me. I shrugged, unable to determine any other meaning, and changed the subject.

Speaking of tomorrow—if I buy you lunch will you help me write back?

So you did get a message.
Yeah and I don't know how to respond.
You're hopeless.
Don't make me beg?
Never.
But tomorrow is too long—buy me lunch today and you won't have to fret.

A lock of hair had escaped my bun and I twirled it around my finger. In fact, it was the same piece of hair I'd been twirling around my finger since I got Skye's message. I dropped it and flexed my fingers, which were already itching for me to twirl it again.

I don't fret.
I can hear you fretting from here.

I was going to type out an angry denial but realized I was twirling my hair again. And chewing on my lower lip. And my eyebrows were all scrunched together. Okay, so I was fretting a little.

But it's Sunday.
It's still a rest day if you bring lunch here and we hang out on the couch.

I really wanted to. I was already wandering into my bedroom to look for my laptop bag, but it felt selfish. It may not be active work, but composing the message meant Pen was doing something for me on her day for herself and that felt wrong. Still, her couch was so much comfier than mine and I hadn't seen her since Friday lunch time. It didn't sound like a long time to go without seeing a friend, but I was desperate for some quality Penelope Time.

I'll take chicken salad on rye from Maisie's.
Pajamas are rest day dress code, so come appropriately attired.

I showed up at her front door in sweatpants and a hoodie an hour later, bags of diner food in one hand and my laptop in the other. When I knocked, Pen called out that the door was open and I walked in to find her sprawled on the couch. She wore a pair of button-up pinstripe pajamas that looked like they'd been ironed, but no one could lounge like Pen. She had one leg thrown over the back of her couch and one arm tucked behind her head.

"It's about time," she said, turning off the home renovation show she'd been watching. "I'm starving."

"Plate?"

"No time," she replied, making an adorable grabby motion for the bag.

I couldn't help laughing at her childlike expression of desperation. "Are you even capable of cooking for yourself?"

She took the takeout box and shook her head. "Nope. It's all takeout and my BFF's kindness or I'd starve."

"I'm charging you for that sandwich," I said, waggling my laptop bag in her direction.

She mumbled something that sounded like "later" through a mouthful of fries and I dropped onto the couch beside her. We moaned in unison at the first bite of overstuffed sandwich and settled in for a good old-fashioned chow session. For all her complaints of hunger, Pen ate slowly, even daintily, and we peppered our meal with our usual banter and a lot of teasing.

The longer we chatted, the lower I sank into her pillowy couch. Pen had saved me the chaise section, which was my favorite and offered a view of her side yard through a double window. She'd put in a new flower bed with hydrangeas and some shrubs with red-tipped leaves. I watched them flutter and dance in a light breeze as my eyelids drooped. I was always more comfortable in Pen's house than my own, partly because there were no projects to distract me, but mostly because of this couch.

Pen slid my computer onto her lap and stretched out across the rest of the couch cushions. She tossed me a wink and said, "You relax and let me work my magic."

I was far from arguing. In fact, I was already half asleep. I smiled my lazy response and pulled my hoodie tight around me. I stared into her perfectly manicured lawn for a while, trying to recall if she'd told me she was putting in a flower bed. I couldn't remember the conversation, but I'd been so caught up in myself recently I missed a lot. I turned to Pen, meaning to ask her about it, but the thought died the minute I saw her.

Adorable was the only word to describe it. With manic intensity, she glowered at the computer screen. Her eyebrows danced as she read Skye's message, the occasional silent chuckle rocking her entire body. It wasn't the attention I saw when she was intent on her professional work. When she was showing a house or walking a client through a closing, she was an approachable expert. The person you could count on to answer any question without making you feel stupid. But she also was attentive to her clients and her coworkers, splitting her attention without missing the slightest detail. But here she was single-minded. I could have smashed through the window and I doubt she'd have looked up. As she typed a response, her tongue peeked out between her lips. Every now and then she would whisper the words she'd written, replace them, and try again. Like I said, adorable.

While she worked, I fell asleep hugging a throw pillow. I jerked awake at some point, finding a thick blanket draped across my body. I tried to sit up, but my limbs were still trapped in sleep. Pen looked over at me with an indulgent smile.

"Sorry," I mumbled, my voice sticky. "You should've woken me."

"Nah. You looked so peaceful."

I fell asleep again before I could respond. When I woke the second time the light through the window was dimmer, carrying the red-orange glow of evening. The room was quiet, and I craned my neck to look for Pen. She was asleep across the length of the couch, her hands tucked under her head a few inches from mine. I watched her for a while, the steady rise and fall of her shoulder matching the softest whistle from her parted lips. It wasn't a snore exactly, just the whisper of her breath across her teeth. It was really cute. I'd definitely tease her about it later.

Pen woke, her breath hitching for a second as she stretched like a cat in the sun. Her flexibility never showed more clearly than moments like this. I was jealous that I couldn't stretch so thoroughly. Her jaw cracked as she yawned and rolled onto her back.

"That was awesome," I said, pulling myself up into a sitting position but keeping firm hold of the fluffy blanket. "I can't remember the last time I took an afternoon nap."

"This is what rest days are all about," Pen said, scratching the hair over her right ear and looking more like a cat than ever.

I let out my own, less impressive yawn. "I could get used to this."

"You're welcome anytime."

Pen's phone rattled around on the coffee table. She scowled and snatched it up. It was kinda adorable how much she hated phone calls. She answered clients' calls reluctantly, but otherwise she was a strictly text message or email gal. She always hid her annoyance when I called her, but sometimes I just couldn't type fast enough to get my thoughts out like I needed to.

"If you need to get that I can go," I offered, hoping she'd decline.

She jammed her thumb into the screen and the cheery jangle of her ringtone cut out abruptly. "Nope. It's my dad."

As happy as I was to be staying, Pen's dad was really sweet. "How is he?"

"Forgetful apparently, or he wouldn't be calling me," she replied, tossing the phone back onto the table.

"When was the last time you talked to him?"

She shrugged and tucked her hands behind her head. "Not long enough that he's forgotten I call him, not the other way around."

I couldn't help but laugh at her grumpiness because I didn't miss how she peeked over at the screen to see if he'd left a voice mail. "Maybe he's checking to see if his daughter's a millionaire yet. How did the showings for the Georgetown place go?"

"Looky-loos," Pen replied. "What a waste of a Saturday. If I'd known they had no real interest in the property, I wouldn't have bothered."

"That sucks. I'm sorry."

"This one'll take a while, I guess." She didn't look too bummed about it, but I knew she'd be sweating the sale again soon. "Wanna watch a movie?"

"Who gets to pick?" I asked. Pen's tastes went toward action flicks. Usually the ones from our youth, with scantily clad damsels in distress.

"You're the guest."

"Yeah, but I'll pick an '80s rom-com and you'll snore through the whole thing."

"Excuse me, ma'am." She glowered at me. "I do not snore."

"You were literally snoring two minutes ago."

"Was not."

"Was too."

She tossed a pillow at me and I managed to catch it before it smacked me in the face. I tucked it behind my head and pasted on a smile that was almost as smug as Pen's normally was.

"Your violence only serves to prove my point."

She hopped off the couch and slouched into the kitchen, her bare feet slapping against the hardwood floor. "I'm not sharing my popcorn with you."

She did though. And she reheated some vegetarian chili and poblano corn bread for us. I knew her complaints about not feeding herself were exaggerated. We settled on *Ladyhawke* as the '80s intersection between action and romance. Fortunately for me, she'd never seen it so she didn't know the romance heavily outweighed the action. And the trademark '80s cheesiness was cringeworthy. It was actually a pretty bad flick, but sweet enough to make me cry. Plus, Michelle Pfeiffer. Not much more needed to be said.

By the time Michelle rode off into the sunset with her soulmate, the moon in Woodbridge was well up. I peeled myself off the couch reluctantly and folded the blanket. My bones felt like jelly from so much relaxing and I hated to make them solidify again.

Pen picked at the couch cushion and said, "You can stay if you want. No one's used the guest room since Dad was here for Christmas."

She stuck her bottom lip out. Unfair. She knew I couldn't resist the patented Penelope Pout. Still, the mention of her rarely used guest room was a clear reminder of where most of her overnight guests slept. I'd seen more than one of them leave when we carpooled. I also saw how her neighbors looked at them and I didn't want any of that shade thrown my way.

"Sorry, Pen," I said, pushing the thought from my mind. "We've got work in the morning and while these sweats were great for a rest day, they don't exactly fit Randy's dress code."

"Yeah," she murmured, still staring at her pillow. "I guess not."

She looked sad and I wondered if she'd been cooped up inside too long. I ruffled her hair on my way out, but she stopped me at the door.

"You forgot your laptop."

"Oh shit."

I'd completely forgotten about the reason for my visit. My stomach dropped at the thought that I hadn't answered Skye in almost a full day. I'd never made them wait that long.

"Stop fretting," Pen gave me a wink as she held out my laptop bag. "I sent it through while you were sleeping."

CHAPTER TWENTY-TWO

I knew there was no chance I could sneak out of work early without anyone noticing, and I was thrilled the only person who caught me was Arthur.

"Nice try, Kieran," he said, slipping through the open door of my office as I collected my purse and briefcase. "Where are you off to?"

"I came in early today so I could get all my work done by four. I'm not doing anything wrong. You can't tattle."

"You always come in early and you always get your work done by four. You're the only one of us in this office who works." He paused to flash his charming smile at our coworker Dawn as she headed out on her third smoke break of the afternoon. She scowled at his comment but continued away from her overflowing desk anyway. "I don't care about that. I want to know where you're going."

I smiled and didn't even try to hide it since my blush would have given me away. I was desperate to talk about Skye. "I have a date."

"At four o'clock?"

"No. It's not until six, but I want to look really good for this one."

"You're going home to shave, aren't you?"

He sat on the edge of my desk and leaned in, for all the world like one of my high school friends asking for the scoop.

"No. I'm not the kind of girl who goes home with someone on the first date." Chloe notwithstanding, I had a strict fourth date rule and I was not going to break it again. "But it doesn't hurt to smell nice."

"If you think that's important, you're definitely not going out with a guy."

I should have argued but he could judge his own if he wanted to. "As a matter of fact, they are not a guy."

"Oh! Another hot enby, huh?"

Sometimes I regretted teaching him some basic queer vocabulary but it was refreshing to hear a straight, cis white guy refer to a nonbinary person appropriately. And wow did I want to gush. I dropped my bags and jumped up beside him on the desk, pulling up my favorite pic of Skye. Arthur whistled and took the phone from me, grabbing his glasses from his suit pocket to ogle better.

"Nice work, Kieran! They're even hotter than Alex."

I chose to focus on the compliment and held back my cringe. Arthur and Alex had always gotten along, even after we'd broken up. I hadn't wanted our friends to have to choose sides, but if they did, I wanted them to choose mine. I didn't know if Arthur and Alex still hung out, but, in case they did, I agreed that Skye was hotter. And also funnier, wittier, and more charming. In fact, they were so great I had a hard time keeping my cool while we messaged.

"It didn't start off on the best foot," I confided in Arthur. "But things have definitely been looking up."

It had been tough to wait that whole day for their first message but waiting had been a big part of my relationship with Skye so far. Content creators, and I still wasn't clear what one was, were apparently extremely busy because it still took them ages to reply.

The message Pen had sent while I napped Sunday afternoon didn't get a reply until Monday lunchtime. It was still a trend with us. I would reply immediately, as long as Pen was there to help me craft something decent, and then wait twelve hours or more for Skye's new message. At first it seemed sweet and old-fashioned to wait, but then it became annoying. I wanted to be more of a priority to them, but there was no way I could say that without sounding super needy. I didn't want to start a dynamic of me whining and them acquiescing to keep me happy. They were dedicated to their work and that was something I understood. If the trend continued when we got more serious, then we could talk about it.

The whole thing would be cleared up when we met in person anyway. I was much better in person than online. Once they met me, they would fall as hard as I had and then they'd drop everything to talk.

After two weeks of increasingly personal messages and several hints, Skye had finally asked me out for dinner. More than any other person I'd messaged, more than any other date I'd been on, this was one I thought could go somewhere. I was already planning a second date.

"That's so great. I know you two will really hit it off. Only thing," Arthur said, a frown deepening lines around his eyes. "I thought you were going out with Pen tonight. Didn't I hear you talking about it?"

"Oh yeah. I'm meeting her after."

"You have a date after your date?"

"It's not a date. It's Pen!" I hopped down and collected my stuff from the floor. "I was nervous for that first online date…"

"The Disaster at the Newseum."

"Arthur, if you have given titles to each of my disastrous dates kindly do not tell me. Anyway, the date was so terrible I met Pen after to drown my sorrows. It's sort of become a routine for us."

"So you preplan the drowning your sorrows? Sounds like you're setting yourself up for failure."

"Not this time," I said, sashaying to the door. "This time it'll be a chance to gush about how amazing my night was."

CHAPTER TWENTY-THREE

Skye lived in nearby Lorton, so we picked a restaurant there for dinner. Unlike the trendy spots in the city, Giorgio's was a quaint little Italian place tucked away beside a subdivision. It reminded me of Layla's, so I loved it immediately. The hostess gave me a warm smile and led me to a table fit snugly into the back corner. The ceiling was low, giving the table a cozy intimacy. It was a ridiculously charming spot and the perfect place for a first date with someone as deep and sensitive as Skye.

I chose the chair with a view of the front door and ordered a glass of Pinot Grigio while I waited. The waiter introduced himself and told me to catch his eye if I needed anything before Skye arrived. I sipped my wine and spied on the other tables to settle my nerves. Everyone here seemed to be on a date. Right next to me sat a man and woman in their seventies who couldn't keep their eyes off each other.

I amused myself watching them go through the steps of their obviously well-known dance. They chatted so easily. I wondered what on earth they could have to talk about after so many years together. My parents had been deeply in love, but they never had the chance to grow old together. I never met any of my grandparents. My father's parents hated my mother and blamed her for their son's left-leaning political views so contrary to their own. They never came to visit any of us and, when they died, my father didn't attend their funerals. My mother's parents divorced young. She'd barely known her father and her mother had not been a kind woman. It had always been our little family against the world. All my school friends' parents had been divorced or single parents. Pen's mother had died when she was a teenager and her father never remarried. I'd met him a few times over the years, but he and Pen had little contact.

Laying it out like that, I realized how little contact I'd had with stable relationships. Maybe that's why I craved one so much. Why I had married so young. Why I had latched on to the first person who came my way afterward. Why I put myself through this crucible for the slightest glimmer of happiness. I looked back to the door, hoping to see Skye there to rescue me from my gloomy thoughts. All I saw was a small congregation of servers at the hostess's stand.

My phone buzzed and I checked it under the table.

Running about 15 min late. So sorry. Have a glass of wine and I'll be there soon.

"Way ahead of you," I mumbled and sipped my Pinot.

It wasn't the best start, but I could excuse a little lateness. Not everyone could leave work early like me and Skye's work seemed demanding. The waiter came by and I told him that my date was running late. He was kind, waving away my apology, and offered to bring me breadsticks to hold me over. I didn't think I'd need them—fifteen minutes wasn't a long time—but I agreed because he was kind. After he was gone, I did a quick Google search on content creators. It was hard to define the job, but it seemed like they made blog posts and handled social media for rich people.

I munched on a breadstick and wondered what could hold someone late at work as a content creator. Was there such a thing as a Twitter emergency? Did blogs have hard deadlines?

It wasn't the most charitable thought, but the elderly couple had woven their fingers together as they headed for the door like the happiest humans in the universe. I doubted that a love like that started with one of them showing up fifteen minutes late to their first date.

With them gone, I scanned the room to find something else to distract me. I was happy to see a lesbian couple leaning across their table toward each other as they talked. One was small and butch, wearing a pinstripe shirt and suspenders. She had the look of a woman who worked with her hands and took pride in dressing up. Her skin was several shades darker above her neckline than the almost rose-pink showing at her open collar. Her date was taller, her skin glowing a fine sienna in the low light. Her broad build filled her off-the-shoulder dress. Her hand rested on the table between them and I watched her gasp as her girlfriend stroked the palm with her fingertips.

"Would you like another?"

I'd been so intent on my people watching that I jumped at the question. My server was back and, more surprisingly, my glass was empty. I checked the time. It had been twenty minutes since Skye's text and there was still no sign of them.

"Yes," I said as I picked up my phone. "I will. Thank you."

I texted Skye asking if everything was okay and, to my relief, I got an immediate response.

Five minutes away

An apology would have been nice, but they were probably pulling into the parking lot if they were that close. I checked my outfit to make sure I looked perfect for their arrival. Like the woman across the restaurant, I'd chosen an off-the-shoulder dress for the evening. If only I could fill it out as well as she did. Still, it was simple and elegant without being too dressy. I wondered now, however, if I looked like I was trying too hard. This date seemed far more casual in Skye's estimation than it was in mine. Maybe I was putting too much pressure on this.

Ten minutes after Skye's text I stopped watching the door. The group of servers was still there and I caught a few pitying looks my way. There was definitely whispering. I turned my attention back to the lesbian couple, but they were looking at me, too. I caught a sad little shake of the head from the butch.

Just like that, I crumpled. Like any woman, I'd learned long ago how to keep my face neutral while I wept inside, but it was harder this time. With a jolt I realized I'd never been stood up before. Not surprising when one had such a limited dating experience, but it pained me to realize that's what was happening. Skye's texts said they were coming, but it was hard to believe them.

Unfortunately, I couldn't stand up and saunter out, my head held high. The wine and the humiliation combined to paralyze my legs. If I tried to leave now the whole restaurant would see me stumble and that would be much worse than sitting still. Besides, there was a chance that Skye would still show.

Fifteen minutes later, the lesbian couple left. They both looked over at me while they walked out, the butch's hand resting on her girlfriend's lower back. People at other tables were looking at me now, too. The servers weren't hiding their stares and whispers anymore. No one was laughing, so there was a tiny glimmer of hope, but I decided that it was time I gather up my dignity and leave. When my waiter passed close a moment later, I asked for the check.

He arrived with my bill—he'd only charged me for one glass of wine which felt as much like pity as kindness—when the door crashed open and Skye charged in. The cluster of servers stood and stared, not sure how to handle this particular arrival, while Skye scanned the small room. It took them a ridiculously long time to spot me. They stumbled into an empty chair in their haste to cross the room.

"Kieran, I am so…" They collapsed into a chair and slid half out of it. "I'm s' sorry. I'm late."

"I hadn't noticed," I replied in the flattest voice I could manage. The waiter was still standing at my elbow, apparently frozen in place by the turn of events.

"I'm sorry." Skye slid on the chair a little more, grabbing at the tablecloth in an attempt to steady themselves. "Lemme make it up t'you."

The words slurred at the edges and brought the smell of bourbon across the table. I looked more closely at Skye and noticed a few details I'd missed. They were wearing a tailored jacket and a buttoned shirt open at the throat, but the shirt collar was wrapped over the jacket collar in more than one place. The tail of the shirt was peeking out of their jeans and their hair was mussed in odd places.

"Are you drunk?" I demanded in a loud whisper.

"No!" After a beat they turned bright red and stammered, "A little?"

"Did you drive here in that state?"

"No. Took'n Uber."

"Then you can take an Uber home."

The waiter finally came to his senses and turned to leave. In a flash Skye's hand shot out and grabbed his wrist. "Wait. We wanna order. I'll have a glass of wha' th' lady's having."

"If you would be so kind as to let go of me," the waiter said, an edge of anger in his voice.

Skye dropped the waiter's hand immediately and I saw the red imprint on his arm. They slunk back into their chair and mumbled another apology. He left without a word and I prayed he wasn't actually getting that glass of wine.

"I cannot believe you…" I stopped and lowered my voice, leaning across the table so I could speak to Skye without embarrassing myself any further. "Why did you even come here? You're an hour late and drunk. What on earth…"

"Lemme esplain." Skye swallowed, trying to shake the slur out of their voice. How much had they had to drink? "I's working."

"You were drinking."

"It was a work func-tion. I couldn' get out of it. It was a dinner, but I was gonna leave early so I di'n't order any food. I shouldn've had the wine either."

"You don't smell like wine."

"Had a drink wi' my boss." Their eyes narrowed and the red that had appeared in their cheeks and neck was getting brighter. "I've a career to maintain."

"You could have rescheduled with me."

"I di'n't want…" They met my eye and I knew they were lying. They turned abruptly, looking over their shoulder. "Where's th' waiter. I'll take 'at glass of wine now."

I slipped cash into the binder with my bill and stood. "You've had enough and so have I."

As I passed, Skye reached for my hand, but I knew to avoid the contact. When I whipped my hand out of their reach they said, "Please, Kieran. I 's nervous."

That stopped me. "What?"

"I 's nervous to meet you." They slid out of the chair and for a heart stopping moment I thought they'd passed out, but they stood shakily and took a deep, settling breath. "Your messages were so witty and I could n-never match that."

"You did! Your first message to me was perfect."

"It took me a f-full day to write it!" They grabbed at their hair like a person at the extremity of frustration. "I worked on it all night and all day and then you responded back in like five minutes. How c'n I compete with that?"

"Don't you do that for a living? Isn't that what you do as a content creator?"

"I write snarky Tweets for boring musicians and desperate housewives. It makes me…no wait…it *takes* me hours to write two hun'red-eighty characters!"

I could have spared them some shame by coming clean about Pen's help, but Skye chose that moment to lunge at me for a kiss. The waiter hadn't gone far. When I squealed at Skye's movement, he was there with an arm around my date, pulling them away.

"Gimme 'nother chance! Please?" Skye bellowed.

The waiter looked at me and I shook my head, so he held on to Skye as I ran from the restaurant.

CHAPTER TWENTY-FOUR

After two glasses of wine, I decided to leave my car at the restaurant and take an Uber to meet Pen. She was cruising at nearby Workhouse Arts Center, which was holding a Pride Month market featuring queer artists. Abby had invited the regulars from Riveter's since she was exhibiting her paintings there, and Pen had decided it would be a hot spot for the artsy Northern Virginia lesbian population. I requested a quiet ride and hunkered in the back seat. My mood swerved from angry to embarrassed to sad. Had the journey been longer, perhaps I would have landed on one emotion, but it was only a few miles to the gallery.

It was packed and I had a moment of panic, worried that the queer couple I'd watched at the restaurant would be ending their night out here. They had been the first to recognize I was being stood up and I didn't think I could face them again. For a heartbeat, I considered turning around and heading back home, but I needed Pen more than I needed my pride. Humiliation had already happened, and if the couple was there, nothing would change.

Workhouse Arts Center had originally been a prison complex, but the living quarters were repurposed into art studios in the early 2000s. Six buildings holding more than one hundred studio spaces now surrounded a courtyard that was often transformed into an open-air market and exhibition space.

I stormed into the crowd, seeking but not seeing in my anger. I sought out the darkest corners and the most secluded studios because I knew I'd find Pen in one of them. I was right.

She was standing in the dimly lit corner where two buildings met, a lithe twenty-something blonde plastered all over her, trying to see how far down Pen's throat her tongue would fit. I leaned against a brick column nearby and tapped my foot. When they came up for air Pen looked my way with a lopsided grin. The woman giggled and dropped back down onto her heels. She had been on tiptoe, her exposed cleavage as close as she could get it to Pen's chin.

I turned an apologetic smile on the woman and tried to be nice, I really did, but I was back in a wave of anger. The words came out before my brain could stop them. "I'm sorry to be a bitch, but can you fuck off? I need to talk to Penelope."

The blonde blinked at me and it looked like she was trying to figure out who Penelope was. It took an eternity for the penny to drop. When it did, she whipped her head around to stare at Pen.

"You said you were single!"

It probably didn't help matters that Pen laughed and said, "I am."

"Bullshit. You're a lying..." Her tirade was interrupted by a botched attempt to disentangle herself from Pen's legs. Pen wasn't stopping her, but she still had a hard time removing her ankle hooked around Pen's. She finally got free, adjusted her skirt and stormed off, shouting over her shoulder, "Bitch!"

"Come on, Kieran. I was totally gonna score with that one."

My sad mood kicked in as the blonde disappeared into the crowd. "I'm such an asshole."

Pen didn't seem the least bit phased, but when she put a warm hand on my shoulder I lost it completely. One minute I was fine, the next minute I was a blubbering, sobbing mess right there in the open-air gallery. My humiliation was truly complete.

"Penelope Anne Chase," shouted a familiar voice.

I looked up in time to see our favorite bartender storming over from her place behind a nearby table. Abby wore a paint-speckled apron and a nametag identifying her as a vendor. I'd expected to see her here, but I certainly didn't want to cry in front of her. I turned to the wall and tried to quiet my sobbing against the bricks.

"What the hell did you do to Kieran?" I heard Abby growl over my sobs.

"Nothing! It wasn't me!"

Abby's anger became a flood of mumbled curses and threats. Her hand, weighed down with at least six elaborate rings, landed next to Pen's on my shoulder.

"What's wrong, sweetie?" She asked me in a cooing voice. "What happened?"

I couldn't answer through my hiccupping sobs, so Pen leaned close and told Abby that she guessed my date hadn't gone well. Abby made several consoling sounds but stopped short of saying, "Again?" With my tears explained, she apparently felt safe leaving me with my best friend. I thought my crying would stop, then I remembered the servers staring at me as Skye tumbled into the restaurant and the whole thing started again.

Pen's hard-soled shoes scraped along the concrete and then her arms were around me. The air I'd been gulping suddenly smelled like lavender and sandalwood. Breathing was a lot easier when the air smelled so sweet. The night was chilly and my exposed shoulders were like ice, but I didn't notice until Pen's cheek pressed into one. It warmed me through to my broken heart, which managed to beat at a steadier rhythm. I fell into her embrace, allowing her to pull me into the circle of her arms. People were probably staring, but I didn't care. The only thing I cared about was Pen soothing all the battered parts of me.

"Better?" she whispered against the top of my head.

It wasn't. Not really. I could crawl away from here tonight and still feel like shit. The only place it was okay was here where she hugged me and listened about my terrible night and, if I was lucky, teased me about it until it didn't hurt so badly. If I said I was better now, I'd lose the comfort of her arms around me and I wasn't strong enough for that yet. Then again, I thought as a tear rolled down my cheek onto her shoulder, my mascara was doing nothing for her beige jacket.

"Oh god, Pen!" I shot up straight and saw the stain. She'd never be able to get it out. "Your jacket. I'm so sorry."

She looked at the smear of makeup and laughed, turning those kind eyes on me and making me feel warm all over again. "Don't worry. I know a good dry cleaner."

I couldn't open my mouth because tears were threatening again. I pressed my lips together and swallowed a sob. She led me to a nearby metal bench and sat so close her hip was touching mine.

"Hey," Pen said, taking my hands in hers. "I can still sleep with that chick. You don't have to cry." She winked. "It'll be fine."

My guffaw was as abrupt as it was unexpected. Leave it to Pen to make me laugh on a night like tonight. Still, the tears were threatening and all I wanted were Pen's arms around me again. I curled into her embrace without the slightest protest. She wrapped me up and pressed her cheek against the top of my head. I closed my eyes and took a long, slow breath. As I let it out, lips pressed against my forehead and then my eyebrow.

I could feel Pen's lips against my forehead. I could feel how gentle and strong they were against my eyebrow. She left them pressed against each spot for the space of two heartbeats. I held my breath each time, worried I'd sob again and scare her off. I'd thought the band of her arms around me was bliss, but it was nothing compared to this.

In an instant, the whole world felt right again. It was warm and soft and smelled good. The sounds of the party—the voices and music—all faded into a distant hum as I curled tighter into Pen's arms. I slipped my hands under her jacket and up her back, gripping hard at her shoulders. My hands were cold against her warm shirt and I felt her sharp intake of breath against my cheek. When I tried to pull my hands away, she squeezed me tighter. Sooner than I would have liked, the world around us came back to life.

"All kidding aside," I said. "I'm sorry about ruining your chances with that one. She's cute."

"You don't have to be sorry. I can make it work. Keep crying on my shoulder for another minute and I'll be the best friend in the world."

I whispered just loudly enough to be heard over the beat of her heart in my ear, "You already are."

There was a rumble like a purr in Pen's chest. It reverberated through me and shook the last of the anger away. The tears were gone, but they left emptiness behind. I hadn't been this tired in a very long time.

"And now she'll know it and I can definitely get traction with that."

"You know what," I said, prying myself out of her arms with difficulty. "I bet you could."

Abby came over to check on me, but I wasn't in the mood to talk, so I scanned the crowd and let Pen reassure her. I was pleased to see no one was looking our way. Perhaps women breaking down in the arms of the first person they found was a regular occurrence here. It seemed to be the theme of the night. Across the courtyard, seated on a metal bench identical to ours, was another woman sobbing into someone's shoulder. I couldn't see either of their faces, but one had long, blond hair and the other had the gayest haircut I'd ever seen. Short with lots of product in an asymmetrical cut. She wore a plaid shirt and bulky men's jeans.

The blonde came up for air and I realized it was the skinny girl that had been draped all over Pen when I came in. I shot Pen a look, and it was clear she'd seen the display. She shrugged, though it wasn't in her nature to give up so easily. Then, as I watched, her face hardened into a mask of confusion. I looked back to the bench and now the butch's face was visible. It was a very familiar face. I had a feeling that, if I saw her walk, she would still walk just as gay as she had leaving Pen's townhouse.

"Um, Pen, isn't that…"

"Sure is."

"For someone who isn't gay," I said as the blonde went in for a kiss as aggressive as the one she'd been laying on Pen. The kiss was returned energetically if somewhat sloppily, frightening a yuppie straight couple nearby. "She's really leaning into it."

We watched them make out for a little while. It wasn't the prettiest thing in the world, but then watching someone else make out rarely was. When I realized there was little chance Pen would actually go home with the blonde, I sighed and squeezed her hand.

"I guess you've earned yourself a toaster oven, Pen."

"Excuse me," she said, her eyebrows knitting together. "That joke is a reductive stereotype that denies lived experience and sexual fluidity."

She held her straight face for a full two seconds, then started to laugh. I scowled at her. "That's my line."

I wasn't able to hold my scowl nearly as long as her. Soon we were both laughing and banging our hands on the bench. Abby gave us a long eye roll and that only made us laugh more. This was exactly what I'd been looking for tonight. Pen being her normal, hedonistic self and teasing me for being my normal, overthinking self. It was the sort of dynamic I had never had and, given recent events, doubted I ever could have with anyone else. Our relationship was the most special part of my life and I could cry with gratitude for it every day.

Pen grew quiet first. "Want to talk about the date?"

"No." I'd tell her eventually, but I was exhausted emotionally and physically. "I just want to hang out with you for a little while. Is that okay?"

"Of course."

"Then I'll send you off to fight for another notch in your headboard. Deal?"

"Deal."

CHAPTER TWENTY-FIVE

Hank Prince was a single guy who'd worked sixty-hour weeks for years to buy his first investment property. It'd been difficult to set an appointment for his closing because he travelled a lot for work and often at short notice. He was very polite and even apologetic both times he'd had to reschedule. When we set the third appointment, I mentioned his appraisal would expire if we pushed the date again. He promised to not make any more trouble for me, even if he had to fake being sick to get out of work.

In the end he didn't have to, but he had to do the closing without his Realtor present. The only time he was free was a Tuesday afternoon, but Pen had helped him find this fixer-upper. When I told her the new date was a rest day she offered to come in but he refused, even enlisting my help to get her to stay home.

Our mutual battle against Pen's stubbornness helped build a rapport before we'd met, and I had a feeling from the tone of his emails that he was going to hit on me. He didn't waste any time, asking me to drinks before he'd even picked up his pen. To his credit, he was very polite when I turned him down.

"I understand," he said, rubbing a hand over his prematurely bald crown and sparse copper hair. "Seemed worth a shot. I thought it would work to my advantage that I own two homes now."

"Actually," I said, sliding the deed signature page across the table to him. "You only own one home until you sign right here."

He laughed and scribbled his name. He was one of those clients whose signature got sloppier the deeper we progressed into the packet. I could never abide someone who couldn't maintain good penmanship. Sure, thirty signatures was a lot, but it showed a lack of commitment. Anyone who got distracted while spending a quarter million dollars wasn't worth my time.

I noticed some of the wind had gone out of Hank's sails. It was inappropriate for him to make a pass, but this was a big day for him and I didn't want it spoiled by any awkwardness. Hoisting on a fake smile, I tried for friendly humor.

"For the record, it's not you…" I didn't finish with the cliched "it's me." Instead I finished with, "I'm taking a break from dating at the moment."

"Why's that?" he asked as he signed the name affidavit.

I slapped my notary stamp on the page more firmly than necessary. "I've had some bad luck on a dating app."

He laughed sourly. "I've been there. It's the worst."

I tortured myself by allowing the image of Skye stumbling drunkenly into Giorgio's to play in my head for the first time in over a week. "Yes, it is."

"Keep your chin up. The right one's out there."

"I've thought that before and I've been wrong."

"I'd rather trust the wrong person than give up." He seemed to realize that he might have insulted me and stammered, "Not that taking a break is giving up. You just need time."

"Maybe so." I straightened the paperwork and slid one copy into a thick folder for him. "Congratulations, Hank. You've got another house."

Excitement lit his eyes and I couldn't help but smile along with him. Taking the keys, he left the office, tripping over his chair in his haste to get back to work. While I was sorting my own paperwork and dreading an afternoon trip to the courthouse, Hank stuck his head back in.

"Maybe you should try it the old-fashioned way," he said.

"Excuse me?"

"Meet someone in real life and be disappointed without standard text messaging rates applying. You know?"

I laughed and that made him look shyly away. "I've had the exact same luck with that."

The courthouse visit was miraculously brief and I made it home before rush hour traffic snarled the roads. I made a bowl of rice and quinoa with roasted beets, mushrooms, and Brussel sprouts. While the veggies roasted, I whipped up a dressing of yogurt, dill, and lemon and thought of Hank's suggestion to meet people offline. In retrospect, I realized he probably meant himself, since he'd waited a long minute in the doorway, but that didn't mean he was wrong. I'd met Alex in a bar and Nick in high school. In person. Neither of them had been anonymous faces at the other end of an Internet connection and maybe that was why we'd formed a real human connection.

The problem, of course, was that I'd tried this game before. Hank's advice was the same as Pen's when I asked her to help me write a profile, and my experience now was the same as it had been then. I went to bars, restaurants, stores, and every manner of outdoor event. I'd talked to people I thought were cute and I'd let them approach me. Nothing ever came of it, just like online. I met more people on Swingle, but I also had more disasters. Which was better?

I scooped grains into a bowl, but the sight of all the leftovers filled me with defeat. All I wanted was someone to share a meal with. Okay, honestly I wanted to share a whole lot more and the desperation I'd felt months ago was reaching crisis level now. But the truth was that I craved love more than sex. I craved someone I could talk to at the end of the day. Someone to lie on the couch with and share my bad '80s movie obsession.

The phone rang as I started up *Adventures in Babysitting*. What could I say? I'd had a lifelong crush on Elisabeth Shue and damn if she didn't look even better now than she had in 1987. Pen's name appeared on the screen and I answered on speaker so I could eat my dinner while we talked.

"Hey sexy," her voice rang through the line with the sort of energy a day off always gave her. "How'd the closing go?"

"He hit on me."

"Of course he did. That's why he scheduled it for a Tuesday. So I wouldn't be there and he had a clear shot. What an ass."

"It was fine," I said, plopping onto the couch. I'd set the AC to blast and curled up in my sweats and thick socks, cradling my dinner bowl in my lap. "He was sweet when I turned him down."

"I'm surprised he didn't cry," Pen said with more edge to her voice than I'd expected. She must've really not liked the guy.

It seemed prudent to change the subject. "How was your day off?"

"Scanned some listings for a new client and binged a docuseries on a serial killer."

On screen, a muted Brad raged at his sister for using the last of his pimple coverup to paint her picture of Thor.

"You know it's not a day off when you work. That makes you a workaholic."

"What about the documentary? What does that make me?"

"A basic white girl."

"Can't argue there." After a minute in which I scraped up the last of my dinner, Pen asked, "Why haven't we been hanging out recently?"

"We're having lunch tomorrow."

"Yeah, but we haven't been going out after work. It's been two weeks since you've scared off one of my hookups."

I laughed and snuggled deeper into the couch cushions. "I do miss that."

"Remember the chick who walks so gay? While you've been home pouting, she and that girl you threw out of my lap moved in together."

"I haven't been pouting."

"You've definitely been pouting."

I might've been pouting. "What do you mean moved in together?"

"I mean, she's not a toaster-oven joke anymore, she's a U-Haul joke."

"Wow, you're pulling out all the lesbian stereotypes, aren't you?"

"Clearly they're all based in reality."

I laughed along, but a moment later I stopped, staring at Elisabeth Shue's excellent '80s hair but not really seeing it at all. "Wait. You're serious, aren't you?"

"Of course I'm serious. Keep up. The kid moved in last weekend. She's not a kid, really, she's twenty-eight, but still feels pretty young to me."

Pen explained how the gay walker's name was Marlene and how she approached Pen at Riveter's on Saturday night to thank her. She'd never been so happy in her life and it was all because of Pen. I was only half listening to the story. The only part that stuck with me was how happy those two women were. It gave me hope. Here the kid had been devastated by an imagined betrayal and Marlene was just getting her gay feet under her. They were both floundering and yet they'd found their way to each other despite the odds. I found myself rooting for them in a way I hadn't rooted for any real-life couple in a long time.

As much as their love story, I was charmed by our part in it. Recapping with Pen afterward had become the best part of all my dates. Hanging out with her made me feel better about everything. She made me laugh and made me hope. Being with Pen made me feel better about me. Now there was evidence that it made more than my life better, it made the world better.

"Aw, Pen," I said. "We made people fall in love."

"The hell we did. I made people fall into bed. It's not love, they barely know each other."

"I don't believe you. I'm sure they're happy."

"Maybe so, but they don't have what it takes to last. You can see proof." Her hesitation made me realize this was the real reason she called me. "Set up a date with whatever loser you're talking to for tomorrow. Meet me at Riveter's after and you can see they won't last."

"I can't."

"Sure you can. You don't have to make it a big-deal date. Just get coffee."

"I can't because I'm not talking to anyone. I'm taking a break from Swingle."

"Not that again." The words sounded exasperated, but her tone was anything but. There was a sadness there that made her sound vulnerable.

Vulnerable was a rare state for my best friend and I rushed to defend myself. "It's too hard. Everyone is awful."

"You shouldn't give up, honey." All the teasing was gone now and she was sweet mixed with vulnerable. "You deserve love. And besides, I miss hanging out with you after."

I missed that, too. I missed how she laughed when I told her my stories. I missed how she always spun them to make me believe again. Most of all, I missed how she'd hugged me last time. The smell of her skin and her clothes and how I felt so safe there in her arms. Her lips pressed against my forehead. I couldn't get it out of my head.

Pen was not a hugger. Sex she could do without thinking. Hugging was something else entirely. It was intimate in a deeper, more meaningful way, and I wanted her to hug me more. If I got another hug like that, maybe it was worth scouring Swingle for another disappointment.

"I doubt I can get someone to go out with me in less than twenty-four hours. Online dating isn't like that."

"Then come out with me without the date. We can just hang out."

As much as I wanted to go out and have fun with Pen, I didn't really feel like watching her take some stranger home. It felt less invasive on her prowling to meet her halfway through the night with a story to tell.

"Next week," I said to only mild argument. "I'll have a date by next week."

CHAPTER TWENTY-SIX

When I promised Pen I would have a date the next week, I didn't really think it would happen. I'd moved my Swingle app to the back page of my phone where its little icon sat all alone. It felt cruel to abandon that cheery little heart to its lonely corner of shame, but it hadn't exactly been kind to me either. The first thing I did after hanging up with Pen was rescue it from solitary and put it back to its normal spot on page two, beneath my equally ignored Pinterest app.

I'd been getting messages but hadn't checked them for a couple of weeks. Several people I'd ignored now wanted nothing to do with me. I couldn't blame them. After all, Skye had made me wait one day and I was ready to wallow in loneliness forever. Now I knew that would have been a significant improvement over the actual turn of events.

When I tried messaging two of my admirers, they'd already blocked me. Fair. There was one, though, that looked promising and my apology to them went through, meaning they may not have given up on me. Lucky for me, because they were close to the ideal person.

Their name was Charlie and they were a gorgeous, ridiculously tall enby. Hints of silver streaked the auburn hair at their temples. They had a warm smile and a broad, powerful build. I had to admit, I liked the idea of a partner towering over me and Charlie looked the type. At forty-five they were a little older than I usually went for, but they had a face almost as youthful as Pen's. In fact, there was something in their eyes that reminded me of Pen, too.

I was heading to bed, and had even grabbed my toothbrush, when I realized I hadn't turned the Swingle notifications back on. Without that little chirp to announce activity, I might miss more messages. It was a good thing I took the time because there was already a reply from Charlie. If I'd made them wait again, there would be no way I could talk them into a date the following week.

Their message was charming if a little bland, but I was okay with the strong and silent type. That's how I had described Nick to my mom when we'd first met. She had given me an indulgent smile and shot a glance at my dad. I hadn't understood the look at the time, knowing my dad to be anything but silent, but I had been pretty young. I hadn't realized how much people could change over time.

"Stop thinking about it," I growled aloud, but I knew myself too well to believe I could be distracted once I'd started thinking about Nick.

I managed to hold back the nauseating feeling of betrayal long enough to reply to Charlie. It wasn't a great message, but I was tired and my heart wasn't in it yet. Smashing my thumb into the send button, I pressed the heels of my hands into my eyes and slumped back onto my bed.

"Why do you ruin everything?"

I'd meant it as an admonition to my overactive brain, but it might as well have been directed at Nick himself. My mind knew I was lucky to be rid of him, but every now and then my traitorous heart reminded me how much I'd lost in our divorce.

Nick had been my best friend and the partner to my life's biggest adventures. He'd made his interest known the moment we met, but then he'd done something completely unexpected for a teenage boy.

He'd stopped flirting with me.

Other guys had given me a single compliment and then tried to shove their tongues down my throat. Nick had spent the whole semester earning my friendship. He hadn't made a move. He'd just…listened. He asked me about my hobbies and joined my friend group. I thought he didn't like me and I moped for a little while, but he became a good friend. A year later, when he finally asked me out, I asked him why he'd waited.

"I don't date strangers," he'd told me. "How do I know if I like you if we aren't friends first?"

That had *really* worked for me. I fell in love with him in that moment. We got married two years later, a week after high school graduation. Everyone said it was too fast, but I knew I'd found the best guy in the world. A few months later he got a great job with a military contractor in DC and we moved away from home. It had been so surreal to start married life that young, with no safety net apart from each other.

Northern Virginia was only a three-hour drive from Morgantown, but it might as well have been on a different planet. My parents had lived inside a progressive university bubble, but its borders were sharp and confined. It was not the place where I could find the real me, even in the more open-minded collegiate environment. The DC suburbs were full of people who made me feel normal and welcome, but there were bubbles in DC, too. Nick's company was full of macho men with conservative wives. Nick loved it, but I cringed with every new party invitation.

Around the time I met Pen, the military industrial complex where Nick was thriving was in an uproar over the impending end of Don't Ask, Don't Tell. The conversations at Nick's work functions made my skin crawl. Like how they'd have to have two sets of showers, one for the straight men, one for the gay men to keep the straight guys safe. I started spending more time with Pen and I relished having a friend that shared my worldview. Nick enjoyed his "time with the guys." I don't know when we stopped being each other's best friend.

It was fine until I also realized that I wasn't exactly straight. There wasn't a lightning-bolt moment and I didn't fall in love with someone else. I'd just met Pen at Riveter's for drinks one night like usual and realized that I found several of the women at the bar attractive. That was it. A harmless attraction I had no intention of acting upon. The more I explored my own feelings, the queerer I'd felt. Finally I understood what was weird about me and it was so liberating.

When I realized that my newly understood orientation didn't affect my love for my husband, I felt even better about it. I didn't want to explore sex with women, I just knew this was an important part of who I was. So I shared that, including the assurance that I didn't want anything in our marriage to change, with the most important person in my life. Nick's reaction was nothing like I'd imagined.

"You're a queer?" he'd shrieked.

I'd started using that word about myself in my head, but I'd never said it like that. He'd spat out the word like it tasted foul. The man I loved described me like I was trash, and the pain was unbearable. It hadn't hurt as badly when my parents had died.

"Yeah. So?" I'd replied.

That's when he'd started screaming. In the years since we'd moved to DC he had put on layers of muscle. All his work friends were ex-soldiers, ripped after years of mandatory physical training. He'd become obsessed with lifting weights, eager to fit in with this crowd he'd idolized. Now when he shouted at me the tendons in his neck stood out and his biceps rippled as he waved his arms. For the first time, I had been frightened of him. He'd stormed out of the house and I'd called Pen to my side.

She had such a different reaction to my revelation that I wondered if I'd dreamed Nick's fury. It was like she'd known all along, but that it hadn't been a big deal. When he came home early the next morning to find Pen asleep in an armchair while I slept on the couch, he'd been even more frightening. Pen roared back at his accusations, asking him where he'd spent his night, and he stormed out again. It took me months to discover that he'd been with another woman.

On days like this, when some little incident reminded me of him, I tortured myself wondering if he'd have left me for her anyway. He'd insisted that he hadn't cheated until after that fight, but was it true? Why had it taken so little to lose him?

The chime of another Swingle notification pulled me out of my reverie. I swallowed hard against the sourness in my gut and turned my attention back to Charlie. Nick was in my past, but if I wanted to hang out with Pen next week, I needed Charlie to be part of my future.

CHAPTER TWENTY-SEVEN

Charlie and I eventually hit it off. They were so thoughtful and kind. I couldn't help it, I loved being treated like a lady. Opening doors, pulling out chairs—all that stuff made me melt. I could tell from our conversations online that Charlie was that kind of person and I really, really liked it.

Maybe because they were old-fashioned and liked getting to know someone in person, they agreed to a face-to-face date really quickly. A few days after the first message, I was dropping hints. They picked up on them fast and we settled for an after-work coffee on Wednesday. I'm not sure who was happier to have plans with me, Charlie or Pen, but I had to admit I was more excited for the after party than the main event. I was sure Charlie and I would get along, so I had high hopes for finally having something to celebrate over drinks.

We decided to meet at Georgetown Cupcake for a coffee and treats. It was less formal than dinner and Charlie didn't drink alcohol, so a bar was out. GC was trendy and packed as always, but they had decadent cupcakes and the coffee wasn't bad. It was one of my favorites and Charlie confessed they had an overactive sweet tooth but had never been here. On paper it seemed like the perfect first date.

I arrived first and snagged a table before they filled up. I ordered for us both and did my best not to tear into my red velvet cupcake before they arrived. This was the first time I hadn't been nervous for a date and I couldn't figure out why. Then Charlie walked through the door and the moment I laid eyes on them I knew it wouldn't work out.

They were hot, no doubt about it. With their crisp khakis and ironed button-up under a motorcycle jacket, they looked exactly the part. Their smile was dazzling and, when they crossed the room, I saw that explicitly gay walk Pen had talked about in Marlene. I liked that walk. I liked motorcycle jackets and androgyny and a touch of gray at the temples. I just didn't feel any chemistry with Charlie. Worse, I could tell by the way they greeted me with a stiff hug and a forced cheeriness that they felt the same way.

We made a game attempt at small talk for a little while. They thanked me for my choice in cupcake and coffee for them. I asked about their day at work. They were an architect at a firm in the city and was in the middle of a big project for the federal government. Charlie asked about my day. It was all very polite, but they didn't hide that they would rather go home. Maybe it was the fact that I seemed to be trying harder than they were that annoyed me. Maybe it was yet another failed date. Whatever it was, my cool snapped.

"Okay," I said in a voice even I could tell was confrontational. "What's wrong?"

"I'm not sure what…"

"I don't want to play this game anymore. You are very sweet, so please don't lie to me. This clearly isn't working. What's wrong?"

It showed well on their character that Charlie didn't play dumb. "Honestly? I feel like you duped me into this date. You're nothing like your profile."

They looked sorry, but the words still stung. "That's not true."

It seemed desperate, I know, but I started defending myself out of pure instinct. I even pulled up my profile on my phone, listing the things that were true. Most of what I listed were the things Pen and I had changed after failed dates. I spent a lot of time telling them how the music section was very much me.

"Sure, you're into all that stuff," Charlie said, swirling their coffee cup. "But that's not what you're passionate about. They don't drive you. What drives you?"

It'd been a long time since someone asked me that. Instead of shouting back an angry response and storming out which was, I'll admit, my first instinct, I thought about it.

"'80s movies. John Hughes films that are problematic and ridiculous but remind me of a simpler time in my life."

They didn't say anything, and so I thought a little more.

"Keeping a clean home. I love to tidy and listen to audiobooks while I work. Getting lost in a love story and pretending I'm Cinderella. I love antiques, but not the stuffy ones that smell like aged wood and moth balls. Refinished pieces that have life breathed back into them. Have you ever been to Lucketts Market?"

"Never heard of it."

"I could spend my whole life wandering between those tents to find gorgeous things."

I ran out of ideas and stared at my profile picture. It was the one of me at Wolf Trap, looking back over my shoulder and smiling at Pen. I was doing this all wrong. Maybe it was me. Maybe my lot in life was to be alone forever.

Charlie's voice was soft and kind when they sat forward and asked, "Why didn't you make that your profile?"

"My best friend helped me write it." I looked up at Charlie and shrugged, more than a little embarrassed. "By writing it."

"That's your problem."

"She knows me better than anyone else and she's good at this sort of thing. I'm obviously terrible at it."

"Maybe she knows you well, but the thing about other people, even ones who know us well, they love different parts of us than we love in ourselves. They cherish parts of us we don't necessarily feel the same way about."

I didn't know if I believed them or not, but I knew the only savior for me now was made of red velvet.

I tore off a hunk of cupcake and shoved it into my mouth while Charlie continued, "One of my favorite projects was a sitting room for an eccentric couple. The walls were completely mirrored. There were several low couches and the walls all looked flat, but I put angles in certain places behind the mirrors. You could sit next to someone on the same couch and you would see something entirely different in the mirrored wall because of that one little angle. Two people could never have the same perspective."

"What if they were sitting on the same cushion?"

Charlie smiled and I could tell they'd wanted me to ask that question. "The difference in height if you were sitting on someone's lap would also change the view."

"I have to say, I think that room would stress me out."

"I loved designing it, but I hated being in it. I'm not the kind of person who wants to look at myself that much."

There was a story there and I could see that this could have been an interesting date. Charlie was a fascinating person when they weren't lecturing me about my dating profile. "I'm sorry I wasted your time." Then, because they were encouraging me to be honest, I continued, "I've pretty much given up on online dating. I only tried again because my best friend pushed me to do it. We go out and talk about my dates after and I always have fun crying into my drink with her."

"What's your best friend's name?"

"Penelope." I laughed at the thought of her face twisting when I used her full name. "Pen. She always sees the best in me. She gets me."

"How'd you meet?"

"At work. She's in the office next door. I had a bad day—the worst day, really—and she was there for me even though she barely knew my name. That's the sort of thing she does. She's always willing to bend over backward for people."

"I have a friend like that. He's right about everything. It's annoying."

"Isn't it?" We laughed together and then I just kept talking. I guess I wanted to talk about Pen. "She has this way of dropping a bombshell and then waiting for me to realize how right she is. She always follows it up by teasing me until I can laugh at my ridiculousness."

"You see now why your profile doesn't work? She loves you in a different way than you love yourself."

I was about to agree when Charlie's words echoed in my head and realized something was off. "You keep saying love. We're just friends. Pen doesn't love me."

Charlie smirked. That was the only word for the smile they gave me, with one side of their mouth turning up in a knowing, almost pitying twitch. "Oh yeah she does. You haven't read what she wrote in your profile, have you?"

"Not...everything."

"You should. Pay particular attention to the 'how would your best friend describe you' answer."

Charlie stood up while I tapped around on my phone, finding the section of my profile that I couldn't answer and led Pen to write everything. They took their time sliding their arms into their coat and finishing their coffee. When I finally found it, I was too afraid to start reading. I didn't want it to prove their point, but part of me kinda wanted them to be right. I took a deep breath and scrolled down.

My best friend would say that I am too beautiful a soul for the way the world has treated me. I would roll my eyes and say something sarcastic, but I would secretly hope she's right. That there is someone out there who would love me in the whole, unabashed way I love other people.

I looked up slowly, my ears buzzing. Charlie's face was kind and without a hint of sadness. They knelt beside me and put their hand on mine. I hadn't realized how much it was shaking until their touch settled the movement.

"She loves you, and, more to the point, you love her. Goodnight, Kieran."

The words popped in my mind like a child's bubbles, leaving a soapy film over my brain and making it hard to string thoughts together. It couldn't be true, could it? I searched for a reason to deny the claim as Charlie retreated, but my mind still wasn't working. All I could think about was the way my heart had pounded when Pen had held me as I cried. The way she'd kissed my eyebrow and how it had made me feel whole for the first time in forever. I sat there for who knows how long, churning over the possibilities. In the end, the only clear thought I could form forced me to my feet and out the door.

I needed to get to Riveter's.

CHAPTER TWENTY-EIGHT

I caught a cab and set my mind loose to wander as we inched down M Street. I assumed it would find its way back through the brain fog by the time we turned onto 14th, but it didn't. Charlie's words echoed and the sound of the traffic dimmed and roared like a poorly tuned radio. We'd been sitting outside Riveter's for a full minute before the cabbie finally snapped at me to get out.

Next thing I knew, I was sitting in the nearly empty bar, Abby sliding a glass of Rosé toward me. I managed to thank her, but she was already gone. The sound of my own voice broke the spell and I finally analyzed what Charlie had said. Was it really possible that Pen was in love with me?

We'd been friends for so long, it seemed ridiculous. Could two best friends turn that into something more? We knew all each other's faults. We'd shared things with each other that we'd never shared with anyone else. Didn't that sort of honesty make intimacy impossible?

There was also the little detail that she'd never made a pass at me, but that only proved she didn't want to have a one-night stand. Of course, I had been married when we first met. Pen didn't have a lot of boundaries when it came to sex, but she respected relationships even if she never wanted to be in one. After Nick there was Alex. But Alex had been gone for a long time and still Pen hadn't made a move. She would have said something if she wanted to be with me, wouldn't she? Except she didn't do relationships so this whole thing was moot. She couldn't love me because she didn't do love. Did she?

I couldn't get anywhere with that, so I was forced to look at the rest of what Charlie said. The part where I loved Pen, too. That should have been easier to refute, but somehow I couldn't come up with any evidence against it. When I was sad, I wanted to be around Pen because she made me feel better. When I was happy, I wanted to be around Pen because she was the only one I wanted to share it with. Then there was how I felt recently when she hugged me. If it hadn't been Pen, I would have said that feeling had been attraction. More than attraction. *Desire.* I stopped my wineglass halfway to my mouth, dwelling on the feeling of Pen pulling me close.

"You okay, Kieran?"

Abby's voice came from a long way off and I fought to focus on her face. "What?"

"You shivered. Like a whole body, top of your head to tip of your toes shiver they do in the movies. You cold?"

No, the last thing I was feeling at the moment was cold. Quite the opposite. I was warm in places I certainly wasn't going to tell Abby about. My voice came out as a squeak. "No. Um… no, thank you, I'm fine."

She raised an eyebrow, "If you say so."

I didn't want her asking any more questions, so I changed the subject. "How'd the show at Workhouse go?"

She shrugged and rearranged some glassware. Her voice was nonchalant, but there was a tightness around her eyes. "Not the crowd for my work. Abstract doesn't really sell in Lorton."

"Sorry to hear that." Because I couldn't seem to get my mind off Pen's hug that night, I said, "And sorry to drag you away from your table. I was kinda a mess that night."

"No need to apologize. I'm just glad Penelope was there for you."

"Yeah," I murmured, my eyes slipping out of focus as I remembered her lips on my skin.

"Want me to refill that?"

"What?"

She pointed at my glass, still hovering in midair. It was empty. As I stared through it, I watched the front door open and Pen march through. Her phone was to her ear and her face was a mask of concentration. I saw the answers to all my questions in the way her brows furrowed and her mouth moved in a perfect, graceful arc.

Charlie had been right.

I had it bad.

"I'll take two, thanks Abby."

Pen ended her call and threw herself onto the barstool. My hand shook on my glass.

"Can you believe it? That couple looking at townhouses in Woodbridge? Thanks Abby, you're a doll." Pen took a sip of her Rosé and winked at Abby before she continued, "Now all of a sudden they want to look in Culpeper. Culpeper! Drove all the way down there today and of course they love it. It's in the middle of nowhere!"

She stopped her rant to wave at Abby's retreating form. Pen hadn't looked at me yet but I couldn't take my eyes off her. It may have been the first time I'd ever really seen her. Her long, lean body and the delicacy of her limbs. The curve of her jaw as it swept up to disappear beneath her short, choppy hair. I wanted to trace the line with my tongue.

"Just my luck. I'll be down there a dozen times at least." She stopped to take a long sip of her wine, closing her eyes and groaning in delight. I watched her neck stretch as she swallowed and couldn't suppress a groan of my own. I was in deep shit now.

Pen heard me and looked over, her face flipping from professional annoyance to personal concern like a lightbulb flicking on. "What's wrong? Was the date that bad? You're here earlier than I expected."

I didn't answer, I just looked at her.

A nervous confusion joined her concern. "Was it that good? Come on, don't keep me in suspense."

I'd known from the moment she sat down. The sound of her voice cleared my head and allowed my disjointed thoughts to connect. Everything became perfectly obvious.

"You're in love with me."

Pen froze. Not a muscle in her body, from the prefect roundness of her cheeks to the unpolished emerald of her eyes, so much as flinched. She didn't blink. She didn't breathe. I heard my heart pounding in my ears, but every other living thing in the world went just as still, just as silent as the two of us.

She broke the moment as I'd known she would. Pen didn't thrive in tension and she always dispelled it with humor. The booming crack of her laughter set the world back in motion. She slapped the bar so hard it made both our glasses shake. They clinked against each other, making the delicate sound of windchimes in a light breeze. On her third bark of laughter I heard the forced, confused quality and I took a long, relieved breath. There had been a terrible moment when I'd thought I was wrong. Now I knew Charlie had been all too correct.

"Good one," Pen said, gasping for breath when the laughter died.

She dabbed tears from her eyes with a cocktail napkin. I waited for her to put it down.

When she was silent again, I asked, "Why didn't you tell me?"

She stiffened again, but this time she looked wary. There was an edge to her voice when she spoke. "What are you talking about?"

"Why didn't you tell me you were in love with me?"

I slid closer and reached for her hand. She pulled it out of my reach. "Why do you keep saying that?"

"It's true. Isn't it?"

"Kieran…"

"Isn't it?"

Her eyes flashed and part of my heart heard the warning. The other part smelled lavender and sandalwood and it made my mouth water. I had a sudden, visceral need to taste her skin.

"I don't fall in love, remember? You know that about me. Where is this coming from? What about your date?"

She was trying to change the subject. Pen was so good at deflecting. I had to answer though. She needed to know I was all in. "I met them. It didn't work out."

"I'm sorry to hear…"

"Actually, it did work out. Just not for them and me. They're the one who told me."

"Told you what? How much wine have you had?"

I pushed my glass away and a dollop of liquid splashed over the rim, soaking the napkin beneath it. "I'm not drunk, Pen. I'm more clearheaded than I've ever been. Charlie was right. You love me. You've shown me in a million little ways for years, I haven't been paying attention."

"You're not making any sense. You know how I work. I don't do love." Her words sounded sincere, but the resolve didn't shine through her tone. "I've been your friend, nothing more. I'm sorry. I don't want to hurt you, but it's true."

It stung to hear her say that, but she wasn't meeting my eye. I knew her well enough to know when she was forcing herself to lie. I reached out to touch her and this time she didn't pull away. My hand slid over hers as it had a thousand times before but this time it felt completely new. A pulse of electricity ran from the soft, velvety skin of her hand through my fingertips and straight to my heart. I knew she felt it, too. There was no way something could be so strong without being shared. I rubbed the pad of my thumb across her knuckles, between the silver of her ring splints. A whole new world I'd never dared imagine opened up in front of me as Pen finally pulled her gaze away from our laced fingers and stared into my eyes.

"Look me in the eye and tell me you don't love me."

It was a heavy request, I knew. It may have even been unfair, but I was well past caring. I needed to know. I needed her to say something. She kept quiet for a long time, looking at me and holding my hand. I watched her swallow hard. I watched her try and fail to speak twice—three times. On her fourth attempt, she looked away but not before I saw a well of sadness open in her eyes.

"Kieran, I can't..."

She didn't finish. I knew what I had to do. I had to be the brave one. I reached out with my free hand, the one that wasn't holding tightly to hers, and cupped her cheek. Her face was cold, her skin flushed but touched by color only, not heat. Her face was even more beautiful to touch than to see. I leaned in close, pulling her to me as gently as my pounding heart would allow. I wanted to kiss her. I needed to kiss her. But I forced myself to wait. There were things I had to say first. I stopped my lips inches from hers and looked into those eyes that were too close to escape my gaze.

"It's okay, Pen. I love you, too."

The gentle, intimate moment cracked like thin ice on a river, releasing the torrent below. Pen leapt to her feet, every muscle of her body rigid, every tendon visible beneath her skin. Her eyes went from sadness to feral anger in a flash. She bared her teeth and growled her words.

"Don't you dare..."

She hovered over me like a wild beast ready to attack, but I wasn't afraid. She would never hurt me. She grabbed my shoulders and held me in a bruising grip.

"Never say that to me again."

I blinked and her hands had released me. I banged down hard onto my barstool and only then realized I was off it. I had no idea if Pen had lifted me or if I'd stood on my own. A wineglass smashed on the bar beside me and I looked to see if it was mine. Both our glasses had been swept behind the bar.

When I looked back, Pen was gone. Her absence hit me like a physical blow and my vision went black for a single, gut-wrenching heartbeat. Movement caught my eye. The back door was swinging shut.

I was at the door before it had time to close.

CHAPTER TWENTY-NINE

The moment I stepped outside, the damp heat of another muggy mid-Atlantic summer night wrapped around me. I'd have loved to blame my labored breathing on the weather, but it was the heady mix of fear and excitement that weighed on my chest. I needed to find Pen. To catch up to her and make her talk to me before she could slip through my fingers, but she was nowhere to be seen.

The door led out into an alley behind the bar. The fire escape of Riveter's neighbor loomed overhead. I turned toward the sound of traffic, but she wasn't there. Only the flickering flash of headlights as they zipped past. She couldn't have escaped me that way even if she'd run. Something banged against metal deeper into the alley and I whipped around. There she was, marching toward the bend created by the back of the building on the next street.

"Pen! Wait!"

Her steps didn't slow. Her shoulders didn't twitch. There was no way she'd missed my shout echoing off the brick walls, even with the thudding music from the many surrounding bars. I ran to catch up—not an easy task in my tight black skirt and three-inch heels. My silk blouse was loose enough to flap around me, but a fresh sheen of sweat made it stick to my skin. I was panting hard when I finally reached her side.

"Pen, please stop."

She didn't break her stride or look over at me. Her jaw was set in a rigid line that was both ominous and distractingly sexy. How had I missed that for so long? I had to skip to keep up with her. Despite my semi-regular morning runs, my fitness level was nowhere near hers. Her five hours a week in the pool gave her the long, sure stride of an athlete. If she kept this up much longer, I'd have to stop and catch my breath, and there was no way I was letting that happen.

"Can we talk, please?"

She remained stonily silent. I had to skirt around an empty dumpster and Pen turned the corner, heading into a narrower, darker section of the alley. She must've used this escape route before.

"I just want to know how you feel…"

"Don't!" Pen stopped, whirling to face me, and I came to a skidding stop in front of her. She towered over me, making my skin tingle. "Please. Please don't do this, Kieran."

"Why not?" I asked, stepping closer. She didn't step away. "How do you feel about me, Pen?"

Regret painted her features and her shoulders sagged. Sadness shone through every inch of her and all I wanted was to hold her until the pain was gone and her laughter came back. I wanted to be the one to bring the light back into her eyes.

She swallowed hard and I knew there was more to say. I stepped forward, reaching out to lay my fingertips on her arm. "You still haven't said you don't love me."

Her silence persisted, but it spoke volumes. I reached up, running a hand across her shoulder and looping it around the back of her neck. She didn't stop me or shy away from my touch. I pushed up onto my toes and pulled her down to me. When our lips touched, our bodies were drawn together like metal shavings to a magnet. All the loose pieces came flying together of their own accord.

Pen's lips were as soft as her skin, but as the kiss lengthened, her touch was firmer, more deliberate. Her tongue split my lips and crashed into my mouth. I met her with the groan I'd been holding back all night and clawed her closer to me. She kissed me like a wild beast, desperate and hungry, and I kissed her back like prey begging to be devoured. Pen wrapped an arm around my waist and dragged me to her. The press of her flesh to mine was intoxicating. I ached for more.

Without breaking the kiss, I pulled Pen back against the brick wall behind me. There was a shallow alcove into which I tucked our bodies, but I would have knelt in the middle of the street on my knees to beg for her body. My hands flew to her belt the moment I felt the ragged press of brick against my back. She tore my shirt free of my skirt, her hands diving beneath the fabric. Her splayed fingers slid across my stomach, my sides, my back. My whole body hummed beneath her touch. I wanted her to memorize my form with her hands.

My need made my hands unsteady, but I had her pants open soon enough. I raked my fingers across her stomach, teasing the waistband of her boxer briefs, but she caught my hand and broke the kiss.

"Kieran, are you…"

"Please, Pen." I couldn't stand to hear her try stopping me. Not now. Not when I knew the utter delight of her touch on my skin. "I want you. I need you. Please?"

She was on me again in a flash and with a passion she had not yet shown. Had I known the effect my begging would have on her, I would have led with that. I'd been directing the encounter before, but the lead was firmly in Pen's hands now. Everything was in her hands. They moved across me, exploring every inch of me. She cupped my breasts through the lace of my bra and it took everything in me not to shout prayers into the night sky. Her thumb teased my nipples into hard peaks. Her touch firm and teasing, eliciting sensations my body had needed for so long. All thought of touching her vanished as my mind went blissfully blank.

Kissing Penelope had quickly become my favorite activity. There was a fire in her mouth I longed to quench or be consumed by, either would have been fine by me. Like her hands, her tongue was gentle and insistent. I wrapped both hands around her neck and raked my nails through the short hair at the back of her head. As she surged forward at the touch, I slipped my thigh between her legs, pressing against her heat.

Without warning, Pen grabbed the hem of my skirt and wrenched it up, clearing her path to my core. She pressed herself against me and I rocked into her, swallowing her groans as she rode me. Her hand slid beneath my panties and then it was me groaning unabashedly. Fire from the touch of her skin and ice from the still-cool metal of her ring splints raked across the most intimate reaches of my body, numbing and burning me. She plunged inside me, fearless and frantic, hovering on the edge of control. I clutched at her with clawed hands and bared teeth, needing to feel and taste her all at once. I did my best to keep up with her relentless pace, but it was all I could do to keep myself in this perfect, burning moment. Never before had I found myself in the sway of someone so passionate, so intense. My heart wanted to stay here with her, to match her pace and bring her with me, but my body was already flying apart.

I couldn't hold in this scream. I threw my head back and roared into the dark night. I heard Pen's answering shout and felt her body lock and shake against mine, but I was already ascending again and I had to hold on to her strong shoulders to keep myself from falling.

It was all a blur after that. I was still floating through bliss when she pulled my skirt back down and straightened my blouse. Her fingertips touched my forehead, brushing the sweat-soaked bangs behind my ear. My eyes were still hazy, but I felt the press of her lips on my forehead. She may have said something to me, but I couldn't make out the mumbled words over the pound of blood in my ears.

When I reached for Pen, she was gone.

CHAPTER THIRTY

I woke up ridiculously early the next morning. I'd been too keyed up to sleep well. Pen had left my body satisfied as it hadn't been in years, but rather than curbing my hunger, that first taste only made my cravings stronger. I wanted my hands on her again. I wanted her hands on me again. I wanted the taste of her mouth and the scent of her skin.

Most of all, I wanted Pen to return my messages.

I wasn't proud to admit how many there'd been. She hadn't answered any of them, of course. I didn't dare try a phone call. That had even less chance of success and even more chance of earning her anger. Still, she eventually had to acknowledge what we'd shared.

Didn't she?

I gave up on sleep at four o'clock and pushed myself out of bed. I checked my phone again for messages, and, finding none, dressed for a run. I took a long, winding course through my neighborhood and lost myself in the monotony of my footfalls. No one was awake at that hour and the sun wouldn't be up for a long time. Even the longer days of summer weren't that long.

I chose a playlist heavy on Tegan and Sara and managed to steer my mind away from Pen until a few choice songs from *Heartthrob* came on. I skipped "Closer" a few seconds too late. I was already dreaming of how to get Pen underneath me again.

By the time I turned my run and headed back home, the sun was shooting pink and coral through the morning sky and I was at peace. I knew Pen wouldn't text me back today. She would keep to herself and avoid me, but she would be thinking. Pen was always thinking. That's why I knew everything would be okay.

It took the rest of my run to figure out why I wasn't panicking, but my head finally caught up to my heart. Pen knew how I felt. I knew from the gentle way she'd kissed my forehead that she knew how she felt, too. Pen acted like she didn't care about anyone, but the truth was that she cared about everyone. She made room for so many people in her heart and then pretended she didn't. Even though she'd never admit it, I had proof. Starting the day I lost my parents and ending with how she treated all her hookups. Most people who played the field like Pen would see her dates as disposable, but not her. She might complain about having to be friends with Marlene and her new girlfriend, but I knew she was happy for them. It was all there in the way she rolled her eyes when we talked about them. Despite her disclaimer, none of her hookups ever seemed to resent her. Hadn't I seen one greet her warmly when their paths crossed? She'd even encouraged me to be with Pen, too.

I spent my shower ruminating on how amazing Pen was. I smiled each time I dredged up a new memory of her kindness, both to me and to strangers. Even keeping all her friends separate was a form of kindness. We were each her entire focus when we were with her. We were special.

She needed time to come to terms with this unexpected change in her life. I could give her time. I'd waited my entire life for a love like this—a love with my best friend that was as all-consuming as it was safe. I could give Pen the time she needed to see the miracle of it.

Dressing for work was more fun than usual. Even though Pen would avoid me today, it wouldn't hurt to prepare for any accidental sightings. I slid into her favorite dress of mine, a wrap-around knee length number in cobalt blue with a neckline that plunged just enough to be flirty while covering all the key areas. Despite the peek of cleavage, it left a good deal to the imagination. Pen had a wonderful imagination. While she loved heels on women, she hated them to be too high. A tall heel looked like torture to her and she couldn't stand a woman torturing herself for beauty. I picked a pair that was tall enough to be evocative without being uncomfortable. One day I'd convince her that some women loved wearing high heels and I was one of them.

My stomach was still too fluttery for breakfast, so I packed a yogurt and headed to work early. Sure, there was a little skip in my step. Today was the start of something brand new.

I was locking my front door when I thought of Pen's disclaimer.

I'm not going to fall in love with you. I'm not even going to call you tomorrow. I probably won't remember your name. I'm not saying this to hurt you, I'm saying it to make my intentions clear. I can give you the night of your life, but I can't give you anything more than that. If that doesn't work for you, let's stop this now with no one hurt.

I wondered if I was her only hookup who didn't get the line. The term "hookup" rather than something more intimate annoyed me, but I couldn't stop my brain. That fact became painfully clear as I inched through traffic. Once I'd started down that line of thought, I couldn't shake the uncertainty that settled into my bones.

She hadn't given me the disclaimer. Not exactly. She had laughed when I suggested she loved me. Then she'd said she didn't fall in love at all. Was that the same thing as saying she wasn't going to fall in love *with me*? I'd pressed her and she'd refused to deny it, but she hadn't admitted her feelings either. I chewed on my bottom lip, chasing the thought in circles until my distraction nearly made me rear end a pick-up truck. I shook myself and concentrated on the drive.

That lasted all the way to the office but, once I was there, nothing was enough to distract me from my fears. She hadn't said she wouldn't call me the next day but here it was the next day and she hadn't called. I opened the office and started coffee, resolutely not thinking about how she had given me the night of my life and explicitly not wondering if she would give me anything more. Pen had tried to stop me so many times, maybe I should have listened to the disclaimer.

"You gonna drink that or just stare at it?" Randy asked from the doorway.

It'd been so long since I'd heard him speak outside of staff meetings, that I finally came to my senses. I had been sitting at my desk, my coffee cup in midair, staring into the black liquid. Considering that I'd poured it fresh and now there was no hint of steam coming from the surface, I must've been there a long time.

"Sorry, boss. Lost in thought."

"Whoever they are," he said with a forced smile. "They're either not worth your worry or they're the one."

"What?"

"The only people that ever made me look that happy and miserable at the same time are my wife and my ex-wife."

Somehow that made me feel better. Randy didn't often dispense wisdom. "So which one did I just find? My wife or my ex-wife?"

He saluted with his coffee cup and turned to leave. "It's always fun finding out, isn't it?"

When he was gone, I powered on my computer and set all thoughts of Pen aside. Except for one.

I couldn't help wondering if this was how all the women who'd had sex with her felt the next morning. I allowed myself to think it and then I sent the thought away.

I would feel better about everything when I saw Pen again.

CHAPTER THIRTY-ONE

Pen didn't come to work that day. I heard through the grapevine she'd called in sick. Because of her EDS, Pen made it a point not to call in sick unless there was something serious going on. While those of us at HomeScape took more than our fair share of mental health days, the Realtors worked on commission and Pen was conscious that a day off meant no cash coming in. Healthcare was expensive, even with insurance, and Pen's more than most. Between that and her lavish taste in clothing, furniture, and entertainment, her budget had little wiggle room. The longest she'd taken off in recent memory was two days in the winter when she had surgery to stabilize her ankle. She always bounced back quickly. This time, folks at the office were concerned because they thought she was sick. I was concerned because I doubted she actually was.

She was avoiding me.

She didn't come into the office on Friday either because she was showing houses in Culpeper again. My gut told me I needed to give her space, so I didn't text or call. It took everything in me to stay away from her front door, but I was confident everything would work out in the end.

By Monday my confidence had all but evaporated. Tuesday was her rest day, so I knew I wouldn't see her then, and she still hadn't returned any of my messages. Almost as concerning was how our personal issues were already starting to affect work. I was stuck in the middle of a tricky title search for the Georgetown property and it was stressing me out. The house was old and had gone through what felt like a thousand owners in the previous hundred years. Sorting through inheritance and sale documentation was bad enough, but DC laws were some of the most convoluted in the country. Their real estate laws were even more convoluted than the rest. The city had a history of hazy property tax laws and an unusual government structure. The capital city of a country founded on "no taxation without representation" had no federal government representation. The hypocrisy of America always confounded me.

Usually a difficult title search involved hours of consultation with the Realtor to clear up questions with the seller. Unfortunately, this property's selling Realtor was none other than my best friend and new lover who was not currently speaking to me. I was at sea in a storm both professionally and personally. It wasn't a good feeling.

Uncertainty was starting to nip at me. Uncertainty and a deep dislike of that house in Georgetown despite the beautiful sunroom and the memory of hugging Pen in the garage. My thoughts were full of her scent and the feel of her muscles relaxing under my touch. It was probably the sound of me banging my keyboard that brought Arthur to my door. Aggressive typing was an annoying habit I'd tried hard to curb, especially after Randy complained about having to buy me a new keyboard every year.

"Flowers were delivered for you," Arthur said, causing me to miss the keyboard entirely and smash my pointer finger into the desk. "Try to act surprised when Carol delivers them in a minute."

I didn't have to act, I was surprised. I didn't peg Pen as one for a grand romantic gesture. Turns out she wasn't. My heart skipped several beats before Carol arrived, red-faced and glowing. She said it was excitement for me, but I think it had more to do with the fact that she could balance the overlarge vase on her overlarge belly. She was now a week overdue and desperate to have the baby out. My hands shook as I opened the card.

"No need to be excited, Carol," I said after reading it. Disappointment stained my voice as I explained, "It's from a client."

Not just any client, but Hank Prince, Pen's client who'd made a clumsy pass two weeks ago. Had it really only been two weeks? It felt like a lifetime. After all, I'd fallen in love in the few short days since I'd seen him. I tossed the card in the garbage but kept the flowers. He wasn't the one I wanted to receive flowers from, but I wasn't the kind of girl to waste a bouquet of Gerbera daisies.

Carol shuffled back to her desk, puffing with each labored step, and Art asked, "Dating clients now?"

"Not at all. I'm too professional for that." It was true. I was only unprofessional enough to have sex with a coworker in an alley. "He offered me some advice and was checking up on my progress."

"What advice was that?"

"To look for love in the real world rather than online."

"How's that working out for you?"

I bit the inside of my cheek and eyed my silent cell phone. No new messages. Tears sprang to my eyes. "I'm not sure yet."

"Have any dates lined up this week?"

"I'm not sure yet."

Surely Pen had to get in touch before Friday? Another five days with no contact might kill me. I'd never gone this long without talking to her and now we'd added mind-blowing sex into the equation. I knew she loved me as much as I loved her. Not even Pen could hold out that long, no matter how confused she was.

As Arthur left, I remembered how stubborn Pen could be. How long she could hold a grudge. How she was always determined to make her point and how, if she decided to drop someone from her life, she didn't give second chances. I broke two keys off my keyboard before I left for the day.

I nearly ran over Arthur in the parking lot when I arrived Wednesday morning. I'd been scouring the lot for Pen's car, and I let my forehead drop onto the steering wheel when I didn't see it. I forgot that I was still moving, but I wrenched my head up and slammed on the brake when I heard him shout in alarm.

Part of me had hoped I'd wake up to a message from Pen that morning. Something long and explanatory like an email that she painstakingly composed on her day off. Apparently that was not how she had spent her Tuesday because there was nothing. Still, I'd thought as I took a shower that was too long and too hot to be healthy, she had to come back to work today. She hadn't been in the office since the previous Wednesday. Not even her laid-back boss could let her go a full week without checking in.

Obviously he could. After an extended apology to Arthur and promising to bring him a pair of jelly donuts the next morning, I went to work. I lasted almost a half hour before I wandered over to the real estate side with some bogus excuse about grabbing a file from Pen's office. I sat in her chair and tried to imagine what she was thinking at that moment. Was she obsessing over me the way I was obsessing over her? Did she regret our encounter? Had her lust that night been born of pity or something real?

I didn't get any insight despite spending far too long burrowing into her leather chair. I overheard their secretary, a much less efficient Barbie-doll type whom Carol hated, mention that Pen was showing houses all day. I skulked back to my office to pout.

It had been strange not speaking to my best friend in so long. From that first drive back to West Virginia, Pen and I had spoken nearly every day. We went out for drinks. We had lunch together. On slow days she'd come to my office to gossip. On busy days I'd escape to her office to chat. Now it had been a week and I craved the sound of her voice. I started to think that I'd royally screwed things up.

Digging in my purse, I snatched up my *Goonies* pen and forced myself to go back to work on Pen's Georgetown mansion. I hypnotized myself with the tumbling gold while I waited on hold for the DC Register of Wills. I made a game out of trying to slam the floating bits against the ends of their little tank but couldn't force the satisfying smack I was trying to achieve. I'd done the same thing the day Pen had presented the pen to me. She'd called me ridiculous and threatened to take her present back, but she'd been laughing. Pen had a great laugh. All these years I'd loved that laugh, but I hadn't thought about why. It felt good to hear Pen laugh. Or talk. Or call me an idiot. It hadn't been friendship that had made it feel that way, though. It had been love and I'd been too stupid to see it.

Tears threatened and I clutched Pen's pen as hard as I wanted to clutch the woman herself. I realized that I might have to choose between Pen my best friend and Pen the woman I was in love with. As much as I hated to admit it, there was a chance Pen would never love me the way I loved her. I decided I could deal with that as long as I had my best friend back. People lived like that every day, feeling this burning, terrible unrequited love. I could live like that, too. I could survive as long as she was my friend.

"Horseshit," I breathed into the phone.

"I beg your pardon?" came the scandalized reply.

Too late, I recognized the buzzing that had filled my ear a moment ago as words. Someone had been speaking on the other end of the line while I bargained with the universe over my feelings for Pen. I doubted that my distracted apology quite made up for the request to repeat the long, detailed explanation I'd missed. It might not be a bad idea to send some apology donuts to the Register of Wills tomorrow, too. At this rate, I would need to buy stock in Dunkin' Donuts.

During the slow, quiet post-lunch hours, I finally realized everything was not going to be okay with Pen. No doubt the realization had a lot to do with my first Wednesday in five years that didn't include Garlic Whip at Layla's. I thought of driving over there to see if Pen would show but waiting in a parking lot for someone I knew wasn't coming was a level of pathetic I wasn't ready to embrace.

As I threw the plastic container from my vending-machine tuna sandwich into my office trash can, I remembered how Pen spent her Wednesday nights and all the carefully cultivated confidence I'd carried for the last week crumbled. Pen would go to Riveter's as soon as the sun went down and she would go home with a stranger. Maybe she'd be thoughtful enough to hit one of the other bars she frequented, but she would go out that night and she wouldn't leave alone. She never did.

I picked up my purse and bolted from the office, not bothering to speak to anyone or even switch off my computer.

CHAPTER THIRTY-TWO

Thursday afternoon found me concentrating entirely on my work and not at all on the fact that it had been eight days since I'd seen or spoken to my best friend. I was definitely not thinking about the fact that it had been eight days since I'd had amazing sex with the woman I loved, either. My mind had never once strayed to how and with whom Pen had spent the previous night. I certainly was not stopping every three or four minutes to clutch my chest and bite back tears because everything in my life hurt.

Nope. Of course not.

I was engrossed in the early twentieth-century land-inheritance lawsuit and its impact on the potential sale of a multimillion-dollar row house in one of the most fashionable neighborhoods in the city. That was, admittedly, far more straightforward than the ill-fitting pieces of my potentially broken heart.

The truth was that even if my current task was remotely interesting, I'd have no hope of concentrating on it. I'd barely slept the night before. I'd cried myself to sleep on the couch by seven o'clock, still wearing my work clothes. My brain did me the dubious favor of replaying my encounter with Pen in the alley, which was just as vivid and exciting as the original event.

Dream Pen had me pinned against a brick wall, my skirt pulled up, and I reached out to cup her cheek. Only it hadn't been my hand. Instead of the sun-bleached copper of my skin, I'd seen a rich, deep sepia. My fingers had been longer, with more prominent knuckles and bubblegum pink nail polish. Pen had looked into my eyes and there'd been a different type of lust in her smoldering gaze. The sort of unrestrained, animal lust reserved for someone you'd never see again.

The dream had flashed as Pen touched me and my hand was now creamy white loaded with gaudy rings. Again and the rings had gone, the skin was paler, a fine filigree of tattoos looped across the back of my wrist. On and on it went, my body replaced during each flash of pleasure with a new set of characteristics nothing like my own. I had watched Pen make love to a dozen women until I had been wrenched from sleep by my own anguished shout.

Needless to say, I hadn't been interested in falling into that nightmare again. I'd spent the rest of the night scrubbing the walls of my townhouse so vigorously the drywall showed through in places.

A knock at my office door dragged me away from both my fevered thoughts and my dull work. When I looked up, expecting to see Arthur, I was met instead by the sight of the only person who could make me feel worse.

"Hi, Kieran," said Ashley Britt, somehow managing to look drop-dead gorgeous and awkward at the same time. "Sorry to interrupt your work."

"That's okay. It's pretty boring."

I took a moment to look Ashley over as she stood in my door, waiting for an invitation inside. The drop-dead gorgeous assessment had been wrong. It didn't do her enough credit. I hadn't noticed before—or rather chose to ignore—the fact that she literally had the perfect body. Her legs went on for days and were capped with the smallest waist I'd ever seen. She wore black skinny jeans that must've taken an act of god to squeeze into, but the lack of a single ounce of body fat probably helped. Her shirt's balloon waist billowed around her hips and short cap sleeves showed off her thin arms ending in long, manicured fingers. Every inch of body highlighted by the outfit reminded me of the extra weight I carried in awkward places. I was suddenly very happy that Pen hadn't seen me naked, but that only served to remind me how many times she'd seen Ashley naked.

"I was wondering if you've seen Penelope."

I hadn't invited Ashley in and I was petty enough to make her stand there like an intruder for another moment.

"No." I didn't want to admit it, but I had to. "Not for a while."

I could see the panic flooding into Ashley and it made me feel guilty for my jealousy. I motioned to the chair at my desk and she slid into it. "I haven't either. It isn't like her."

"I'm sure she's fine. Just busy with work."

Ashley ignored the optimistic assessment with all the scorn it deserved. "Is there something going on with her medically? She hasn't broken a bone or something, has she?"

I had been so wrapped up in my angst I hadn't even considered the idea. Pen made such a point of being fine that it was easy to forget her EDS. Had I really been so selfish that I could've missed something serious?

"I don't think so. I'm sure she would've called...one of us if something was wrong."

I'd wanted to say "me," but Ashley, despite or perhaps because of their other arrangements, was Pen's friend, too. If she didn't feel like she could reach out to me, she might've reached out to Ashley. My fear bubbled up and I gripped the arm of my office chair so firmly my hand ached.

"Penelope has never missed..." She smiled at me, confirming exactly what she was talking about. "Our regular appointment, but she did on Monday. I'd already been waiting ages when she texted to apologize."

Several things happened inside me at once. Pen had texted Ashley even though she wasn't texting me, which hurt, but it also wasn't like her to cancel plans after she was already late.

There was also the "regular appointment on Monday." I wanted more details on that. Was this every Monday? Every other Monday? A certain Monday every month? How many of these appointments had there been? Was there a single day of the week that was safe? Of course, she'd missed this appointment, so that was something.

"And she wasn't at Riveter's last night."

"What?" She flinched when I shouted the question. I took a breath and cleared my throat. "How do you know that?"

"Katie and I went there looking for her." I missed my chance to beg her not to elaborate, and she continued, "We were interested in…well, you know our arrangement. My wife, Katie, and I thought Penelope might want to join us, but she wasn't there."

Hope fluttered in my chest, but immediately fizzled. "Sometimes she goes to other bars."

"We texted, but she said she was taking a night off."

That was definitely not like Pen, so I forced myself to ask, "She didn't invite you over?"

"No. Said she was turning in early. On a Wednesday. Alone."

Now I really was worried. Worried and so relieved I could've jumped out of my chair and danced around the office. I didn't want Pen to be hurt or sick, but it was nice to know she wasn't working out her confusion about us with someone else. She hadn't slept with Ashley and she hadn't slept with some random hookup. I dared to let myself hope that meant something. I kept all that relief in the background, however, because I had to acknowledge that Pen might actually be in bad shape. At the very least we needed to know.

"Did you ask her outright if she was okay?"

"You know she hates that," Ashley said. "But yeah, I did."

"And she gave you an earful about it."

I could tell by Ashley's exasperated, bitter look that I was right. She confirmed it with a nod and a raised eyebrow. With each passing moment I was liking Ashley more and more. As much as I wanted to hate her, it was obvious she truly cared about Pen.

"Thanks for letting me know. I'll look into it," I said, wondering how I'd go about that.

Her relief was palpable and it somehow made her even more beautiful. I was pretty sure I could manage to hate her and like her at the same time. That was definitely the direction I was headed.

"That's great." She swallowed and looked away, clearly steeling herself for something unpleasant. "I'll stop by her place."

"No."

I barked out the word before I could stop myself. Fortunately, Ashley misinterpreted my vehemence.

"I know she hates that and I normally would never do it, but this is serious. She probably won't answer the door anyway."

"I...uh...think she's out of town. She's been showing houses out in Culpeper. She's probably there today."

"She goes all the way down there?"

"Not on purpose." Hmm. Pen hadn't told her about that client. She didn't share everything with Ashley then. "I tell you what. I'll call Pen's dad. He's her emergency contact and her doctor would let him know if there's anything serious Pen's not telling us."

"That sounds great!" Ashley hopped out of her chair, looking relieved. "I'll stop by her place on the way home. How about we both do our thing and reconnect later?"

"Great." I couldn't keep the bitterness out of my voice. I'd just dropped another woman into Pen's lap. Not just any woman, but one Pen was certain to screw when they met up. And she was going to Pen's house. Where her bed was. It was the worst option of a thousand terrible options.

When she got to the door, Ashley hesitated. She turned back to me and I could swear she was almost blushing. "This probably sounds strange to you, but Penelope is part of our family. We're worried about her."

She didn't wait for a response but gave me a sad smile and left. Maybe she had picked up on my reluctance to send her to Pen's house and assumed it was because I didn't like the nature of their relationship. It did seem strange that a married couple cared so much about the woman they invited into their bed, but maybe I was being unfair. Maybe, given time, I could understand that dynamic. Right now, there was too much jumbled in my brain to think about that.

I had Mr. Chase's number saved in my cell phone, but I called him from my office phone. He was a chatty guy and I had been stuck with a dying cell phone when I called him before. He picked up on the second ring and sounded genuinely happy to hear from me.

"If it isn't the lovely Ms. Hall." His baritone filled the line, echoes of Pen's higher but equally rich tones evident. "How've you been? Penelope says you're dating. I understand you've had a rough time of it."

My heart slammed against my ribcage. Had he meant the disasters before Pen or the disaster with Pen? Surely she hadn't told her father about our night together, but my romantic misfortunes were adding up.

"Some of the boys around here use online dating, too," he continued, referring to his retirement community. "Don't give up hope. The right one's out there for you."

I swallowed hard, willing myself not to tell him that the one for me was his daughter. "I'm sure they are."

Mr. Chase was an outgoing guy, and I could hear the ghost of Pen's laughter in his weathered voice. I'd met him only once and been shocked by how little he resembled my best friend. Where she was tall and round-cheeked, he was hunched and gaunt. His features were sharp and angular, like an old bird, but there was a warmth to him that was undeniable. And he looked at Pen like she was everything he could have ever wanted in a child and more.

When I asked him if he'd heard from Pen a weariness crept into his words. "I'm afraid not. We don't talk much these days. She's so busy with work and I have a very competitive bridge table."

I explained that she'd been avoiding her friends and the office for over a week, but I cut the explanation short when I heard him clucking in the background. I'd allowed Ashley's concern to bleed over into me so I was frustrated by his indifference.

"I haven't heard from any hospitals, so I'm sure she's fine." There was a muffled sound as he spoke to someone else on his end, the rustle of his hand covering the phone loud in my ear. "Look, I appreciate your concern, Kieran. It's wonderful that Penelope has such devoted friends, but I'm sure there's nothing to worry about. She's been...known to do this."

"She's never done it while I've been..."

"Penelope likes to keep people at a distance, especially if they're trying to force their way in closer. She's had to put distance between herself and more than a few of her lady friends."

There was a knowing hint to his voice and it sounded an awful lot like he was accusing me of being a disgruntled former lover. Was I a disgruntled former lover? Was that all I'd ever get out of that fevered night in the alley? Of course it was, I thought as I said my goodbyes and hung up, but how could he know that?

Before I could analyze it too much, I sent a text to Ashley. She answered immediately, happy that Pen wasn't seriously ill. Unfortunately, Pen also wasn't home. Ashley had waited but there'd been no answer at the door and her car hadn't been in the driveway. She had to get home to her wife, but she promised to try again the next day. It wasn't the best news, but at least she wasn't in Pen's bed and Pen wasn't in the hospital.

By the time our conversation ended, it was five o'clock and my coworkers were trickling out of the building. I closed down my office, appreciating at the very least that I had one day this week where I'd accomplished a little work. When and if Pen ever showed her face again, she would see that her title search was completed and she was one step closer to that big commission.

I was reaching to flip off my desk lamp when Arthur appeared in the doorway. The hall behind him was dark, but not as dark as his expression. His tie was loosened and his coat was ruffled, but he looked like he was ready for a fight.

"She finally did it, didn't she?"

"Who did what?"

"Penelope finally broke your heart."

I'm pretty sure my jaw hit the desk. I hadn't said a word to anyone in the office for obvious reasons and Arthur had never struck me as particularly intuitive. Had my distress been that obvious?

Dropping into the chair so recently vacated by Ashley, he sighed, clenched fists perched on his knees. "I guess I should congratulate her on her restraint. I thought she'd hurt you years ago."

"Pen hasn't..."

"Stop," Arthur barked. The good natured, mildly inappropriate coworker was gone. This man looked like the angry father of a jilted girl. "When are you going to see Penelope for the selfish person she is? She's always taking and walking away."

"But she doesn't," I replied, my own fists balled and ready for a fight. "You don't know her. She's not like that."

Pen hadn't been the one to take this time. I had. She'd wanted to walk away but I hadn't let her. I'd been the one to push. I'd seen what I wanted and I went after it, even while Pen tried to protect me. That didn't make her wrong, it made me selfish.

Lost in my thoughts, I'd missed Arthur's next evisceration of Pen's character. I didn't need to hear it to defend her. Even while my stomach soured with guilt, my voice was calm as I said, "You're wrong."

"Am I?" He still sounded like a father, only this time one who was trying to comfort rather than scold. "Are you happy?"

"I'm..." Okay, I wasn't happy exactly, but I wasn't interested in explaining the situation to Art. He wouldn't understand.

He took my lack of explanation as confirmation. "Exactly."

"This isn't her fault," I said.

"Then whose is it?"

I stared at my clenched fists on the desktop. "Mine."

I don't think Art expected that, but he probably did expect the tears. I hated that he didn't understand why I was crying. He probably still blamed Pen, but I saw the truth all too clearly.

"You're not like her, Kieran." He patted my hand and I missed my dad for the first time in a very long time. "You don't have to be. Don't let her make you into someone you're not."

"That's just it," I choked through my tears. "She didn't. I did."

There was nothing Art hated more than a crying woman, so I was shocked that he didn't run away. Instead he sat there, awkwardly patting my hands while I pulled myself together. It wasn't easy. I'm an ugly crier. Like splotchy skin, snot-for-days-ugly crier. He stuck it out though, bless him.

When I finally cleaned my face up enough to be presentable, he asked, "Want to tell me what's going on?"

Of course I didn't want to. I did anyway. I told him all about the hug after my non-date with Skye and how she kissed my forehead. Then about how she asked me to find another date so we could hang out and about what Charlie said. Arthur was on his best behavior and didn't ask for details when I alluded to the alley.

He didn't look too judgmental when he asked, "So she didn't admit that she loves you?"

All I could do was shake my head. I couldn't even meet his eye. It was high time for me to lean into my self-disgust. It felt good to beat myself up a little bit. I had plenty of reasons.

"She will," he murmured.

That came out of the blue. Pen cared about me, I was sure of that. She loved me. What I hadn't allowed her was the right to love me in a different way than I loved her. She'd told me who she was and I didn't listen. Now I'd lost my best friend.

"I don't think you understand," I started, but I didn't know how to explain.

"Sure I do. Pen's been in love with you for years, you've been too dense to see it."

"Hey!"

"You're pretty oblivious if you haven't noticed how she treats you."

"We're friends," I argued. "She's good to her friends."

"Maybe so, but not like she is with you." He threw one leg over the other knee and leaned back. He obviously had some mansplaining to do. "Haven't you ever wondered why I hate Penelope so much?"

"Because she's popular, hates country music, and embarrassed you playing horseshoes at the company picnic three years ago."

"Other than that," he growled through clenched teeth. The horseshoe game was a particularly sore subject.

"Why?"

"Because she ruins all your relationships."

"She does not!"

Sure, my voice was a little shrill, but he deserved it.

"Nick thought you were cheating on him with her."

"Nick was the cheater. I never did anything with Pen while we were married."

"But when you were having problems, you called her."

"Of course I did. She was my best friend and he bailed." I hadn't told Art where Nick had gone that night and I wasn't going to now.

"What about Alex?"

"What about them?"

Art ran a hand through his hair and I swear he rolled his eyes. How his wife hadn't murdered him before now, I'd never know. "You never let Alex in like you let Penelope in. They always felt like they were competing with her for you."

"I'm so glad my ex talked to you about our problems." I was so pissed I was half out of my chair as I shouted at him, "Maybe if they'd talked to me, we'd still be together."

"No, you wouldn't," he said, refusing to rise to my level of anger. It was so infuriating. "Because you never loved them as much as you love Penelope."

Now I was standing up. I was half a heartbeat away from crawling over my desk to throttle him.

"It's not your fault." He raised his hands, but his attitude was anything but submissive. "You can't help that you love her any more than she can help that she loves you. And she clearly doesn't want to admit she loves you."

That took the wind out of my sails. I slumped back into my chair, my elbows slipping off the armrests. I was just so tired. Why was it so hard?

"She doesn't." I wasn't sure if I meant she didn't want to admit it or that she didn't love me.

"What are you gonna do about it?"

I lifted my head enough to look at his smug smile. "What *can* I do about it?"

"You might try fighting for her."

"I tried that. It…" Well, it had ended in hot sex in an alley, but it had also ended with her ghosting me. "Didn't work out."

Art shook his head, a sweet smile carving lines into his cheeks. I was suddenly very happy he had daughters. I bet he was a great dad to them.

"You tried pushing her to admit her feelings. That would never work with Penelope. You might try letting her know you don't have any expectations. That you'll be there whenever she's ready."

"Isn't that what I've done? I haven't texted her since last Thursday." I'd felt every minute without contact, too.

"Did you tell her why, or did you just shut up?" He correctly interpreted my silence and continued, "Tell her why you've been quiet. Tell her you're giving her time and space."

"I don't think that'll do any good."

He shrugged and stood, straightening his tie. "It would work for me."

He was at the door when I asked, "You think you and Pen are that much alike?"

"Of course. That's why we hate each other so much." He shot me a quick wink and finished, "It's also why you like us both so much. Goodnight, Kieran."

I waited until I parked in my driveway an hour later to pull out my phone.

"What the hell," I said to the empty car. "Maybe he's right."

CHAPTER THIRTY-THREE

Hey Pen
I'm sorry about last week
Not that it happened
But I am sorry that I pushed
Whenever you're ready to talk about it, I'll be here

I miss you

CHAPTER THIRTY-FOUR

Friday went by in a haze. I fell into bed immediately after work and woke up late on Saturday. I hadn't dreamed of Pen, which was fine by me. The longer I went without seeing her, the less her dream face resembled the one I knew so well, and the difference left me panicking. Waking up calm was a treat, though as soon as my eyes opened, I still reached for Pen's pen from its new perch on my bedside table. I clutched it to my chest while mentally preparing for the day to come. My plans consisted of a trip to the grocery store followed by an evening of home-spa self-care. It wasn't exactly a thrilling prospect, but I had to get myself used to my new life. Boring and lonely. I'd never ever felt so single.

I stumbled across a farmer's market I didn't know existed and decided to be bold by altering my plans. After all, a single, friendless lady needed someone to talk to. That someone was a stranger today. A massive crown of broccoli the same vivid green of Pen's eyes caught my attention as did a precarious-looking mound of potatoes. They joined a bunch of spring onions and a pint of strawberries in my bag and I headed back home without stepping foot into the harsh florescent light of the grocery store.

The rest of the afternoon was devoted to making me feel pretty. Nothing lifted my mood like a charcoal mask. I took a long, luxurious bath, shaving my neglected legs and scouring my body with my favorite Himalayan sea salt scrub. It smelled like a pine forest and left my skin feeling raw and fresh. I lotioned and pulled on a loose sun dress that wouldn't irritate my tender skin. After tossing the potato in the oven, I searched for something to watch. The movie I picked was a little outside my usual time period, but there was nothing like *Titanic*. Leo had a face forgettable enough that I could focus all my attention on Kate as the oven hummed and the water that would steam my broccoli bubbled on the stove.

Today the love story barely held my attention. I absentmindedly stroked the soft skin of my arm and let my mind wander. It bounced from subject to subject but always came back to the same thought. I needed to go back to Swingle. There wasn't any hope to this thing with Pen and maybe there never should have been. I'd been lonely for so long, maybe I'd wanted Pen because she was the closest to me in my loneliness. Maybe it hadn't been love, but desperation that drove me into her arms. She'd tried to warn me off, but, in the end, she was the person she would always be. She would always sleep with the woman who wanted her. There wasn't anything wrong with that, but it wasn't the foundation for a relationship.

I picked at my potato and threw half of it away before dropping back onto the couch and returning to my thoughts. Kate and Leo kissed and I realized I'd been trailing my fingertips along my belly. I snatched my phone off the coffee table, intending to pull up the Swingle app, but I selected my photos instead. After a little scrolling, I found the picture I'd taken of Pen when we went for lunch at an outdoor café. The sun illuminated the side of her face, making it glow like pale gold. She was laughing, the skin around her eyes, usually so taut and pristine, was pulled into a bundle of deep lines. Her chin rested on the heel of her hands and I could feel the burn of her eyes through the screen. No one ever looked at me the way Pen looked at me.

My hand drifted lower down my belly as I stared at Pen and listened to the sounds of Kate and Leo getting to know each other in the back seat of an old car. The flesh around my fingers heated in anticipation and I told myself they were Pen's fingers, burning and freezing me as they had on a muggy night with the press of brick into my back. My fingertips grazed the band of my panties and I hesitated before plunging forward. Pen stared at me through the phone and I lost myself in her emerald eyes. I slid two fingers beneath the cool fabric just as the doorbell rang.

I groaned and forced myself to stand, pausing the movie on the image of Kate's hand pressed against a foggy car window. I cursed my visitor all the way to the door, only remembering at the last second to make sure my dress had fallen back into place. If I could get rid of whoever this was quickly, I might be able to hold onto this moment.

I opened the door and every molecule of air left my body.

It was Pen.

She'd been walking away. Her body was turned away from the door and she had one foot in the air, hovering above the top stair, but I would have known that body anywhere. Her shoulders slumped and she turned to face me.

"Hi," she said, staring at her own feet.

It wasn't just Pen. It was Pen wearing a heather-gray men's three-piece suit that fit her like a glove. The vest hugged her body, emphasizing her breasts yet making her look utterly, deliciously androgynous. Beneath it was a crisp white shirt and a thin black tie held in place with a silver bar. Every coherent thought I had evaporated as the lustful side of my brain took over all control of my body.

When I didn't answer, she looked up with worry redrawing those lines around her eyes.

"I got your text," she said. "May I come in?"

My tongue was stuck to the roof of my mouth, but if I didn't leave it there it would be on the floor. I stepped aside and let her in. She kept her hands in her pockets and her eyes on the ground.

"Can we talk?"

I wasn't at all convinced I'd be intelligible, but I nodded and led her to the living room. I sat on the couch, giving her plenty of room beside me, but she hovered behind the armchair, picking at its decorative buttons. She glanced over at the TV and froze. I'd forgotten all about Kate and Leo's private moment and rushed to switch the screen off.

"Sorry to interrupt your evening," Pen mumbled. "I should've called first."

The formality of her tone should have frightened me, but it had the opposite effect. Pen was nothing if not a gentleman dyke, as she liked to refer to herself, but she wasn't the type to dress up and go to a woman's house to break her heart. As her dad had said, she bailed when things went further than she wanted them to.

"You know you're always welcome, Pen."

She looked up, meeting my eyes for the first time and they were something to behold. I had lost myself in a photograph of her eyes, the real thing was likely to be the death of me. I slid my hands under my thighs to keep from reaching out. I'd screwed up last time by moving too fast and pushing too hard. This time I'd be patient. Let her take the lead.

"You, um…" I managed, "Look good in a suit."

She smiled with almost her old charm and smoothed a hand down her tie. "I wear suits all the time."

"Not like this." I couldn't help but stare at the way the collar exposed enough of her neck to make me want to see more and the tie clip was perfectly centered on her chest. "You said you wore men's suits, but I've never seen it."

"I said I wear them on special occasions."

"So…this is a special occasion?"

Sure, there was a hint of hopefulness in my voice. It sounded a little like desperation, but it was definitely hope. Pen shrugged and seemed to steel herself.

"I'm sorry for disappearing," she started. "I didn't mean to make you worry."

"I wasn't that worried."

"My dad said you called to check up on me. And Ashley's been stalking me for a couple days now."

"In my defense, I told her not to go to your house." My reasons for that weren't important.

A twinkle formed in the corner of Pen's eye, telling me she knew the reason. "I spent two nights waiting in a neighbor's driveway to avoid her. It was getting annoying."

"She cares about you." I hated myself for saying it, even if it was true, so I followed it up with a little more truth. "So do I."

Pen swallowed hard and finally sat down in the chair, propping her elbows on her knees to lean toward me. "So you don't hate me?"

"Of course not."

Pen let out a long breath and ran her hand through her mop of hair. It bounced back messier than before. She looked like a little kid, amazed that they'd wormed out of trouble. Silence stretched between us long enough that my nerves flared again.

"Did you," I started, hoping she would interrupt and start the conversation. She let the pause stretch, too, so I asked, "Want to talk?"

She nodded but continued staring silently at her entwined fingers.

The words burst from me before I could stop them, "Let's start with something easy. Why'd you come by tonight?"

"I...um...."

She stopped to rub the crease on her trouser leg but didn't start talking again.

I chuckled to break the tension. It didn't work. "My goodness! Penelope Chase, speechless around a woman? What's the world coming to?"

When she didn't roll her eyes or laugh at my teasing, snakes of fear writhed in my gut. "Pen?"

"I have a speech." She rubbed her palms on her thighs, then against each other. I never thought I'd see Pen with sweaty palms. "I practiced it on the drive over."

"Okay," I swallowed back my doubt and puffed out a breath. It didn't make me feel better. "I'm ready."

"Are you? I don't think I am."

"Not gonna lie, Pen. You're starting to make me fret. You know how rare that is for me."

That earned a laugh. Well, not a laugh exactly. A slight lift of the corner of her mouth, but it was something. She traced the lines of her palm with her fingertip and said, "I had three speeches, actually. One was for if you slapped me when you opened the door. Another was for if you tried to kiss me when I opened the door…"

She trailed off then, her eyes flicking up to settle on my lips. My stomach fluttered in a decidedly pleasant way as she stared at them and I wished I had thought to kiss her while she stood on my stoop. Or let her press me against the front door. It would've been much more pleasant than when Chloe had done it. Or maybe it would've ended the same way.

I cleared my throat in an attempt to clear my mind. "And the third?"

"The third was for when you acted like Kieran."

The syllables of my name on her lips made my heart race. "Is that the one I'm getting now? Because not even I know how Kieran would react to all this."

"Neither do I."

I took a chance and asked, "How does Pen react to what happened?"

"I don't really know that either."

Not the best answer, but at least she wasn't saying she never wanted to see me again. I straightened my spine and said, "Since you don't seem to have a speech ready after all, mind if I start?"

Her eyes flickered to my lips, then my eyes, then away again so fast it made me dizzy. She gave a sharp nod and rubbed her palms together again.

"I owe you an apology." Guilt pushed the scant remnants of my dinner into my throat. "Will you come sit over here? I need to tell you something."

She hesitated for a long time, staring at the couch cushion like there was a trap hidden underneath it. Finally, just when I thought I had asked too much, she slipped across the room and settled beside me. I could smell her perfume again and my mind reeled. I reached out and put my hand over hers with the lightest touch I could muster.

"I was…pushy at Riveter's. You weren't ready for what we did and I shouldn't have forced myself on you like that."

"I was definitely consenting."

"Yeah, but that doesn't make it okay that I chased you down an alley. You needed time and space and I should have respected that. I'm sorry."

She laughed and turned her hand over, lacing our fingers together. "This is supposed to be my apology, you know?"

"There is nothing about that night you need to apologize for." Sitting with her like this, talking about the way we'd touched each other, sent a shiver through me.

"Yes, I absolutely do need to apologize." Her face hardened and she looked away from me again, the guilt painted in the smooth curves of her cheek. "You're not…"

She shook her head, and she was quiet so long that I whispered, "I'm not what?"

"You're not the kind of woman I wanna screw in an alley."

The words had come out in a rush, leaving a blaze of red across Pen's cheeks. I smiled, cupping her cheek in my free hand and turning her face up to look at me. "Where do you wanna screw me then? 'Cause I'll go anywhere."

"I'm being serious, Kieran."

"So am I." I let go of her hand and held her face with both hands, keeping her close. "I'll do anything for you. I love you, Pen. Don't you see that?"

She didn't speak. She reached out and hooked her fingers behind my neck, pulling our lips together inch by agonizing inch. When they met, my body lit on fire. Her lips were softer than any I'd ever known and the press of them was like a drug shooting through my veins. Her tongue brushed against my lips and my mouth flew open to invite her in. She kissed me now the way she had that night, not just with desire, but with tenderness. With devotion.

I couldn't sit still any longer. I pressed forward into the kiss, pushing myself into her lap. She accepted me there without hesitation and I straddled her hips, fitting our bodies together.

It was as though they had been meant for nothing else. Pen slid her hands up my back, holding me close. The strength of her arms and the gentleness of her touch made me groan and arch my back. She released my mouth and buried her face between my breasts, covering my skin and the thin fabric of my dress with warm, wet kisses.

Running my fingers through her hair and feeling her lips on my flesh reminded me of our first night and I forced myself to pull back from her touch. It was incredibly difficult, but I was going to do everything right this time.

When she looked up at me her pupils were wide with lust and she clearly was having trouble focusing. I touched her cheek with the very edge of my fingertips. "Pen, I want you and I love you, but, if you need time…"

"I don't."

"Maybe we should talk first?"

She slid a hand up my thigh and under my dress, her grin widening the closer she came to the soft cotton of my panties. "We can talk later. Right now, I want you too much to form words."

Her hand arrived at its destination and I was the one who couldn't form words. My eyes rolled back in my head as sensation burst across my skin, leaving gooseflesh as it traveled through my body. As quickly as it had arrived, her hand moved away, but the ghost of her touch haunted me far longer. Her lips found my neck and brought me out of my daze. I slid my hands underneath her jacket, massaging the bunched muscles of her shoulders as I slipped the fabric off. She had to lean forward to shrug out of it, so I slipped off her lap and grabbed her hand.

We left the jacket crumpled on the floor of my living room. The vest and her shoes stayed in the hall and her pants landed in the doorway to my bedroom. I loosened her tie but didn't take it off. I used it to pull her across the rug to the foot of my bed. She reached for my dress, but I pushed her hands away. The alley had been about me—tonight would be about her.

I wouldn't have guessed based on her silhouette that Pen would have been able to get by without a bra. When I finished unbuttoning her shirt and peeled it away from her body, I was happy to be proven wrong. There was nothing beneath her starched shirt but pale skin, liberally spattered with freckles. She had incredible breasts, round and perfect and pale as starlight in my dimly lit bedroom. I pushed aside her shirt and tie and took her nipple into my mouth. I couldn't see her throw her head back, but I felt how her body shuddered when I closed my lips around her. The way she responded, flesh and sound, to every flick of my tongue and teeth was like the sweetest wine I'd ever sipped. I let myself get drunk on her and then moved to her other breast. By the time I let her go my head was spinning.

I was barely conscious of pushing her back onto the bed and ripping off her boy shorts. The sight of her lying on my bed, shirt and tie open and the rest of her nothing but skin and muscle made me stumble. It was the first time I'd seen her naked and I took a moment to memorize what I could, but the roar of blood in my veins quickly drowned out my curiosity.

Pen raised herself onto her elbows and looked at me, a little smirk playing across one side of her full mouth. My body hummed to touch hers again. I don't remember telling my limbs to move, but I found myself straddling her, taking her head in my hands and kissing her too desperately to be graceful. I needed her. I needed my hands on her and inside her. I doubted that even a night full of her touch would be enough to quench the fire raging inside me.

She made quick work of my clothing. I must have moved or helped in some way, but I wasn't conscious of any of it. I was conscious only of her scorching touch and her cooling lips. Of the way her body moved beneath me and the way mine moved in response. My vision was already blurring when Pen put a hand on my hip, trying to roll me underneath her. I pushed her hand away and her shoulders back onto the mattress.

I held onto her tie, wrapping one end around my fist, as I trailed kisses down her cheek to her neck and then to her chest. She tried again to push me off her and I grabbed her hand, pressing it down into the feather down duvet.

"Don't make me use this," I said with a smile, brandishing the end of the tie where it dangled from my grip.

Her eyebrow shot up and her smile widened enough to show me she was considering one more transgression just to earn a punishment. "You're a top?"

I placed a kiss in the valley between her breasts. "Maybe." I placed another on the bottom of her ribcage. "How else will I make sure..." I swirled my tongue in her bellybutton, earning a sharp intake of breath. "That you won't run away after?"

My next kiss landed on her hipbone and I made sure my breast grazed between her legs as I moved. Her whole body bucked in response. I slid across to the other hipbone, pressing myself against her as I did. Her head fell back to the mattress and she gripped the duvet beneath her with both hands.

The first taste of her was like honey. The second was a cool glass of sweet lemonade on a hot day. Every one thereafter was like liquid summer. I drank her in, greedy to keep every drop. She moaned and quaked as I took her with my mouth. When her body tensed and she screamed, I couldn't suppress a shudder of my own. I could listen to this amazing woman make those sounds for the rest of my life and never be satisfied. I barely let her still before I threw myself back on top of her and replaced my tongue with my hands.

I pressed her down with the length of my body, our mingled sweat making our skin slip off each other in delightful ways. I couldn't stop kissing her. I couldn't get enough of her tongue against mine. Even when her body shook again and she shouted into our kiss, I couldn't stop. My body was possessed by her. By the need to please her.

It wasn't until she laced our fingers together that I realized I had been holding her arm down. She gripped me hard, pressing our palms together until there was as little space between them as there was the rest of our bodies. I slowed the movements of my other hand, caressing her gently. Her breath caught. It was such a soft sound from such a hard woman that my eyes immediately prickled with unshed tears. My next touch earned a sigh. Her eyes had been shut tight, but they peeled apart like a rose opening its petals to the sun.

She looked into me. Not at me or through me as she so often did, but into me. The green of her eyes shone wet and bright in the moonlight through the windows. She looked into me and smiled and my whole world shattered. Everything I thought I'd known about her had been wrong. I wanted to spend the rest of my life finding out the real woman behind the armor she put on for the world. A tear fell from my eye and I prayed that she would show me that woman. Pen reached up and cupped my cheek, then her eyes rolled back and she whimpered her final release.

Our bodies stilled and we lay there for a long time, our fingers and bodies intertwined. I was half-asleep or half-drunk on Pen's pleasure when she rolled me onto my back. Her breath was hot on my thigh and the touch of her mouth was gentle as a bird's wing. I had no idea that she could be so gentle. I could think of nothing else as she explored me with her tongue. Her mouth led me through wave after wave of pleasure. She was reverent, kneeling there at the foot of my bed with her head buried between my thighs. A lifetime passed in pure bliss and I was hardly aware of her pulling me beneath the blankets and wrapping me in her arms.

CHAPTER THIRTY-FIVE

I awoke to the smell of brewing coffee. For a long, luxurious moment I spread all my limbs out and rolled my naked body against the sheets. True to my routine, I'd changed the sheets yesterday morning. I'd never been so happy for that habit. When I pressed my face into the mass of pillows and tangled bedding all I could smell was Pen. Lavender, sandalwood, sex, and sleep sweat. My head spun. I wanted to wallow in those sheets and breathe in that scent all day long.

Most people would have been upset to wake up alone after a night like mine, but I wasn't. Sure, it would have been infinitely better to see her sleep-tousled head on my pillow, but Pen was a light sleeper. Staying in bed too long made her joints ache. More to the point, she'd told me long ago that she never stayed overnight in a hookup's house. It implied she wanted to see them again, even if it was just in the morning. She always left after they fell asleep. Pen hadn't left when I fell asleep. Around three o'clock I'd raked fingernail marks into her back, so I was certain she'd stayed the night.

The coffee was a clear sign, too. When she brought women back to her place, she made a point of sending them home early. Her one hard-and-fast rule, one she never broke no matter how much the other party begged, was that she never made coffee when there was a stranger in her house.

"Coffee is a conversation beverage," she'd explained once. "I don't have conversations the morning after. I don't even have goodbyes."

Since Pen was brewing coffee, I assumed she had a conversation in mind. I was nervous about that, sure, but the smell of Pen's skin on my sheets made me brave. Brave enough to smile when I heard her footsteps crossing the living room floor. Not brave enough to keep smiling when I saw the somber look on her face. I pulled the sheet up to cover my suddenly cold skin.

"Hey," she mumbled.

"Hey yourself." I slapped on a flirty smile, but even I could hear the tremor in my voice.

She was wearing a pair of my running shorts and an old food-festival T-shirt. Both hung off her, highlighting the difference in our body sizes. She held a pair of coffee cups that sent steam curling into the air between us. After an indecently long time drinking in the sight of her wearing my clothes, I finally noticed the rest of her. Every inch of visible skin from neck to shins was covered in bruises, some fresh red-purple but most of them fading to a sickening green-tinged yellow. Pen followed the path of my gaze and said nothing. When I looked back up into her eyes, they were cold stone again.

More as an excuse to avoid that distant gaze than a desire for clothing, I leaned over the mattress and snatched up the first thing I could reach. It was Pen's shirt, crumpled now but the collar still smelling of starch. I pulled it around my shoulders as Pen crossed the room and sat on the other side of my bed. The shirt didn't fit well, especially around my chest, so I couldn't button it. When I moved toward her she held out a coffee cup, stopping my progress. I took the hint along with the coffee and settled my back against the padded headboard.

"We...um," Pen cleared her throat and her hesitation was adorable in the way only a blushing butch can be. "Didn't get to finish talking last night."

I sipped my coffee and let her collect her thoughts. She was a skittish cat—if I spooked her now I'd ruin everything.

"You're right, Kieran." She took a long breath and locked her gaze on me. I fell into the green fields of her eyes. "I am in love with you."

Hearing her finally say the words made my heart roar and my lungs burn. "I'm in love with you, too."

"I'm sorry," she mumbled.

Not exactly the answer I wanted.

"For what?"

Pen looked down into her coffee as though there was some answer in the black contents. "I'm sorry you love me back. This was a lot easier when I was the only one with feelings."

I couldn't stop myself. I reached out and cupped her cheek. I wanted her to look up at me, but she refused to acknowledge my gentle pressure. I pressed my forehead against the crown of her head and whispered, "I'm not. This—you and me—this is the best thing that ever happened to me."

Her hand rested on top of mine, but she kept her head lowered. "You don't know what it would mean to be in a relationship with me."

I took a deep breath and plunged into the conversation we were circling. If I didn't make my expectations clear now, I was in for a lot of heartbreak. "I know it would require monogamy and I know that's not your thing." Pen stiffened under my touch, but I plowed on. I thought of Ashley and the kindness in her eyes when she called Pen family. "I think we could negotiate a middle ground."

Pen sighed. I was expecting some sort of relief, but that wasn't what I heard in her voice. "It doesn't have anything to do with that. Although we do need to talk about that, too."

"What are you talking about then?"

Pen looked up and, for the first time in her life, I saw shame. Maybe even embarrassment. The emotions didn't sit well on those soft features. "You don't know what it's like to be with me. To date a person with a chronic illness."

"I can't imagine how your EDS…"

"Can't you?" She growled, cutting me off. "Look at me." She swept a hand over her body.

"You bruise easily…"

Pen pulled aside her collar to show me a particularly livid bruise at the spot her shoulder met her neck. It was fading to yellow at the edges, though the center was still a dark red-purple. I could see the outline of teeth in the center of the bruise. I hadn't bitten her last night and she assured me in whispers and kisses in the small hours of the morning that there had been no one else since our night in the alley.

I'd bitten her in the alley, I was sure of it, but not that hard. And it had been over a week ago. This bruise was still the color of raw meat after ten days. I gasped at the thought of what I'd done. How I'd marked her flesh. The more I studied the bruises, the more I could attribute to myself. I reached out with trembling fingers and touched the bite mark. Her skin was cold.

"Pen, I'm so sorry. I hurt you."

"It doesn't hurt, Kieran. Not at the time. It hurts for days after. That bruise will last a month."

"A month?"

"This is what I'm talking about." She raked a hand through her messy hair. "This is what it's like to live with Ehlers-Danlos."

"I can handle a few bruises."

"Can you handle the dislocations?" She pulled the arm of her shirt up to show her shoulder. There was a fine stippling of red dots circling the joint. "Friday I took my annoying couple to Culpeper for more showings. We went to six houses. I dislocated my shoulder from opening so many doors in one day."

"You can dislocate your shoulder opening a door?"

"Not one, or even two. Not as long as I do it right. I twist too much or press too hard on the door when I'm opening it, my shoulder comes out. If I turn my wrist the wrong way on a doorknob, I can dislocate that, too. If I'm not careful going up stairs, or coming down them, I can dislocate my ankle. I have to think about every single movement I make with every single one of my joints."

"That sounds exhausting."

"I don't take days off because I'm lazy," she said, refusing to surrender my gaze. "I take Tuesday and Sunday at home because I usually don't have the strength to get out of bed. I tire easily. I need rest. More than most people need."

"But you swim so much."

"If I don't strengthen the muscles around my weak joints, they give out. Swimming is the only way I can exercise without risking injury."

"Okay, I get that, but we can work with that. I can respect your routine. I can respect your need for time to take care of yourself."

"It's not only those days off." Pen slid farther onto the bed and started picking at the stitching of my duvet. I forced myself to sip my coffee and not read too much into how her body moved closer to mine. "Sometimes I'm too tired to go out. Sometimes I go out and I'm too tired to stay."

"I don't need to go out all the time. I like a quiet life."

"And what happens when it's your birthday and I need to go home before the entrée is served?"

"You really think that'll be more important to me than your health?"

"In time it will." She tucked her foot underneath her leg, but the more she settled in, the more distant her expression. I could see the walls around her. She was showing them to me and daring me to try climbing them. "It won't take long for you to get annoyed by my limitations."

"I can't promise I'll be perfect, Pen." If she thought I'd be intimidated by these barriers she built around her heart, she had another thing coming. "Couples fight. We might fight about that, I don't know. But let me be a bitch first before you get mad at me for being one."

"It wouldn't make you a bitch." She was running her hands though her hair again and it was getting more and more messy with each pass. "That's what I'm trying to tell you. It's a burden. Dating me will be a burden."

Now she was just pissing me off. "Pen, what's this really about?" She raised her hand to her head again, but I grabbed it before she could pull her hair out. "Why would you think this way, baby?"

It was a calculated move, calling her baby. She hadn't been in a relationship before, had anyone ever called her a pet name? If there was anything I could do to highlight the intimacy between us, I'd do it. I had no problem fighting dirty for her heart.

Pen was quiet for a long time, staring at me. Eventually she sighed and slid her fingers between mine. "I need to tell you about my mom."

That stopped me in my tracks. Pen had never talked to me about her mom. She'd made it clear early in our friendship that subject was off limits. I didn't even know her name.

"Okay," I said as gently as I could. My stomach was in my throat. "Tell me."

It was a long story, but I hung on every word. I didn't even try to hide my curiosity.

"She was beautiful. Dad says I have her nose. I remember her eyes mostly," Pen said. "And how frail she was. When I was a kid, I thought she was made of glass. I didn't hang off her like other kids hung off their moms. I made it my mission to protect her. Walking in front of her and opening doors. She called me her knight in shining armor."

She leaned over and set her coffee cup on the bedside table. She hadn't taken a single sip.

"One day she picked me up from school and saw me on the playground, showing the other kids how I could bend my arm all the way back so I could touch my own elbow. They were all either screaming or cheering."

"You can do that?"

"I'm not supposed to, but yeah." She pulled her right hand back with her left until the fingers of her right hand were flat to her forearm. The sight made me a little queasy. I would've been one of the kids screaming. "I was ten at the time. All EDS kids play around with their hyperflexible joints. It freaks out other people but it doesn't hurt us, and kids don't know how bad it is for them."

She released her arm and wiggled her fingers. Her smile wasn't for me. It was for ten-year-old Penelope and the kids she freaked out on the playground.

"Mom sat me down and told me all about Ehlers-Danlos. She had EDS and she'd guessed I had it. Dad didn't want to get me tested 'cause he thought it would freak me out, but mom knew I wouldn't stop pushing my joints if I didn't know it was bad. That's how I found out why she was so frail."

"But you're not frail. Why was she?"

"Because of me."

"How could you have had anything to do with her health?"

That's when Pen took a long, shuddering breath and started the real story. I tried not to interrupt her. It was like watching poison leeching from an old wound.

"My mom had a different type of EDS. More severe than mine. Hers was vascular so there were more heart complications. She didn't walk until she was four. In her early twenties she was diagnosed with a complication called aortic root dilation. It put her at high risk for aneurysms, so her OBGYN advised against pregnancy. There was a good chance that she wouldn't survive childbirth."

I took her hand when her voice wavered, but she composed herself quickly.

"Dad told me they had a lot of fights about it. He wanted them to adopt but she wouldn't hear of it. My mom had always wanted to be pregnant and she won. She was very stubborn."

"I'm glad she did," I whispered.

Pen smiled at me for a heartbeat then continued, "They tried for a long time. I think there were some miscarriages, but they wouldn't talk about it with me. When I finally stuck, it was…Dad said it was the worst and best eight months of his life. Mom was in constant pain and so weak she was in bed for weeks at a time. He said she'd lie there, pale as a ghost, rubbing her belly and talking to me. They took me early and I was fine, but Mom was in the hospital for a month after I was born."

Pen fell silent. She sipped her coffee, giving the impression she was searching her memories, but it was obvious she didn't have to search far. These feelings, these memories—they were close to the surface. They were a bruise that would never heal.

"Most of my childhood she was fine. I didn't start thinking of her as frail until she got hurt more often. One of my first memories was sitting on her hospital bed when I was four or five, playing with her and trying not to jump too much. It was hard because she was always in good spirits. It started to get really bad when I was eleven, though. She would be in the hospital or in bed for weeks or months at a time, then she would be fine and act like nothing had been wrong. She was always smiling and laughing. She couldn't work after that, so she made it her job to be the perfect mom. She was."

This time when Pen stopped, I thought it'd be safe to ask, "What was her name?"

"Connie." Pen sighed and shook her head. "She didn't live long enough for me to get to that phase where you call your parents by their first names though."

It was a pretty name. A name that made me think of sunshine and spring flowers. I was starting to get a picture of this woman in my head and I liked everything about her. She reminded me of Pen.

"For my fourteenth birthday we had a big picnic in the park. The sun was shining and the grass had just been cut. They'd trimmed the lower limbs on an oak tree. You could still smell the sawdust in the air. My friends and I played soccer and ran around the playground. Mom kept chasing us with drinks and treats, telling us all to be careful. Dad was hanging out with the other dads, grilling or something.

"It was hot. I remember that, too. I was sticky with sweat the whole time, but it was so much fun. We gathered around the picnic table and mom brought out this huge sheet cake loaded with candles. Everyone was singing 'Happy Birthday.' Then mom fell."

The image I'd had in my head had been a perfect scene out of some '90s movie. It ended abruptly with that. With the image of a slightly dowdier Penelope hitting the ground and cake splattering over everything.

"It was weird because as soon as she went down, everything went silent. None of us kids knew what to do. Then she climbed back to her feet, apologizing about the cake. She fainted again, but Dad caught her. She said she felt like she had the flu."

I tried to imagine what it would've felt like to see my mom crumple at my birthday party. At fourteen I would've been more embarrassed than anything else.

"Dad and I took her to the hospital in our station wagon while the other parents cleaned up. She spent the entire ride turned to face me, apologizing for ruining my party and promising to make it up to me. By then I knew all the nurses at the hospital from Mom's frequent visits. They heard what happened and threw me another party in the waiting room. Dad was pacing around the whole time while they made me a party hat out of latex gloves and yellow sticky notes."

"Sounds fun."

She nodded but I felt like an idiot. Of course it wasn't fun. I wish I didn't know how this story must end.

"When the doctor finally came out, he took Dad a little ways away, but I could still hear. Mom had an AAA. An ascending aortic aneurysm. I looked it up when we got home. The main artery from her heart got thin in one spot and swelled, then threatened to burst. They got her to surgery but her vessels were too fragile."

"Because of the EDS. Because she didn't have enough collagen."

Pen nodded. "I was watching Dad when the doctor was talking. When he said Mom was dead…" She had to stop and shook her head like she was trying to clear it. Her voice was huskier when she continued, "I saw his eyes."

She stopped again for a long time. I squeezed her hand but she wouldn't look at me. "What about his eyes, Pen?"

"He was relieved."

"What do you mean?"

"When the doctor said Mom was dead, my dad's reaction was a moment of pure relief. I knew then what it was like to live with someone with EDS. Sure, he was sad after. It crushed him a moment later. He fell to his knees and cried for what felt like hours, but his real reaction was relief. She had been a burden and he was glad it was over. He used to get so annoyed when we had to cancel plans because of her pain or her dislocations or her bad heart. He was free from that burden."

"Pen, I…"

"I know he loved her." She looked at me and her eyes were dry. Dry and determined. "He loved her but she was still a burden. Love isn't enough. Not when the person you love is so limited. Maybe at first it is, but eventually it's too much. I can't put that burden on you. No one wants to live that way."

I watched her speak herself into silence, unleashing her greatest fear into the world with me its only witness. She bent her head, exposing the back of her neck as though she were placing it on the block for me to chop off. It took me a while to realize that was exactly what she thought would happen. That I would see this story how she saw it—as all the excuse anyone would ever need to lock one's heart away for good.

I wasn't naïve nor dismissive enough to believe her preference for casual sex was all due to this one moment in her life. But I also wasn't naïve nor dismissive enough to believe that trying to process both her own and her father's grief hadn't had a profound impact. She may have chosen a life without romantic entanglements, but she'd also chosen to suppress her feelings out of fear.

My heart cracked in a thousand places for fourteen-year-old Pen. It cracked in a thousand more for the warmth she was denying herself. How different would her life have been if she hadn't seen that flash of emotion on her father's face? How different would it be had she interpreted it the way I did?

I brought our lips together gently, a brush of supple flesh against supple flesh. Her lips were warm and dry against mine. I pressed a kiss to her right cheek, above the spot my thumb caressed. After her right cheek I kissed her left, then each eyebrow in turn, and finally the center of her forehead. Then I tucked her face into the crook of my neck, her cheek resting against my shoulder. When she started to sob, I held her close, the tears falling onto my neck and trickling down the open front of my shirt.

She cried for a long time while I stroked her hair. She choked and sobbed and I held her tight, dropping the occasional kiss into her messy hair. I wondered when she had last cried for her mother. If she had ever allowed herself to cry like this. I hoped she had for her sake, but I knew how precious it was that I made her feel comfortable enough to open this old wound.

When she cried herself dry, she slid closer, wrapping her arms around me. The light through the curtains made the room glow and the grip of her arms made me glow. Her breathing slowed until I could almost believe she was sleeping. Our breaths were synchronized, our chests rising and falling in perfect rhythm.

"I'm so sorry that happened to you, Pen," I started. When she didn't pull away or tense up, I went on, "That must have been hard for both of you. And your dad never remarried."

"No. Once I thought he had a girlfriend at his assisted living facility, but she married some older dude with an eyepatch."

"Chicks dig a pirate." She snorted at my joke, which I took for a good sign. "He never said why?"

"We haven't talked about it. I heard him tell my grandma once that he wasn't looking for another mom for me."

I took a deep breath and dove in. It was now or never and I wasn't going to let her use this as an excuse to not date me. "You'd already had the best mom out there. And he'd already had the best wife. Some loves can't be replaced."

She sat up but didn't have the distant look she'd had before. Also my unbuttoned shirt had come partly open during our embrace. Some of the best parts of my body were now showing and I wasn't above distracting her with my tits to get her attention.

"Can I offer a different explanation for how your dad reacted?" She didn't stop me, so I plowed on. "Your mom had been in a lot of pain for a while. In and out of the hospital. You saw that but imagine how much more he saw. You can barely sleep and you don't hurt as much as she did. He must've stayed up night after night trying to soothe her pain."

"Imagine his relief that he'd finally get to sleep through the night."

"Or his relief was that he didn't have to see the woman he loved hurting anymore." Her eyes were distant, and so I continued, hoping she was watching that scene in her mind with different eyes. "It sounds to me like his first reaction was the least selfish he could have. He thought of the end of her pain first, and the start of his second."

The room fell so quiet that I could hear the rustle of my pulse moving the shirt collar at my neck. I could see the thought seeping into her mind. I could see her processing the possibility.

"He loved her so much he could never think of another woman in his life," I whispered.

If Connie had been anything like Pen, and I knew in my bones that she had been, she was the kind of woman who got under your skin and wouldn't go away. The kind of woman who could never be replaced. The kind of woman you would drive yourself crazy over after only one night.

"It must have killed him to see her hurting. Knowing that she was finally at peace…well…if it were me," I had to bite back a sudden, overwhelming nausea at the thought of losing Pen. "If it were me, I'd want the woman I love to be free of pain. I can see how that would be a relief. Even if he's spent the rest of his life missing her."

Pen stared into my eyes and I tried to show her that I understood her dad. That I felt the exact same way he did, only I felt it for the daughter his wife had been willing to shorten her life for. I don't know what Pen saw there, but she wasn't running away. In fact, her thumb had begun absentmindedly stroking my bare thigh. I soaked in the touch, hoping it was a sign she wasn't preparing to bolt.

"Maybe," she said after a long time.

It was a major admission, but I wasn't going to let her get a big head about it.

"Duh," I said. She wrinkled her brow at me and I smiled in return. "I'm the smart one in the relationship."

I expected her to flinch at the word, but she didn't. Maybe this could work out after all.

"I guess that makes me the pretty one."

I feigned outrage, making sure the shirt fell back, revealing one naked breast. As I'd expected, Pen's gaze went straight to it. Her thumb moved a little further up my thigh. It only took a moment for her to shake out of her daze.

"I guess I never thought of it that way."

"Of course not, you were fourteen. You didn't know what it meant to be in love yet."

"I may be older, but I'm not a whole lot more mature." She stopped the motion of her thumb and slid further back on the bed. "This is going to be hard for me, Kieran. And not just because I'm used to going to bed with whoever I want, whenever I want. I've never been in love before."

"I know your entire outlook won't change overnight." I had to stop to catch my breath because she looked into my eyes and all the words I'd planned to say stuck in my throat. One side of her lips twitched up. She knew what she was doing to me. "But maybe you'd consider trying being exclusive. For me?"

"There are a lot of things I'd be willing to try for you."

I waited for a "but" to continue the sentence. Something along the lines of "but I'm not that kind of girl" or "but that's too much to ask." None of those "buts" came. She just looked thoughtful for a long moment.

"I don't know how good I'm going to be at this."

"But you'll try?"

"Of course I will. I love you, Kieran."

The words ripped apart the last of my doubt and made my eyes prickle. If I'd known this was possible, I'd have called her over to help me with dating apps years ago.

"Then you're already amazing at this." I lay back against the pillows and let my shirt fall all the way open. "And I love you, too."

She was practically drooling.

"So Sunday is one of your rest days?"

"Mmm Hmm."

"And you spend the whole day in bed?"

"Mmm Hmm."

She crawled up the bed toward me.

"Then I need your help. Get over here."

"Sure," she said, flinging her T-shirt across the room. "What's up?"

"I'm horny."

"Whoa," she said mimicking the panic in her voice from that Tuesday night a few months ago. "We're not that kinda friends, remember?"

I wondered if she'd felt that night how I felt now. Hopeful and a little apprehensive, but willing to do anything—to be anything—for this woman. I hooked a hand around the nape of her neck and pulled her down.

I groaned as her body sank into mine. "We are now."

EPILOGUE

Sitting in the conference room, I tapped my *Goonies* pen on the thick stack of documents in front of me. I hated waiting. Like really, really hated it.

"Ugh, what is taking so long?" I growled to my pen.

I was whining. I knew it. But this was the end of my workday and I wanted to get out of there. The heater overhead rumbled to life, shaking the ceiling tiles. Not that it was doing any good. The office was freezing. I wrapped the loose ends of my cardigan around my torso.

Across the room an old, faded, ceramic Christmas tree blinked dully. Half the little plastic lights were opaque with age and the bulb inside didn't quite have the umph to make them glow. The plastic menorah next to it on the table didn't look any more robust, with gold paint chipping off in places. The thin coating of dust on both decorations made them look sad, but it wasn't that surprising this late into January. Carol was still out on maternity leave and no one else was willing to take over her role of de facto housekeeper. I knew Art and Randy were expecting me to do it, but they could take their traditional gender roles straight to hell.

"Sorry, Kieran," Art said as he eased into the room. "Copier jammed."

That at least sounded legit. Our copier had probably been around as long as the office Christmas tree, but that didn't ease my impatience. Nor did the fact that he made a big show out of straightening his papers before sliding them into a folder emblazoned with the Three Keys logo. His grin was cartoonishly large when handed me the folder. My hands only shook a little when I took it.

"Okay," he said, holding out his hand, palm up. "Time for the big moment. You ready?"

"Not exactly," I said, squeezing the folder to my chest.

"Shoulda thought of that before you signed all the docs."

"Yeah," I grumbled. "I guess."

His expression was kind, but also wary. He was nervous about this big change in my life, as he'd informed me every day since I put my house on the market. I fished the ring of keys from my pocket and inspected them. I hoped it looked like I was checking to ensure they were all there, but I wanted to give them one last look.

Art rolled his eyes and said with affected annoyance, "I've got plans with a beautiful woman tonight, Kieran."

I stuck out my tongue and slapped the keys into his palm. "So do I, Arthur."

"That's Arty the Party to you, kid." He tossed my...no *the* keys into the air and grabbed them. "Congrats. Seriously. This is a good move for you."

"Really? I didn't think you..."

"I don't." He scooped up the two copies of my closing documents. "But you're happy, so I'm happy."

An hour later I was sitting alone in the quiet corner of Riveter's bar, tapping my fingernails against my frosted martini glass. I took a sip every now and then, but mostly I was lost in thought.

Nick and I had been married when we bought the townhouse, but it had been my inheritance that financed it. Without the life insurance money, we would have continued moving from one crappy apartment to another, skirting the edges of DC to find a place we could afford.

The townhouse had been Pen's listing and it took a lot of convincing to get Nick to agree to the location and the price. Staying after he'd left had nearly ruined me, both emotionally and financially, but it was mine and I wasn't going to let him take everything. Now it wasn't mine anymore and I wasn't sure I liked that.

"Pardon me, ma'am. You look like you could use a friend."

Pen's throaty voice sent electricity across my skin that settled low in my belly. The heat of her body and the brush of her breath against my neck as she leaned over me to whisper in my ear didn't hurt either. Six months on and her presence still made my toes curl with desire. I hoped the feeling never went away.

"I'm afraid I'm waiting for someone," I purred, bringing the glass to my lips.

"Are you sure that someone isn't me?"

Pen's arm snaked around my side, her fingers pressing into my belly. If we'd been home, she would have trailed them up to cup my breast, or maybe further down. She'd taken me like that more than once at her kitchen counter. *Our* kitchen counter I corrected myself. As of one hour ago, we were officially cohabitants of Pen's deliciously comfortable house. Damn, how I wished we were there now.

I craned my neck to look over my shoulder at her. Her eyes danced with mischief in the low light. She got sexier every day.

"Mmmm. Maybe it is. Can I buy you a drink?" I cut a glance at her martini sweating on the bar beside me. "I had the bartender make that one for my girlfriend."

Pen dipped her mouth to capture mine. Her sweet, insistent lips drew me in, stealing my breath away. Her arm tightened around me, pulling our bodies close as our tongues became reacquainted. She'd spent all day with potential buyers for a new Georgetown property and I'd missed her like hell. I found my fingers sliding through the hair at the base of her neck, my nails scratching across her scalp of their own accord. Just as my body melted into hers, she drew back from the kiss, my bottom lip between her teeth.

"Damn y'all," Abby said from the other side of the bar. "You should charge admission."

Pen's throaty laugh helped ground me, but I'll admit my head was still reeling from the kiss. *Hello to you, too.* She dropped onto the stool next to me and snatched up her martini, taking a deep, appreciative sip. Abby was still leaning in with her elbows on the bar, the personification of the heart-eyes emoji. She wasn't wearing a wig tonight, her real bangs so long they swooped down to her chin and the back spiky.

"You couldn't afford us," Pen teased. "But I'd hire you to serve drinks. This is a damn fine martini, friend. You're the best."

Abby slapped a towel over her shoulder and scoffed. "Tell my girlfriend. Or make that ex-girlfriend."

"You and Josie split up?" I asked, reaching out for her paint-speckled hand. "I'm sorry. That sucks."

She shrugged, but her disappointment was all too clear. "Wasn't meant to be."

"Looks like you're not the only one nursing a broken heart," Pen said, nodding to the other side of the room.

Marlene, still walking as gayly as ever, slumped through the door and plopped onto a barstool. She was practically living on that stool these days, ever since her ex had moved out of her place. Pen's matchmaking had lasted through the summer, but it hadn't survived the holidays.

"At least tonight she's wearing a clean shirt," Abby said. "Even if it is still flannel."

"You've been noticing her shirt, huh?" Pen teased.

I was about to slap her arm when I noticed a faint pinkness forming on Abby's cheeks. She stammered a half-hearted denial and hurried off to fill a drink order. She avoided Marlene's weak smile, but she stopped long enough to drop a bottle of beer in front of her.

"She didn't have to ask the order," I murmured. "Damn, how'd you know, Pen?"

"I'm very good at reading people." Her reply included a suggestive smirk. "For instance, I can tell that you're freaking out a little about selling your house."

"What? No...that's not..." I spluttered, then I squeaked, then I sighed. "Maybe a little."

Pen leaned over and brushed her lips across mine. "It's okay, baby. I understand."

"You do? 'Cause it's not that I don't want to move in with you." I was practically in her lap. "I love living with you." Not just because waking up next to her every morning meant more chances for morning sex. "It's..."

"A big step."

"Yeah."

"And a little scary?"

"Not scary exactly." I twirled my martini glass, watching the olive sway in the drink. "I have a lot of good memories in that house."

Pen purred, her eyebrows dancing. "Me too."

"Perv."

"You know you were thinking it." She took a sip of her drink. "Remember that time on the dining room table?"

A spike of desire snaked through me at the memory. We'd broken one of the green chairs I'd bought at Lucketts, but it had been worth it.

"And the kitchen floor," Pen cooed.

"I liked the time on your kitchen floor better."

"Our kitchens aren't safe, are they? We shouldn't have people over for dinner." She laughed and raised her glass. "To big steps and good memories."

I touched my glass against hers. "To living with the love of my life."

"I'll drink to that."

We drained our glasses and made out a little while Abby refilled them. I was wondering if I could drag her into the alley for old time's sake when she sat back and cleared her throat.

"Speaking of big steps."

Pen avoided my eye, tearing off a corner of her bar napkin and rolling it into a tight ball. She tossed it onto the bar and took a deep breath, reaching into the breast pocket of her jacket. She'd been wearing men's suits almost exclusively these days. This one had been tailored to fit her tightly across the chest and I took the opportunity to ogle her breasts. I was pretty sure she was wearing the red lace bra, which hinted I was in for a fun night.

Then I saw what she took out of her pocket and my stomach dropped. Apparently someone else was in for a fun night.

The first few weeks we were together involved some soul-searching conversations about what we wanted from each other and the relationship. The more we shared, the more I opened my mind to the possibility of a…less than traditional arrangement. The conversations culminated in a ceremony of sorts. Some months ago, I'd crafted an elaborate art project. It was a wooden block, painted in gold and covered in decorative buttons and bangles with the words "Hall Pass" in bold calligraphy.

I knew I had Pen's heart, but I had decided that her body was hers to share. As long as she told me where she was going and came home to me after, she was free to enjoy a limited non-monogamy. It had been a huge moment in our relationship and had served to bring us closer together rather than further apart.

She'd only used it three times in the months since. Twice with Ashley and Katie and once for a night out on the town "for old time's sake" as she put it. I'd been surprised how little it had bothered me, though I had declined to join in her second trip to Ashley's. It was one thing to let her sleep with others, but I wasn't quite ready to join in.

"Oh," I said as she slid the pass across the bar to me. "Is there someone here or are you heading out?"

I'm pretty sure I kept the disappointment out of my voice. It wasn't that I minded her using it. I'd thought we'd spend the night together since it was official that I'd moved in. No more escape routes. Just her and me in our house.

"Kieran." Her voice was like a caress and she continued in that low rumble she knew had a devastating effect on my willpower. "I'm not using it. I'm returning it."

Her gaze was hypnotizing and I mumbled, "You're…Wait, what?"

"I appreciate the trust you put in me." She ran a fingertip down the length of my jaw. "And I appreciate your craftsmanship."

"Craftswomanship," I slurred, staring at her plump lips.

She leaned in and grazed her teeth along my earlobe. "Whatever you say, darling. I appreciate all that," she whispered. "But I don't want this anymore."

My eyes rolled as her breath tickled my neck. I grabbed the knot of her tie and pushed her gently away. She was distracting me and I needed to clarify. "We agreed to discuss it again after a year. You have six more months."

"I don't need them."

When she tried for my neck again, I planted my palm against her chest, not pushing but creating a barrier.

"Stop distracting me."

She sighed and sat back, reaching for her drink, the devilish smile still in place. "But you like it when I distract you."

"I do." I grabbed hold of my drink to keep my greedy fingers from reaching out for her. "Very much. But what changed? You know it's okay. I trust you."

"I know you do and I love you for it." She snatched up my free hand and kissed my knuckles before I could stop her. "Nothing changed, I just don't want it anymore."

I raised an eyebrow at her.

"I want *it*, but only from you. I'm not interested in anyone else at the moment."

"And if that changes?"

"Then you get to indulge your crafty side again, but Kieran," she trailed off, smiling at me. She did that sometimes. Just... looked at me with this goofy grin that was so utterly her and so utterly out of character at the same time. "I want to come home to you every night. That's all I want."

My smile was so wide it made tears prickle my eyes. "That sounds...really great."

Pen leaned in, but instead of kissing me, she whispered against my lips, "I love you, Kieran."

"I love you, too." She brushed her lips against mine and I slipped a hand under her suit jacket. "Let's go home."

Bella Books, Inc.

Women. Books. Even Better Together.

P.O. Box 10543
Tallahassee, FL 32302

Phone: 800-729-4992
www.bellabooks.com